SPECIAL MESSAGE TO READERS

This book is published under the auspices of

THE ULVERSCROFT FOUNDATION

(registered charity No. 264873 UK)

Established in 1972 to provide funds for research, diagnosis and treatment of eye diseases. Examples of contributions made are: —

A Children's Assessment Unit at Moorfield's Hospital, London.

•

Twin operating theatres at the Western Ophthalmic Hospital, London.

•

A Chair of Ophthalmology at the Royal Australian College of Ophthalmologists.

•

The Ulverscroft Children's Eye Unit at the Great Ormond Street Hospital For Sick Children, London.

You can help further the work of the Foundation by making a donation or leaving a legacy. Every contribution, no matter how small, is received with gratitude. Please write for details to:

THE ULVERSCROFT FOUNDATION,
The Green, Bradgate Road, Anstey,
Leicester LE7 7FU, England.
Telephone: (0116) 236 4325

In Australia write to:
THE ULVERSCROFT FOUNDATION,
c/o The Royal Australian and New Zealand
College of Ophthalmologists,
94-98 Chalmers Street, Surry Hills,
N.S.W. 2010, Australia

Jan Jones fell in love with Jane Austen and Georgette Heyer aged twelve and later decided to write her own Regency novel.

Jan is on the committee of the Romantic Novelists Association but spends most of her time writing novels and women's magazine stories.

You can find out more about Jan on her website: www.jan-jones.co.uk

FORTUNATE WAGER

Secrets and subterfuge abound in Regency Newmarket . . . Caroline Fortune wants only to train horses and to continue her progress towards independence. So she projects a cheerfully argumentative persona in order that the suitors, dredged up by her mother, will leave her alone. Lord Alexander Rothwell is happy to do so. He's in Newmarket purely to fulfil an obligation; irritable because he believes he's investigating a mare's nest, he wants to return to his political career in London as soon as possible. So, when Caroline finds Alexander left for dead at her brother's racing stables, they are both considerably disconcerted . . .

Books by Jan Jones
Published by The House of Ulverscroft:

FAIR DECEPTION

JAN JONES

FORTUNATE WAGER

Complete and Unabridged

ULVERSCROFT
Leicester

First published in Great Britain in 2009 by
Robert Hale Limited
London

First Large Print Edition
published 2010
by arrangement with
Robert Hale Limited
London

British Library CIP Data

Jones, Jan, *1955 –*
    Fortunate wager.
    1. Horse trainers- -Fiction. 2. Love stories.
    3. Large type books.
    I. Title
    823.9′2–dc22

    ISBN 978–1–44480–482–9

Published by
F. A. Thorpe (Publishing)
Anstey, Leicestershire

Set by Words & Graphics Ltd.
Anstey, Leicestershire
Printed and bound in Great Britain by
T. J. International Ltd., Padstow, Cornwall

To the Romantic Novelists' Association
for their love and support
and to my
Friends and Writers Group ditto

1

Newmarket. April 1817

Caroline was reading in the window seat when Scroope opened the door to the sitting-room. She hastily arranged the first volume of *Emma* underneath *The Racing Calendar* and looked up enquiringly.

'Lord Alexander Rothwell,' announced Scroope.

An immaculately dressed gentleman strode into the room. He glanced around. 'You appear afflicted with deafness,' he said to the butler. 'I asked for Mr Harry Fortune, not one of the young ladies. Or is this a ploy on behalf of your mistress to ensure that all marriageable men in the vicinity are intro-duced to her daughters whether they will it or not?'

Scroope turned brick-red with outrage. Caroline bit the inside of her cheek to stop herself laughing. She had seen Lord Rothwell from afar during the tedious half-season she had done last year before her godmother fell ill and she had left London to nurse her. Now she confirmed her impression that the second son of the Duke of Abervale was tall and well

1

made, had dark-brown hair with a meticulous fall of curls across the left side of his brow, and eyes of light hazel. A personable figure and a very tidy estate. No wonder he had been so sought after. The only slight flaw was that his face held an impatience suggesting he was often bored witless by other people's stupidity. Caroline knew how he felt.

'I was under the impression,' said Scroope, his jowls quivering accusingly as he looked at Caroline, 'that Mr Fortune was in here. Along with Miss Taylor.'

Caroline assumed her most guileless smile. 'Certainly he was, but poor Louisa came over unwell, so Harry felt obliged to see her safely home.'

The butler stiffened. '*I* was not aware of any such occurrence.'

'No?' said Caroline, even more innocently. 'It must have been while you were absent from the hall.'

'Fascinating though these domestic details are, they do not get us any closer to your brother's present whereabouts,' snapped Lord Rothwell. 'He is not at his Penfold Lodge stables where I was expecting to transact a matter of business with him, neither is he here. At what hour do you expect him?'

'Oh, I never expect Harry,' said Caroline. 'It makes it all the nicer when he does appear.

I daresay the alarm over my friend's indisposition caused his appointment with you to slip his mind. May I ask him to wait on you?'

Her visitor's eyes grew sardonic. 'That will not be necessary. If he hasn't the courtesy to be at Penfold Lodge himself, I shall simply take my horse regardless of his groom's pettifogging objections. Perhaps you would tell him so when you have the happiness to see him next.' He turned to leave.

A quick alarm jumped in Caroline's breast. 'Has there not been some mistake? We . . . That is, my brother does not train any of your lordship's horses.'

Lord Rothwell's well-shaped eyebrows rose. He put up his quizzing glass and surveyed her from top to toe. Caroline returned the look in defiance of the edict that advised young ladies to be modest at all times. She knew well enough what he was seeing: brown hair that refused to curl, regular features with nothing to lift them out of the ordinary, an ill-fitting gown in blue-spotted muslin, slightly scuffed indoor slippers. In other words a plain girl, indifferently dressed, too unfinished for society's taste and not rich enough to be worth cultivating.

'You are conversant with all the inhabitants

of your brother's stable?' he said sarcastically.

'Yes.' She caught the flicker of surprise in his face and schooled herself not to show any satisfaction at having bested him. 'Harry runs Penfold Lodge for our cousin, you see, and since he has never been much of a hand at letter writing — '

'The reports fall to you. As do making his excuses whenever they are called for.' Lord Alexander Rothwell's disapproval was etched into his countenance. 'I should have thought you too young.'

'People generally do,' agreed Caroline.

He held her eyes a moment longer, then shrugged. 'I won a horse from your brother last night. His groom is adamant that it cannot be released to me without Mr Fortune being present to confirm the transaction.'

'I am glad to hear it.' But despite her light tone, Caroline's stomach dropped away. That was why Harry had slithered off this morning. And she had been sorry for him and Louisa for having to snatch these stolen moments where they could! Which horse had he lost? They couldn't afford to give away any of them. She covered her anxiety with the superficial chatter she had developed to distract Mama from the fact that she wasn't doing whatever it was she had been asked to do. 'I am sure if the case were reversed, you would tell your own men to act in exactly the same manner.'

'I, Miss Fortune, would have left instructions to — ' Lord Rothwell broke off as he registered the unfortunate juxtaposition of syllables in her name. 'Dear me, now I understand why your older sister was so precipitous in accepting that wet fish Mitton's offer of marriage. At the time I assumed it was to escape your mother's relentless thrusting of her into the bosom of society.'

Caroline gasped. He really was astoundingly rude. 'Mr Mitton has many good qualities,' she said, standing up. 'He and Honoria are exceedingly happy together. If you will excuse me while I change my shoes, I shall accompany you to Penfold Lodge to resolve this muddle.'

'*You?*' He looked unflatteringly sceptical.

She drew an exasperated breath, not caring whether he heard: he was the most uncivil man she had ever met. She was furious with Harry for having staked one of their horses in a wager when he had promised *faithfully* that he would never do such a thing again, and just at this moment she wanted nothing more than to be rid of the pair of them. 'It seems the most expedient solution. Especially in view of the fact that the first sweepstake is due to start in little over an hour and you will doubtless wish to attend it.' She didn't give him a chance to argue (or ask how she came to be conversant with the times of the races on Newmarket Heath), but swept past him and ran up the stairs to her chamber.

Within a very few minutes she was ready. So, alas, was Scroope. He barred the doorway, righteousness incarnate. 'Do I understand, miss, that you are proposing to walk through the streets with a gentleman unrelated to you *without even a maid?*'

Caroline sighed. Scroope was a new addition to the household. New and extremely tiresome. 'It is but a step to Penfold Lodge. And if you can find a maid in this house prepared to set so much as a toe out of doors when Newmarket is populated by the racing fraternity, I will gladly take her.'

The butler's jowls quivered. 'Mrs Fortune would never forgive me if I allowed you to go out in such an improper fashion.'

'Nonsense. Whatever *your* feelings on this head, Mama's maternal anxieties will be completely allayed when she hears Lord Rothwell escorts me.'

The gentleman in question instantly swung around from where he had been adjusting the tilt of his high-crowned hat in the mirror. 'Good God, you are right. How considerate of you to alert me to the danger.' He clicked

6

his fingers at the young footman standing glassily to attention at the foot of the stairs. 'You. Is your presence by that newel post vital for the next fifteen minutes?'

'No, sir,' said the footman, flustered. 'That is — '

'Then you may follow us to Penfold Lodge and prevent either of us from compromising the other on the way.'

Caroline knew she should be mortified by Lord Rothwell's accurate reading of Mama's character, but was having difficulty not laughing at the incensed look on the butler's face. 'I shall call on Mrs Penfold whilst I am there, Scroope. One of the Lodge servants will escort me back.'

They traversed the short distance rapidly, his lordship evidently not considering it necessary to modify his normal pace simply because a female walked alongside him.

'Are you always so rude?' asked Caroline.

'I find it separates the wheat amongst my acquaintance from the chaff. Are you always so direct?'

'Indeed no. Young ladies with no accomplishments, small portions and average looks cannot afford to be.'

He glanced at her, surprised again. 'And yet you are to me. May I ask why?'

'*Because* I have no accomplishments, a

small portion and average looks, of course. The 'my lords' of this land are rarely interested in commoners, however much Mama may wish otherwise, and so it is better to be businesslike, is it not?'

'It is unfortunate your brother is not of the same mind,' said Lord Rothwell. 'You would then have been spared a walk.'

'Think nothing of it. I like to walk and would not have been able to otherwise. Harry has done me a favour with his forgetfulness.'

Caroline spoke unconcernedly, but she was increasingly certain that her brother had 'forgotten' Lord Rothwell on purpose. Dearly as she loved Harry, she cherished few illusions about him and knew he was apt to be unrealistically optimistic when in his cups. This was not the first disastrous wager he had made. Every time he swore he would not do it again.

At Penfold Lodge, there was a surface calm which did not deceive Caroline for one moment. Her quick eyes noted a closed door on a stall that had been empty that morning, two strangers whom she assumed were Lord Rothwell's grooms, and all their own men, even those who should by now be taking their break, standing in attitudes of unconvincing idleness in the yard. 'Good morning, Flood,' she said. 'I understand there has been a little trouble.'

The head groom's stolid, weatherbeaten face relaxed. He jerked a thumb at one of the men in front of the closed stall. 'The trouble, Miss Caro, is that this here nasty, cheese-faced runt said he had orders to take away Rufus. So I said I didn't have no orders to let him. So then his lordship turns up but with no sign of Mr Harry nor no note or letter neither. So that's where we stand.'

Caroline's hand flew to her breast in alarm. '*Rufus?* What exactly were the terms of your bet with my brother, my lord?'

Rothwell spoke impatiently. 'I wagered my bay hunter against his chestnut stallion that I would throw sevens before he did.'

Dice! The part of Caroline that wasn't panicking was furious. Harry hadn't even bet at cards where he had some skill, but at dice which everybody knew was purely luck! 'Then I am afraid I see the problem only too well,' she said, keeping her voice composed. No wonder her brother had escaped with Louisa, leaving her to sort this out. She was venturing onto very shaky ground here. The only thing she could think of was to trust to his lordship's sense of honour. 'I regret to inform you, sir, that you have been misinformed. Rufus does not belong to Harry, and so was not his to bet. Rufus is mine.'

9

Lord Rothwell looked bored. 'Naturally he is. Has been since last week, I daresay, and the ink barely dry on the transfer papers. I confess I am disappointed. I expected a better ploy.'

Anger flickered in Caroline. 'I assure you it is true. Lady Penfold left him to me in her will last year. She was my godmother. If you care to ask at the Jockey Club, they will tell you he has been entered under my assumed name of 'Mr Lodge' for the past three meetings.'

'S'right, my lord. That's what I *tried* to tell this thieving cat's-paw of yours, only he's seemingly got dung in his ears and couldn't hear me,' said Flood. 'Mr Harry don't own a chestnut stallion at all.'

'Then what the devil was he doing accepting the wager?'

'I might ask what you were doing proposing it when he was evidently in his cups,' countered Caroline.

'I beg your pardon?'

Caroline gave him back stare for frosty stare. 'It stands to reason that he must have been, my lord.'

For a moment they locked wills. Caroline could feel the flags flying in her cheeks but she was determined not to give way. A scandal such as this, touching on Harry's honour, could ruin him completely.

'Is it common knowledge?' Lord Rothwell snapped at last.

Relief thundered in her veins. 'That I own Rufus? I believe so. Certainly amongst the regular race-goers.'

'Your magpie here knew for sure,' put in Flood. 'Seen him making enquiries last October.'

Lord Rothwell's eyes swivelled to his groom. 'Is this true, Jessop?'

'No, sir,' said the undersized man virtuously. 'I'd have telled you if it was.' He shot a malevolent look at Flood.

Caroline found his lordship's gaze on her again and read fury, chagrin and exasperation in it. Now she had made her point, she could almost feel sorry for him. He would be roasted unmercifully once his friends discovered he'd been gulled. *Stop that, Caroline! Stay on the attack!* 'Perhaps you would like to inspect the rest of our stock?' she invited him. 'To prove that the only chestnuts on the premises belong to other people?'

His lips thinned. 'I believe I would.'

'Not him,' said Flood, jerking a thumb at Jessop again. 'I'm not having the likes of him loose in my stables.'

'Back to the White Hart, Jessop,' said Lord Rothwell. 'Saddle my riding horse. I shall not be long.'

The groom sent another vicious look at Flood and hurried away. The second lad gulped and followed.

'You allow your groom extraordinary licence,' observed Lord Rothwell.

'Flood has been at Penfold Lodge these thirty years. I would not dream of questioning his judgement when it comes to stable matters.' Caroline halted at the first paddock where the foals frolicked up to the rail, expecting treats. She was surprised to see a softening of her companion's features as he watched their antics. Perhaps the man was not wholly inhuman after all. They continued on past the two-year-olds ('The chestnut *filly* and the bay colt are ours, the other two belong to my cousin.') to the last field where the older horses grazed. Rufus ambled over, blowing gustily down the front of her pelisse.

Lord Rothwell compressed his lips. 'You have made your point. He is evidently your horse.'

'Only since Lady Penfold died,' said Caroline, feeling she could now afford to be generous. 'But I helped her grandson birth him and then I cared for him when Bertrand was sent overseas with his regiment, so we have always had a special bond.'

'Helped birth him? But this horse must be five or six years old. You were surely very

12

young to be playing midwife?'

'Thirteen. I daresay I was a great pest. Bertrand was killed in the Peninsular, which is why Penfold Lodge passed to Lady Penfold's great-nephew.' She took a shaky breath and turned her face away, berating herself for not yet having conquered her sense of loss, gave the stallion a last rub along his neck and headed back towards the stables.

'And these are all you have?'

Caroline forced herself to sound business-like. 'Apart from two mares running today, yes. Our facilities are excellent — Lady Penfold was something of a stickler where her horses were concerned — but we do not have much room at the Lodge, and thought it sensible to stay small for the first few years. Harry is a good trainer, especially of young horses, but it is awkward enough having him in direct competition with the Fortune string without giving Papa even more excuse to accuse him of overreaching himself.'

Lord Rothwell gave a short laugh. 'Sense is not an attribute I would have awarded to your brother after last night's exhibition.'

'It was very bad of him to mislead you by omission. I daresay it never crossed his mind that he might lose.' *Please*, she thought, *please let him be magnanimous*.

There was a heavy silence. 'I am prepared

13

to forget the matter.'

Swift relief coursed through her.

'Provided, of course, that Fortune keeps to the second half of the bet.'

Caroline perceived that she had celebrated too soon. Her heart sank into her boots. 'There was a second part?'

'Why yes, that he could take any horse in my stables and turn it into a race winner by the last day of the Second Spring Meeting.' Lord Rothwell looked at her blandly. 'He was most insistent it could be done.'

He would be. And sadly, the brag had Harry's bravura stamped all over it. There would be no getting out of *this* bet.

'You must see that as a conscientious owner, I could not pass over such a chance,' continued Lord Rothwell.

'No indeed. Very laudable of you.' Heavens above, if Harry was making that sort of boast, it was astonishing that they didn't have a stableful of his cronies' no-hopers! Caroline picked up her pace as they returned to the yard, trying to think how best to deal with this new development. She moved distractedly to the closed stall. 'Who is in here, Flood?' she said, lifting the hasp.

'Imbecile girl!' yelled Lord Rothwell, hauling her back. 'Don't you know never to approach a strange horse without hearing its

14

history?' As if to underline his words, a loud crash, as of a furious hoof hitting a timber wall, was heard from the stall.

Caroline's heart banged wildly in her chest. Not at the horse's kick, which had been startling enough, but at Lord Alexander Rothwell's grip on her arm. She would never have believed he could move so fast or be so strong. There were disciplined muscles under that fine waistcoat and moulded coat. *Calm down, Caroline. No sensibility on show, remember?* 'Ah, that will be the second part of the wager, I take it,' she said, praying for her voice to sound detached. 'You had best let me have the horse's details for our records.' She stepped across to the tack room and reached for a ledger with hands which shook a little. 'Did your bet encompass terms? Is Harry to provide you with this winner at his own expense for the next month?'

Lord Rothwell had also regained his aplomb. He brushed a fleck of dust from his coat. 'You are either impressively cool, Miss Fortune, or abysmally ignorant. Send the reckoning for the usual livery and training costs to the White Hart.' His eyes glinted. 'The mare is called Solange. Four years old. Also known as the widowmaker. Good day.'

Caroline watched him stalk through the archway. 'And good day to you also, my lord,'

15

she muttered. 'Flood, if you see my brother before I do, you had best tell him to get himself measured for a coffin.'

⋆ ⋆ ⋆

Alex strode up the High Street, irritation compounding what hadn't been a good mood to start with. Giles would be in whoops. Doubtless the mistake would be all over Crockford's before the day was done. Be damned to Fortune! Why couldn't he have said straight out the chestnut wasn't his? He hadn't been that foxed. A twinge of conscience interposed. Maybe he had been. Maybe they both had been. But what the devil was there to do other than drink and gamble when one was away from the distractions of London or the obligations of one's estate on the far side of the metropolis in Surrey. Alex ground his teeth. Only two days into this ridiculous task and he'd already had to bite his tongue not to defend himself against the scorn in that chit of a girl's eyes. It wasn't what he was used to. Lady Jersey had a lot to answer for.

Alex crossed the road and wheeled sharply right. The yard of the White Hart was crowded with post-chaises and horses, but Jessop came up at once leading Chieftain, the brown gelding Alex favoured for crowded events such as race meetings. A flick of Alex's eyes showed him one of his hacks, also saddled and ready. Damn the man's impertinence. 'I shan't need you,' he said curtly, then swung himself onto Chieftain's back and set off at a smart trot up the street towards Newmarket Heath.

Once there, Alex blessed the gelding's easy strength and placid temperament as they forged a path through spectators and competitors alike. More than one gentleman was having trouble controlling a highly strung mount made over-excited by the crowd. Out of the corner of his eye he saw Giles d'Arblay's man in the grooms' enclosure, taking a pull at a tankard. Alex tightened his lips. Giles was far too lax. Let him catch one of his own grooms drinking whilst in charge of the horses and there would be trouble.

He guided Chieftain towards the starting post, exchanging greetings with spectators on horseback and nodding courteously to acquaintances who were manoeuvring curricles into optimum viewing positions.

'Giles!' he called, espying the blond locks and classic profile of his friend.

The Honourable Giles d'Arblay extricated his horse from amongst a knot of others. 'Not riding your new acquisition, Alex? I'm disappointed. I was going to challenge you to a few furlongs before you'd got the measure of him.'

Something in his laughing face gave Alex pause. 'You knew? You knew about the ownership when you suggested the bet?'

Giles grinned ingenuously. 'There was always a chance Fortune would be greenhorn enough to pay up.'

'Instead of which *I* have been made to look a fool. Why, Giles?' Alex spoke mildly, his attention apparently on the runners lining up for the sweepstake.

Giles shrugged. 'I lost a fair amount of money on that damned chestnut last year. Offered to buy him afterwards, but Fortune had the infernal cheek to tell me he wasn't for sale. Thought losing him to the son of a duke might teach the scoundrel a lesson.'

'Using me as an instrument of revenge, in fact.'

'Can't change the habits of a lifetime. Look out! They're off!' And with a whoop, Giles was plunging after the racers with the other like-minded bloods.

Alex followed more slowly, unable to conjure up any enthusiasm for a race where he had nothing at stake. He could hear Giles hollering, exhorting the rider of the horse he had backed to greater efforts, and was vexed by his friend's insouciance. Surely a gentle-man approaching his thirtieth birthday should not still be playing off the same tricks that had amused him a decade earlier?

⋆　⋆　⋆

In the Penfold Lodge stables, Caroline and Flood opened the top half of the door to the grey mare's stall.

'Hello, Solange,' said Caroline in gentle tones.

The horse rolled a bloodshot eye at her.

'What do you think?' Caroline asked Flood. 'Has she been ill-treated?' She couldn't really believe it. Not after the way Lord Rothwell had smiled at the foals.

The head groom subjected the mare to an experienced scrutiny. 'No marks, but she's as nervous as a grave digger on All Hallow's Eve, that's for sure.'

'We'll just talk to her, then,' said Caroline, leaning her elbows unthreateningly on the half-door. 'Get her used to our voices. How did those men get her here?'

Flood snorted. 'Push, pull and prod. Bloody near come in sideways, she did. So many sparks flying off her hoofs it's a wonder we wasn't burnt to the ground. The youngster was terrified. Reckon he was only there to

19

hang on to the rope and take the blame if she got away.'

Caroline was thoughtful. 'You said you'd seen Jessop before?'

'Know him of old. Ugly customer. No feel for animals, up to all the tricks going, none too choosy about his company and too friendly with the bent legs about the course for comfort. Never stays with anyone for long.'

'Lord Rothwell is not much of an employer if he takes on men like that.'

'Most likely done through an agent. His lordship'll find him out soon enough if the whispers that he's planning on making a stay here are right.'

Caroline wasn't quite sure what she thought about that. Normally the *ton* moved on once a race week was over. The idea of Lord Alexander Rothwell striding impatiently around the town after everybody else had gone was vaguely disturbing. 'Would you say the mare is calmer?' she said. 'Shall I rub her down? It cannot be comfortable for her having her coat stiff with dry sweat, and it may be that she will find the presence of a female in her stall less threatening than that of a male.'

'I'll slip her in some water first. Mr Harry'll have my ears if she lashes out at you.'

Caroline continued to talk to the mare as Flood filled a bucket and pushed it through the floor-level hatch designed for the purpose. Solange seemed quite quiet now, and bent her head to drink.

Caroline watched for a moment more, then entered the stall. Mama was forever enumerating her failings, but lack of courage had never been one of them. She took a handful of hay from the rack and unhurriedly began to rub it across the grey mare's flank.

'Keep an eye out for bruises, Miss Caro,' warned Flood, his hand on the hasp of the half-door ready to fling it open at need.

'I can't see any. But she does most decidedly need a good brush.'

'I'll see to that after you've done. Them grooms where she was must have been too chicken-hearted to go near her.' He sounded disgusted that members of his own calling could have put up such a poor show.

Working steadily, and talking softly the while, Caroline had finished one side and nearly completed the other when shouts from the yard announced the return of the men from their break. Instantly Solange's head whipped up and a challenging scream broke loose from her.

God in Heaven! Caroline was suddenly trapped against the wall facing a horse composed entirely of sinew, teeth and ironshod hoof. She kept mortally still. 'Quieten them,' she said on a thread of breath.

Flood cast her an agonized glance, but could do nothing to rescue her. He scrambled for the door. The grooms' voices fell abruptly silent. Caroline's heart thumped as tension slowly shivered out of the grey mare. Solange rolled her eyes one last time, snorted and lipped her hay. Caroline edged out of the stall and sat down in a rush on a bale.

'Lord, Miss Caro, I thought you were a goner for sure there.' Flood pushed the hasp back down with a grunt of relief.

Deep breath. Several deep breaths. It was a long time since she'd last felt that threatened by a horse. 'She's not partial to noise, then.'

'You could say.'

Caroline's eyes met his. 'Which means,' she mused slowly, 'if we're to win the bet and turn her into a respectable member of horsekind to boot, this stable will have to be kept quieter than a faro table in Heaven for the next month.'

A grim smile appeared on the groom's face. 'Trust me for that, lass. 'Widowmaker' indeed. They'll be eating their words by the time we're through.'

They had better be or it would be bellows

to mend with Harry, thought Caroline. She was still trembling with reaction to Solange's potentially lethal transformation. Her mind recalled the sardonic amusement in Lord Rothwell's light hazel eyes as he'd made his adieux. He had known full well what he was leaving them. Good God, it was tantamount to murder! What sort of man played that kind of trick? She dearly wished she could see his face if he ever learnt that it wasn't Harry who trained the difficult horses, but Caroline herself.

2

Later that day, some three miles distant from
Penfold Lodge, Lord Alexander Rothwell
was the Duke of Rutland's guest for dinner.
As he took a glass of wine and surveyed the
company in the salon, a woman glided up in a
whisper of expensive silk. 'I declare, Cheveley
is the most perfect setting. Don't you think
so?'

'It's a damn sight more pleasant than being
stuck in Newmarket. Good evening, Sally.'

Lady Jersey made a dramatic gesture
through the long window at the wooded
grounds. 'I am sure the dear duke will be
pleased to give you the run of his estate while
you are here.'

'Very likely, but I would not presume, and
it would please *me* more to be heading back
to Town. I'm surprised you aren't there
yourself.'

The uncrowned queen of London society
pouted. 'Alex, you promised.'

'I know I promised and I will keep my
word. Unless you are of a mind to release me?
It's going to be cursed tedious kicking my
heels here when there is no racing — and I

really wanted to get to the House. You know I have hopes of entering Parliament later this year.'

She tapped his hand playfully. 'All the more reason to bend that handsome head of yours to our little conundrum. I hear you have made an excellent start by manufacturing an excuse to be out on the training grounds at all hours.'

Alex's eyes narrowed. 'Where did you hear that? Giles, I suppose.'

Lady Jersey laughed. 'The dear boy. I haven't been so entertained this age. So kind of him to bear you company in your tedium.'

Alex wasn't quite sure how Giles inviting himself to spend a few weeks in Newmarket at his friend's expense could be construed as *kind*, but perhaps Sally was consulting a different dictionary from Dr Johnson's. He tried a different tack. 'Sally, you are one of the richest women I know. Why the deuce should it matter to you if one man is paid to pull a race and another wins a couple of thousand on the strength of it?'

'It was one of my husband's horses that was affected.'

'Allegedly affected. The rider was not his usual man and all horses have off-days as even you must know. He gained the next day because it won with lengthened odds.'

'He was very much disturbed, which in turn disturbs *my* peace. I have been trying to hit on a nice present for him for some time. You are it.'

'But, Sally, he and the other Jockey Club notables are far better placed to investigate this than me. They *run* the Newmarket course.'

'You will not change my mind, Alex. Giles has already tried to persuade me and he has ten times your address. I am convinced this needs an outsider. They see so much more of the game.'

'But why me?'

'Because you're clever. And honourable.'

'And I just happen to owe you a rather large favour?'

'That too. How is your dear sister, may I ask?'

Alex bit down his frustration. 'Enjoying the delights of matrimony with an untarnished reputation, thanks to you.'

'Remember it, my pet. And now you must excuse me whilst I have a tiny word with the duke.'

Alex drained his glass and beckoned for another. A society matron not yet fixed in London for the season espied him and tugged at her daughter's arm. 'Oh, God,' he ground out to the startled footman and strode towards a group of gentlemen who were bemoaning their fortune on the day's racing. He'd rather listen to hard luck stories than be forced into conversation with a simpering doll whose only interest in him was measured in acres. Why the devil did young ladies find it so impossible to hold a rational conversation?

But as the circle widened to admit him, it occurred to him that he had spoken at length with a young lady only this morning who had neither simpered nor deferred. Quite the reverse, in fact. However, Miss Caroline Fortune was clearly an oddity. And plain and with an ambitious mother into the bargain. He doubted they would have occasion to converse again.

★ ★ ★

Dawn was not yet breaking when Caroline awoke next morning. As always, she dressed by the light of a single candle, then opened her casement and climbed silently down the thick ivy. Keeping to the shadows, she sped across her father's paddocks and swung over the rail onto Penfold ground. Even after all these years, she felt a jolt of release every time she crossed the boundary. No more rules. No petty restrictions. Here, her views were listened to as if she were a real person, not a changeling child planted in a handsome family. Here she was valued.

'Morning, Miss Caro,' said a voice from the shadows of the stable.

'Morning, Flood.' There was a soft whinny. 'And good morning to you too, Rufus. Who is going to be a clever boy and win us lots of money in the sweepstake today? I wish I could be there to see you.'

Flood chuckled. 'Them days are long gone, lass.'

'More's the pity. Newmarket is so annoying in that respect. Still, I am safe enough on the heath this early. I would not be able to get away with it any later, even dressed like this.' She looked ruefully down at her short jacket and comfortable breeches. 'Growing up is the very devil, Flood.'

'It is, girl, but it's to be hoped you don't used language like that in your ma's drawing-room.'

'Trust me for that, Flood. I'd never hear the end of it. No, I am a proper young lady in company, however much I would rather be a stable boy.'

'Aye, you'd have made a grand one for sure. Ah well, time's a-passing if you're to give the two-year-olds a proper run. I've got Fancy ready for you.'

Caroline shook herself out of memories of years past when, abetted by Harry and

Bertrand, she had dressed as a boy and roved the race meetings with them, even racing in private matches a couple of times. She walked over to mount the bay colt and noticed Solange looking over the half door. On impulse, she reached up and patted the mare's neck. 'We'll go round the paddock later, and then I'll take you out for an early ride one day next week,' she promised. 'You'll love it. Just you and me flying across the training ground. No dogs barking, no nasty men shouting, nothing to alarm you at all.'

'Mr Harry might have something to say about that,' warned Flood.

Caroline laughed softly. 'Let him try.' She urged Fancy out and was soon trotting up the silent lane. There really was nothing so wonderful as riding a swift horse through the empty morning.

Undoubtedly by design, Harry was not in the yard when Caroline arrived back, nor did he join her in the kitchen for her customary rapid breakfast. She didn't dare linger so had to return home by similarly devious means without telling him exactly what she thought of his behaviour yesterday. It was not until Mama had driven off on her round of visits that he appeared at Fortune House.

'You had better be coming to apologize,' she said severely.

Harry ducked his head. 'Ah, Caro, I knew you'd handle his lordship better than I would.'

'That goes without saying. It would have been better still had you refrained from conversing with him the evening before!'

'Didn't realize I was. That is, I didn't realize he was Lord Rothwell.'

'Goodness. What a splendidly informal place Crockford's Club must be.'

Her brother reddened. 'I may have been just the tiniest bit castaway . . . '

'No, really?'

'Deuce take it, Caro, I'm not a saint. You know that.'

'Yes, I do. But, Harry, you promised you would never stake one of our horses again!'

'I didn't; *he* did.'

'There was no need to accept the bet! And don't tell me that you didn't think you would lose, for you never do and eight times out of a dozen you are proved wrong. I don't know why you go to these ridiculous gambling clubs at all.'

Harry kicked at the empty fender. 'Dash it, everyone does. There's nothing in that. Not that I'd as lief stay at home of an evening if I could only marry Louisa and bring her to Penfold Lodge.'

Caroline was unsympathetic. 'Adventures

like this are hardly likely to persuade Alderman Taylor to accept your suit.'

Her brother threw himself down beside her. 'Nothing short of a title would do that,' he said gloomily.

Caroline sighed. 'I suppose if you wish, you may escort me to Bury St Edmunds to call on her on Saturday. If the weather is fine we can take a nice long stroll around the town.'

Harry brightened at once. 'Best of sisters.'

'Correct. I will write her a note. Meanwhile, you should be at the stable. What if Lord Rothwell calls to see Solange?'

'Why would he? He thinks his bet is as good as won.'

'As well he might! Just over four weeks in which to train an untried horse is preposterous!'

'Peace, Caro; *all* the entrants will be untried. I retained that much sense.'

Caroline was a little mollified. 'As it happens, she does look built for speed. But she is so nervous at the least noise . . . '

'So Flood told me. I tell you, I was looking over my shoulder all morning to hear the place so silent.'

'It's working already though. I was surprised myself at how well. She passed a quiet night and let Flood groom her without a murmur. I only took her up to the first field and back today, but I'll walk her around the paddock properly tomorrow. You can judge how she goes on. Which course have you set for the race?'

'The Rowley Mile. Rothwell himself said that any longer a course would be unfair, but that this should sort out the sprinters. I must say I'm looking forward to wiping the superior look off his face. He treated me as if I were the veriest cub! As if he were decades older than me rather than just a few years.'

'Harry, you make *me* feel decades older and I am six years younger!' She drew a breath and added casually, 'By the by, what happens if we lose?'

Harry got up. 'Heigh ho, I'd best get on, I suppose.'

'Harry!'

Her brother didn't meet her eyes. 'Don't fret, Caro, I know you'll bring her up to scratch. The only competitor to worry about is a half-thoroughbred of Grafton's. The rest are nothing.'

Caroline fixed him with a bayonet gaze. 'What if we lose?'

'A thousand guineas,' he mumbled.

'*How much?*' She stared at him, appalled.

He flushed. 'I was foxed. You don't know what it's like. It's damned tricky not to get carried away when everyone around you is playing high and saying how lucky you are and what a touch you've got and so on.'

'Are you telling me that Lord Rothwell led you on? I don't believe it!' Whatever other impression he had given yesterday, a shark preying on brash young minnows hadn't been one of them.

'No-o, I think it was a friend of his. There was a crowd . . . ' Harry's voice trailed off unhappily.

Caroline knew better than to remonstrate. It wasn't Harry's fault that their father and elder brother had always crushed him for being so lightweight. It wasn't his fault that he'd been born with laughing eyes and the red-gold Fortune hair that had passed *her* by completely but which made him so fatally attractive to women that he'd played up to it, desperate for the approval he didn't get at home. It wasn't his fault that in order not to be bullied at Harrow he had landed himself with a devil-may-care reputation. It certainly wasn't his fault that he'd fallen head over heels in love with Caroline's closest friend. Unfortunately, Louisa was the daughter of a prosperous goldsmith who was looking rather higher for his only child than the son of a Newmarket trainer, gentleman or no.

'Sit down,' she said. 'We'd best begin calculating how to make up the money should we fail. How did we do yesterday? You didn't spend *all* our winnings last night, did you?'

'Certainly not,' said Harry. 'I banked two hundred guineas this morning.' He crossed the room for *The Racing Calendar* and in picking it up knocked *Emma* to the floor. He grinned. 'Caro, you must be the only girl I know who uses novels to conceal the fact that she reads racing periodicals, rather than the other way about.'

'Stop wasting time. Let's see now, there was a light rain overnight which has taken the edge off the ground. What odds were the legs quoting on Mermaid this morning? And I do think Bobadil has a splendid chance in the Claret Stakes, don't you?'

★ ★ ★

Alex rang the bell of Fortune House in a towering temper. Was this blasted trainer never at his place of work? How the devil was Alex to keep an eye on the everyday doings of the racing fraternity if his excuse for doing so was continually absent? He barely suppressed his impatience as, for the second time in two days, the flabby-jowled butler opened the door to announce 'Lord Alexander Rothwell'.

At least Fortune was here this time. He was

34

sitting on the sofa next to his sister, his close-curled red head bent near to her smooth brown one, both of them poring over a journal. They looked up, startled.

'Goodness,' remarked the young lady, recovering her aplomb. 'Mama will be desolated to have missed you a second time, my lord.'

Alex curbed the insubordinate twitch of his mouth. 'She need not have that disappointment if your brother was ever to be found at his place of business,' he said quellingly.

The chit opened her eyes wide. 'But he has been there. Perhaps you are not aware of how early trainers and stable hands have to start their work. Indeed, I was about to request a small nuncheon for him before he goes up to the heath. Will you join us?' She signalled to the butler.

Alex's eyes went to the ormolu clock ticking on the mantelshelf.

She noticed, blast her. There was a decided gurgle in her voice as she added, 'If you think it proper, naturally. I am afraid Mama will not be back to lend us her countenance for some time yet.'

'If she were, I wouldn't be here,' said Harry Fortune frankly. He came over to Alex with his hand outstretched. 'I beg your pardon. I was not expecting you at Penfold Lodge today, otherwise I would have remained there.'

The cub had charm, Alex gave him that. He shook the proffered hand and sat down.

'Did you come to enquire about your horse? She hadn't killed anyone up until an hour ago, but of course it's early days yet.'

His sister gave a strangulated sound which she managed to turn into a cough. Alex's exasperation rose again. The pair of them were so damnably young!

She was talking once more, crossing the room to the tray by his elbow. 'Will you take a glass of wine, my lord? Harry, you will have to do without ale. Scroope appears to think it inappropriate in view of the company.'

About to refuse, Alex looked up and experienced a slight shock. Plain though Miss Caroline Fortune undoubtedly was, she had lovely eyes, something that hadn't been apparent yesterday when they were filled with scorn. Now they were honey-brown and suffused with a merriment that was really quite difficult to snub. She was also, he realized with indignation some thirty minutes later, remarkably managing. Without at all meaning to, he had consumed two glasses of claret and a plate of meat and pickles whilst talking over training methods quite different from those he was accustomed to. All of which found him leaving the house with Mr Harry Fortune in a far mellower mood than when he had arrived.

'I expect I'll see you on the heath later,' said Fortune cheerfully. 'Rufus is running today.'

That reminded Alex of something. 'Your sister said she helped birth him. Can that be true? How old is she?'

Fortune grinned. 'In years? Eighteen. Came out last season.'

'I do not remember her being in Town.'

'You wouldn't. Honoria is the beauty, you see. Caro was quite in her shade. She'll go up again when Selina comes out next spring, but I daresay it'll be the same story. Great gun, though. Worth all the rest put together.'

Alex walked back to the White Hart with a vague feeling of dissatisfaction that he was quite unable to account for. He discovered Giles in the yard, inspecting a dun gelding.

'What do you think?' said his friend.

Alex scrutinized the horse. 'Too short in the back.'

Giles turned to the groom. 'Tell your master I'm obliged to him, but Lord Rothwell thinks him too short in the back.' The groom nodded and led the gelding away. Giles fell into step with Alex. 'Had a good look around the stable, then?'

Alex lowered his voice. He didn't want the entire coaching inn knowing what was going on. Jessop was too close to them as it was, polishing unnecessarily at a spotless girth strap. 'Didn't get a chance. Fortune wasn't there.'

Giles looked at him sharply. 'Then where have you been this long time?'

'I ran him to ground at Fortune House. His sister insisted on plying us with victuals.'

Giles snorted. 'Trying to keep you sweet. Doesn't want you quarrelling with her brother again.'

'That would be impossible. I might as well argue with the sun for shining.'

'Damned cheerful country hick. Doesn't stop him being our man. He pocketed so much yesterday that it couldn't all have been luck.'

Alex felt a surge of vexation. 'Giles, you know my views. I believe this whole crazy notion to be a mare's nest of Sally Jersey's. There *is* no double dealing at the Newmarket races, let alone anything perpetrated by someone as feckless as Harry Fortune.'

'Feckless? You didn't see how much blunt he collected.'

'Deuce take it, for all his youth, the cub is a *trainer*. He is out on the grounds day in day out. Naturally he watches the other horses as well as his own. His 'luck', as you call it, doubtless results from the application of his knowledge.'

Giles shrugged. 'Then I like him even less. There's something damnably ill-bred about using science in the sport of kings.'

'What nonsense you do spout. I'm away to the heath, not that one can spy anything amiss with all the crowds and the dashing between courses. I never knew such a place for so much confusion. If Lady Jersey had ever attended a Newmarket meeting herself, she would know so and not expect me to work miracles on her behalf. 'The outsider sees more of the game' indeed.'

'But as she hasn't, and doesn't know what goes on, you may enjoy yourself without worrying and later tell her you noticed nothing out of the ordinary.'

'Giles, when I promise to do something, I do it.'

His friend shrugged. 'As you will. It makes you a damned uncomfortable companion though.' Then he brightened. 'Hey, here's a thought — why not save yourself some trouble by asking one of the grooms to skulk around on your behalf? Jessop would do it for extra coin in his hand, I'm sure. What's more, he's native to the course here and would know in a moment if there was anything smoky.'

'No.' Alex didn't hide his instant distaste for this suggestion. 'The fewer people in this affair the better.'

'Ha! More that you hate being obliged to the lower orders,' observed Giles. 'You could ask him with ease for I was going to take him up there anyway. You don't mind, I suppose? My man's down with some infernal stomach complaint.'

'You'll be riding. Why do you need a groom?'

His friend looked at him askance. 'For the spare mount if mine goes lame, of course. Where's the fun if you can't follow the race?'

'At the finishing post?' said Alex drily.

'Paltry. You can't just wait for excitement to find you in this life, Alex. You have to go out and extract it whenever possible.'

'You are incorrigible.' Alex clapped him on the back and rode off, waving away his grooms. That was Giles all over. Even on the brink of ruin he would bet the devil he could trot around the rim of Hell without falling in. If he would only put one tenth of the energy he expended on amusement into tending his lands instead, he wouldn't find himself in precarious straits quite so often. Giles, however, had never viewed the long run as near so enticing as the next minute's sprint. Talking of which, Alex felt gloom descend on him once again. He really was not looking forward to spending the ensuing days peering at jockeys and their agents to see whether any of them had been nobbled and by whom.

⋆　⋆　⋆

The gloom was justified. After the most frustrating week's racing Alex had ever suffered, he leaned his throbbing head against the cool windowpane on Saturday morning, wincing at the sun just beginning to shine palely over the rooftops opposite. He couldn't believe he'd been so stupid as to drink heavily *again* last night. First at Crockford's and then damn near a whole bottle of brandy back here in his rooms at the White Hart. Sheer self-pity because most of his acquaintances were departing and he was not.

Soft hoofbeats grazed his ears. He focused morosely on a lithe stripling trotting a bay along the High Street. The boy had a superb action, seeming at one with his mount. Alex had been going to ride today to get the stench of failure out of his head, though admittedly not this early. He'd have to forget the idea. The only thing he could contemplate with any degree of complaisance right now was premature death. He managed to swallow some water without gagging and then crawled back into bed cursing all women and the obligations they exacted on honourable men. Somewhere in his twisted dreams Lady Jersey laughed heartlessly at him, his sister eloped with whole strings of fortune hunters, his one-time mistress taunted that she was leaving him for someone less boring — and then they all turned into Caroline Fortune who informed him he'd brought everything on himself.

He did not feel that much better when he got up some hours later.

'I'm off fishing,' said Giles. 'Coming?'

Alex cast a jaundiced eye through the window of the inn at the offensively bright sunlight. 'You'll never catch anything.'

'Lay you a pony I do. Besides, Rutland invited me. Can't not go when I've been asked.'

'I'll see you at dinner if I happen to be still alive. Remind me to block my ears the next time you suggest a night-cap on top of whatever hellish brew they were serving at Crockford's last evening.'

Giles chuckled unfeelingly, calling in unnecessarily strident tones for his valet as he left their private parlour. Alex allowed himself another moment of self-pity. If he'd been at home, his butler would by now be hovering at his shoulder with a covered tankard. True, the contents in general smelled appalling and tasted worse, but it did the job.

Oh, he was wasting so much time here! He should be in London, studying the proceedings in the House, mixing with the influential personages who were sponsoring his admittance and finding him a seat, impressing them with his intelligence and gravity.

A waiter came in to clear away the remains of Giles's breakfast. He looked sideways at Alex. 'The master always says what a gentleman needs who's been a bit on the go, is the hair of the dog that bit him.'

'Your master is a publican,' pointed out Alex crushingly. 'Such sayings are to his profit.' A crash from the street, followed by horses neighing and an ensuing loud altercation made his head throb unbearably. Was there nowhere quiet in this inn? He picked up a printed pamphlet exhorting the reader to visit sundry Local Attractions for the benefit of their Health and Amusement. A description of the Abbey ruins at Bury St Edmunds caught his eye. 'How far to Bury St Edmunds?' he asked the waiter.

'A matter of fifteen miles, my lord. But it's a good road all the way.'

'Then ask them downstairs to get my curricle ready, please.' Yes, cool monastic solitude sounded very good to him at that moment.

3

Caroline sat on a bench near the Abbey Gate, her eyes closed and the spring sunshine warm on her face. Harry and Louisa had applied to see what was left of the ruined abbey (which wasn't much after Henry VIII had had his way and then the townsfolk had used the resultant rubble as a handy source of building materials), but at the last minute Caroline hadn't been able to face it and had said she would wait outside for them. Louisa had pressed her hand, thinking her friend was being discreet, but the truth was that Bertrand had brought her here before he left to rejoin his regiment in the Peninsular that last time. She had been back several times since, of course, but the sight of two small boys bowling a hoop down the street as they arrived and their sister pleading with the nursemaid to be granted a turn too had brought him too vividly to mind for her to continue.

It had been a lovely day. Bertrand had included his grandparents and the rest of the schoolroom party in the outing and they had sought permissions and brought a picnic, but she had known right from the expedition being mooted that it was her he especially wanted to address. He wanted to say something particular, something he couldn't give tongue to in the stables in the early morning with her dressed in breeches and the men all around.

'Keep visiting my folks, won't you,' he'd said, after the ancient stones had been clambered over, clothes dusted down, raised pies and cold chicken eaten and they had moved slightly apart from the others. 'They'll need some life about the place once I've shipped out.'

'Of course,' Caroline had replied. 'I would even if I didn't want an excuse to keep escaping from home. And I'll look after Rufus and see to his training for you as well.'

'For *us*,' he'd corrected her. 'And don't forget to carry on with our betting account. Flood will put the money on and bank the winnings if Harry can't.' He'd coloured and fiddled with his gloves. 'Caro, I know you're only fourteen and I'm quite a bit older, but you're the best friend a chap could have and I've always thought we might . . . That is, I've been rather hoping that in another couple of years we'd . . . '

A well-spring of happiness had nearly unmanned her. 'Oh yes, Bertrand. Yes, please.

I've never wanted anything else.'

He'd looked relieved. 'That's all right, then. I'll sell out once we've seen off Boney. Don't much fancy the army in peacetime. Those brats are making a hash of flying the kite, aren't they? Shall we give them a hand?'

Reviewing the conversation now, Caroline could see it lacked a certain something as far as romantic declarations went, but Bertrand Penfold had always been more at home with jokes than with deep feelings, and to a girl who had idolized him since he first put her up on a pony when she was an adventurous three-year-old and he a good-natured twelve, the unspoken understanding between them had been all she'd needed. *Oh Bertrand, if only you hadn't —*

'What the devil are you doing here alone?'

Caroline's eyes flew open. The children and their nursemaid were gone. Instead, Lord Rothwell towered in front of her, his eyebrows drawn together in a fearsome scowl. 'I am not alone! I'm with my brother and Miss Taylor.'

His lordship looked around in sarcastic disbelief. 'Who are where exactly?'

Caroline stood, furious with him for jerking her out of her memories. 'Not that it is any of your business,' she snapped, 'but Harry and Louisa have applied to see the abbey ruins. I

46

felt a little fatigued so said I would wait here for them.'

'You've been crying,' he said abruptly.

'*I have not!*' She turned away from him and sat down again, trembling. 'Pray do not let me keep you from your promenade.'

To her rage, she felt the bench shift under his weight. 'I had the ruins in mind myself, but must also admit to feeling a little fatigued. I daresay it was the drive. I shall contemplate the scene for a while, the better to armour myself against any ghostly Franciscans.'

'They were Benedictine monks, not Franciscans, and I wish you would have the goodness to armour yourself somewhere else.'

'Oh no, this position suits me very well. But please do not feel obliged to make conversation. Handsome architecture of the sort I see before me is far better appreciated in silence.'

'Insufferable,' muttered Caroline.

'How strange. That was always my sister's opinion when constrained to accept a companion. You are out of luck. I have first-hand experience of the bacon-brained notions young ladies get in their heads if they are carelessly chaperoned and their thoughts not given a proper direction.'

Caroline swung around. 'How dare you!

Miss Taylor is with *my brother* and it is not only his sense of honour and the esteem he bears her which prevents their behaving scandalously — she herself knows perfectly well what is owed to her father and his position in society!'

He looked startled. 'What the devil has Miss Taylor to do with anything? I have never even met her. I was referring to *you*. It is perfectly obvious from your countenance that you either have a clandestine appointment and your companion has missed it, or he kept it and you quarrelled.'

Caroline could hardly speak she was so incensed. 'Lord Rothwell, you overstep the mark indeed! Even if what you suppose were true — which it isn't and I take considerable umbrage at you even thinking it might be — you barely know me! Do you commonly walk around prosperous market towns dealing out scolds to chance-met acquaintances? I should not be surprised at anything your sister does if you are the arbiter of her conduct!'

'If I had been I should not be here now,' he fired back cryptically. He seemed to recollect himself. 'No young lady should be sitting on a public bench alone.'

'I have told you, I am *not* alone. Also this is Bury St Edmunds, not a fashionable London trysting place. I assure you that even if some disreputable character was so misinformed as to think it worth his while making me the object of his gallantry, I am perfectly capable of administering a set-down!'

'Now I know you are too young to be out alone. How the devil do you imagine that an untaught female could — Good God!'

This last was said in so altered a tone that Caroline followed his gaze. Fierce satisfaction swept through her at the sight of Harry and Louisa emerging in perfect propriety through the Abbey Gate. 'An apology would seem to be in order, don't you think?' she said icily.

But Lord Rothwell was feeling for his quizzing glass. 'What a diamond,' he murmured.

Caroline swallowed down her chagrin. She was familiar with gentlemen being struck dumb by Louisa's fair beauty and cheerful countenance. She did not know why the surrender of Lord Rothwell's senses should be so particularly bitter.

Harry widened his eyes at the sight of her companion and looked a query at her. She shrugged to make it plain that his being here was none of her doing.

'Lord Rothwell,' said Harry. 'How pleasant to see you. Miss Taylor, may I present Lord Alexander Rothwell. He is the owner of the spirited grey mare I was telling you about.'

Louisa flashed a delighted smile and held out her hand. 'I am sure you will not be disappointed, my lord. Penfold Lodge is a most superior stable.'

Lord Rothwell raised Louisa's hand to his lips. 'Amazingly so, considering its manager is so often elsewhere. On this occasion, however, one can see why.'

Caroline was used to the difference that a pretty face made to a gentleman's conduct, but Lord Rothwell's instantaneous transformation into a man of manners grated even so. 'Your own estate is profitable, I suppose?' she asked pointedly.

A glint appeared in his eyes. 'Happily yes, but I have a bailiff to look after it in my absence.'

'And Harry has an experienced head groom. It has been charming to meet you again, my lord. Such a shame we must be on our way. Goodbye.'

But Louisa gave a sharply indrawn breath and with a start of alarm Caroline saw the rotund figure of Alderman Taylor rounding the bend of Angel Hill. In a flash she had taken her friend's arm and swung her so that they were facing the two men. 'We are meeting everybody today, are we not?' she cried aloud. 'Good day, Alderman, you are looking very well. May I introduce you to Lord Alexander Rothwell whose horse Harry has just taken on for training. Lord Rothwell, Alderman Taylor is well known as the finest goldsmith in Bury St Edmunds.'

Lord Rothwell instantly went so rigid with hauteur that she thought he might topple over. To make matters worse, Louisa's father greeted him far too effusively. He was an astute businessman and in general a man of great sense, except in his obsession with Louisa making a brilliant marriage. Caroline found herself hoping that Lord Rothwell would not depress his pretensions too severely.

' . . . quiet, of course, my lord, but I flatter myself that we have several superior attractions here for a man of taste and fashion such as yourself. I very much hope, for instance, that we will have the pleasure of seeing you at our assembly next week?'

Lord Rothwell gave the smallest of stiff inclinations of the head. 'I shall certainly give the matter my consideration.'

Alderman Taylor beamed. Caroline rushed into speech before he could expose himself even more. 'Are you on your way home, Alderman? Will you give Louisa your arm? Then Harry may escort me back now instead of returning for me later as we had planned.'

Louisa's father looked from Harry to Lord Rothwell. 'Oh, but surely . . . '

Caroline kept the bright smile on her face. 'Lord Rothwell plans to visit the ruins. If I have it correctly, he expressed the opinion that great architecture is best experienced in silence and solitude. And I believe the gentlemen have finished their discussion. Is that not so, Harry?'

Her brother had barely opened his mouth to reply when Lord Rothwell cut in. 'I certainly have no more to say. Good day, Miss Taylor, Alderman, Fortune.'

Caroline bit her lip as he strode away. She had deserved the snub of his not taking leave of her, but she did hope his dislike would not extend itself to Harry.

'The carriage is at the Angel Hotel, Louisa,' her father was saying. 'Well, well, the Duke of Abervale's son, eh? I daresay there will be time enough before the assembly to have a new gown made up.'

'Papa, you spoil me. Do you not think it is splendid that Mr Fortune has attracted such an illustrious patron?'

'Yes, yes, now come along. We must get back to your aunt. Blue, do you think? Or pink? Your mama always looked very handsome in pink. Good day, Miss Caro. I am much obliged to you for walking in this direction with Louisa. Good day, Fortune.'

Caroline and Harry were left on the path. Caroline tucked her arm in her brother's as they moved towards the inn where he'd left the curricle. 'He'll come around, Harry.'

Her brother gave a bitter laugh. 'I can't compete with a title, Caro.'

'You don't have to. Not in Louisa's eyes.'

'Two more years until she's of age. Anything could happen. Wouldn't blame her if it did. Dash it, you saw the way Rothwell looked at her.'

'I have seen the way every gentleman of our acquaintance has looked at her since she was ten years old. She loves *you*.'

'I wish he hadn't happened to come by today even so. What was that all about? You looked to be at daggers drawn.'

'Lord Rothwell,' said Caroline trenchantly, 'did not consider it proper for me to be sitting alone on a bench in broad daylight in the most respectable thoroughfare in Suffolk!'

'What a slow-top. Good thing he doesn't know about you shinning down the ivy every morning and riding on the heath in my old clothes.'

Caroline glared. 'It would not signify if he did!'

Harry wiped the grin from his face. 'No, of course not. Wish the parents would consent to you living at Penfold Lodge all the time so you didn't have to, though. It's damned gloomy with only Bertrand's mama there. Those knitting needles of hers are driving me to distraction.'

'You can't wish it more than me. I shall announce another visit soon, and perhaps they will reconsider entirely after next season when I have failed to take yet again.'

Harry perked up. 'Yes, very likely. For Selina is near as well-favoured as Honoria and is bound to go off, don't you think? Mama won't want you hanging around a third time when Eliza comes out.'

Caroline was obliged to swallow her immediate response to this. Harry was the best of brothers, but there were times when he was a little more forthright than was necessary. 'I will come back with you now at any rate. The more I am to be found at Penfold Lodge, the more everyone will expect me to be there. We shall win them over by attrition yet.'

★   ★   ★

Alex strode furiously through the imposing stone gate and presently found himself viewing the remains of the once-great abbey with nothing like the reverence such an ancient place should have induced. It was beyond anything! How dare that wretched chit use him to protect her miserable brother from the consequences of his ill-considered assignations! What sort of friend encouraged a young lady in an intrigue which ran counter to her father's wishes? Wishes that Alex had every sympathy with! Miss Taylor was a veritable beauty and lively too, if her animated countenance was any guide. It was a crime to waste her on a hey-go-mad puppy like Fortune when even a moderate portion should ensure her success in the marriage mart. Why had she not been presented already? Surely not simply because her father was in trade? The *ton* was littered with instances where money had been bartered for a title. The *beau monde's* dislike of the shop could not always afford to extend itself to marriage settlements. And a goldsmith was a very superior craftsman indeed. He must ask Miss Fortune for elucidation the next time he spoke to her.

On which thought Alex foundered. His frown returned. He wasn't *going* to be speaking to Miss Caroline Fortune again. She had forfeited the right to his notice by her appalling behaviour. She was quick enough, he'd concede her that, and in any other young woman he might even admire her loyalty and spirit, but she *presumed*, which was a worse crime in Alex's book even than being vulgar.

The waiter was in the coffee room when he returned. After commenting that he had found Bury St Edmunds a very pleasant town, Alex remarked that he had met with some residents who had mentioned an assembly.

'At the New Subscription Rooms, my lord? Very smart they are, by all accounts. The next ball is on Wednesday, I believe.'

* * *

Harry leant against the side of the stall, watching as Caroline unhooked Solange's tether. 'You don't think you are dressed too fine for this?'

She dusted her hands on the skirts of a walking dress that owed a lot more to her mother's love of unnecessary flounces than her own taste. 'Oh, I do hope so. I've been trying to render this wretched gown unwearable for weeks.' She took a grip on the mare's head collar. 'It's a lovely afternoon, girl. Would you like a stroll around the field and a mouthful of nice fresh grass by day instead of in the dark? Show your admirers how beautiful you are?'

Solange whickered into her hair. Flood met

her eyes. 'I'll be right alongside you, Miss Caro. Soon as she turns restive, you take to your heels and leave her to me and Mr Harry.'

Very slowly, and talking gently all the while, Caroline led the mare across the yard to the first paddock, which they had cleared of the other horses. It shouldn't be any different to walking her around the field early in the morning, but there would be more to see and more movement to catch her eye and possibly make her bolt. There was certainly a moment when shouts from the street sent shivers quivering up and down her legs, but Caroline kept talking and after a minute of indecision, Solange moved forward again. As Flood shut the gate, Caroline let her go and leant on the bars, ashamed that her own legs felt so weak.

Flood grinned. Then his face changed. 'What's that varmint doing here?'

Caroline turned to see him hurtle down the path and twist his fist into the collar of an undersized man lurking in the stable archway, almost lifting him off his feet. She and Harry followed curiously.

'Let go! I'll have the judge on you for assault,' whined the man. Caroline recognized him as Lord Rothwell's groom, Jessop. 'I'm here with a message for his lordship.'

'He ain't here, you lying little guttersnipe,'

growled Flood. 'Which you knowed all along. And even if he had been, the likes of you don't come no further onto our property than the road. Why didn't you tell one of the lads you'd got a message, eh?'

'Didn't give me a chance, did you?' Jessop wrenched himself free and looked murderously at Flood. 'You're going to regret this.'

'Not as much as you will if you set one toe inside this yard again.'

Jessop spat on the ground and turned away. Flood watched him leave.

'I know him,' said Harry with a frown. 'He's been hanging around the betting ring on the heath all week.'

'Up to no good, I'll be bound,' said Flood. 'Always on the edge of trouble, that one.'

'But what was he doing *here*?' said Caroline.

'Wanted to know how we were doing with the mare of course. Either under orders or for information on his own account. Wouldn't put it past him. Mr Harry's ain't the only money riding on this bet.'

'Already?' said Caroline, appalled. She looked back at the paddock anxiously, but Solange had moved over to the far side and was cropping the grass. The raised voices didn't seem to have disturbed her. Even so . . . 'The next time I see Lord Rothwell, I'm going to have words about that groom of his,' she said with decision.

Harry and Flood exchanged grins. Caroline ignored them.

* * *

As it happened, she saw his lordship at church the very next day. She and Harry were sitting dutifully alongside the rest of the family waiting for the service to start when there was a disturbance in the doorway. Everybody's heads craned discreetly in that direction. Lord Rothwell and another gentleman were apologizing to the sidesmen for their tardiness. Now they were being ushered to the pews reserved for the nobility. Caroline felt her eyes widen. She had thought Lord Rothwell well turned out, but his friend was positively exquisite! His coat and pantaloons were an exact match for each other in pearly grey, his waistcoat was figured cream silk, his neckcloth fell in snow-white folds, his gold locks had been styled by a master and not a speck of dirt sullied his highly polished top-boots. Hers was not the only mouth agape. Every young woman under All Saints' vaulted roof was casting admiring glances. And didn't he know it, thought Caroline, observing the tiny air of satisfaction in his bearing. The exquisite allowed himself a contented look around the packed church before sitting down on the other side of the aisle from Caroline.

What a dandy, she thought, and was cross with herself for having followed the herd. She leant back as his gaze reached her, not wanting to pander further to his self-esteem. For a fraction of a second his eyes rested on Harry instead — and to Caroline's astonishment a look of vitriolic dislike flashed across his face.

She blinked, but now Lord Rothwell was easing himself onto the bench and cutting his friend off from view. Had she imagined that look? Surely she must have done. Why would anyone hate *Harry*? She murmured an enquiry of her brother as to the gentleman's identity.

Harry glanced across. 'Who? Oh, that's Giles d'Arblay. Goes it a bit at Crockford's.'

So *he* obviously didn't think there was a problem. Caroline slid another glance sideways. Lord Rothwell was staring ahead so rigidly that she knew he was aware of her. How silly. But she certainly had no wish to distinguish him after his rudeness yesterday. As the service wore on, however, the humour of the situation struck her. There they were, both pointedly ignoring each other whilst seated not three feet apart. By the Nunc Dimittis she was hard pressed not to scream with laughter.

In the catching-up bustle outside the church, which Caroline privately thought was the major reason most of her mother's acquaintance attended the devotions, she was surprised to see Mr d'Arblay make a point of distinguishing Harry, asking him how many stable-hands Solange had crippled so far. 'Only two,' replied Harry in the same cheerful tones, 'and they both have a spare foot, so we haven't lost any work through it.'

Giles laughed and declared Harry to be enviously game. His eyes wandered past Caroline and settled on Selina. It being obvious from her close bonnet that she was not yet out, although she might as well be, the amount their mother took her about '*to get her accustomed, you know,*' he made her an elaborately regretful bow and moved on. Harry spotted some friends and strolled away from the family party likewise.

'Miss Fortune,' said a cool voice.

Caroline could hardly believe her ears. Lord Rothwell was addressing her! 'I beg your pardon,' she said affably. 'I didn't see you there.'

Was that a twitch at the corner of his mouth? 'Kindly apprise your brother of my intention to call at Penfold Lodge tomorrow morning. I would do it myself, but I perceive your mother to be issuing invitations of some description and would as lief be away before she progresses this far.'

Did he *mean* to offend or was he so arrogant that he simply didn't care?

'Certainly I will let him know,' replied Caroline, anger giving her words an edge and reminding her of another cause of offence, 'but pray do not bring Jessop with you. He has difficulty enough comprehending the words 'not on our property'. Flood was obliged to eject him only yesterday.'

Lord Rothwell looked sardonic. 'Doubtless he was visiting an acquaintance amongst your grooms.'

'They say not. Our men do not think very highly of him. Or his morals.'

'And what do you mean by that, may I ask?'

'Merely that he gave every impression of spying — in order to put himself at an advantage, perhaps, when it comes to the betting for Solange's race.'

Caroline had not thought his lordship's expression could grow any more austere. She was wrong. 'I trust you do not think I had anything to do with his being at your brother's establishment?' he said, white-lipped.

'Why, no. There would be no need. An owner, you know, must be welcome to see his horse whenever he chooses.' A loud shout of indecorously unSabbath laughter drew her attention to the knot of young men and reminded her of Solange's idiosyncrasy. 'But only the owner, if you please, not his friends.'

'I must say, you express yourself very freely for one who merely writes the reports for her brother.'

'That is because Harry has too much bonhomie to enforce his own rules. I have no popularity to lose. Oh, I see Mama approaching. Would you care to be introduced?'

'Your servant, Miss Fortune,' he said, in tones of total dislike, and left.

4

Monday morning, six o'clock. Alex reflected savagely that the majority of his acquaintance were no doubt asleep at this moment, most of them asleep in busy, lively, important London. But here was he, staring at the ceiling of a Newmarket coaching inn, thoroughly awake and already suffering from a surfeit of boredom. He rolled out of bed and irritably rattled open the curtains, ready to aggravate himself some more by looking out on a tedious, empty day.

His preconceptions received a sharp shock. Tradesmen's carts trundled along the High Street. Shutters were folded back and the street washed down. Maids were abroad marketing. Maids! Alex disremembered seeing such a homely sight in Newmarket before and couldn't help recalling Caroline Fortune's pithy remark about servants not setting foot out of doors during a racing week.

Were his fellow bucks and bloods that perilous? Surely not. But Alex was fair-minded and reluctantly conceded that when in Newmarket, gentlemen were free of their families and tended to give themselves over entirely to pleasure. Crowded hugger-mugger into the town's many inns and hotels, they were unfettered by the common restraints of polite life. And thinking wryly of all the times he'd paid off Giles's fancies in other places, he thought the more respectable females of Newmarket might just have a point.

For now, he stood at the window of his room and watched the comings and goings of a market town. It was oddly soothing. His attention sharpened as a nice chestnut with a long white star on its forehead trotted by. The youth riding it had a familiar action, one Alex had seen before. On the heath, presumably, one of the hundreds of horses and riders he had been scrutinizing this week. He frowned, trying to pin the memory down. But the entrance into his chamber of a maid to light the fire — and flustered to find him already out of bed — distracted him and chased the matter from his mind.

With no racing or cock-fighting or pugilism on offer, Giles did not put in an appearance at breakfast, relieving Alex of the necessity of finding an excuse as to why his friend should not accompany him to Penfold Lodge. Not, he qualified to himself, that he was letting a chit of a girl dictate his actions. That would be preposterous.

Fortune was there for once, out in the

paddock. Watching unnoticed, Alex approved of the non-hectoring way the young man treated the horses. It was a fanciful conceit, but the beasts seemed to *want* to do their best for him. But, Lord, the place was quiet. No shouts from the stable-block, no ribald banter such as was to be found in other establishments. It was enough to give one gooseflesh.

'We find it serves,' explained Harry with a shrug when Alex greeted him. 'Will you come to the house and join me in a tankard of ale?'

As they strolled towards the yard, Alex noticed a chestnut with a long white forehead star in the field. He paused. 'Didn't I see that one this morning trotting along the High Street?'

His companion stumbled on a tussock of grass. 'I daresay,' he said. 'Most trainers take their horses up to the heath to exercise them. Here, Maiden,' and he stretched out his hand to the filly.

'Lad riding her had a nice action. Very smooth.'

Harry patted the horse's neck. 'Yes, we're hoping for a result in next year's Guineas with Maiden. You want to watch out for her.'

Fortune was hiding something. A trainer did not give out that sort of tip without good reason. Alex's nerves tingled. As they walked on, he directed a close look around the stable and yard, nothing every man there. The sight of Solange with her nose in a bucket of feed, unperturbed by the head groom brushing her down was a considerable facer. Alex gaped. How the devil had Fortune managed it in so short a time? The mare looked . . . normal! 'That lad,' he said casually when he'd recovered, 'the chestnut's rider. Is he here? I'd like to commend him on his style.'

'Eh? No, sorry, he rides out for me now and again but I haven't got enough work to keep him full time. I believe he's got several jobs on the go. You know how it is.'

Alex did indeed. His thoughts turned grim. The boy was good and would be in demand. If he was in and out of other stables, he could well be gathering just such information as would turn a pretty profit at the betting post. Maybe Giles was not so wide of the mark with his prejudice against Penfold Lodge after all.

★　★　★

Caroline sat on a hard chair in the New Subscription Rooms, watching the dancing and stifling a small yawn. Since Harry had relayed Lord Rothwell's comments about seeing her ride Maiden on Monday, she had thought it prudent to rise an hour earlier to

67

exercise the horses. Bertrand had always said she needed less sleep than a rabbit in a farmer's sights, but even so she was feeling just a trifle over-extended now.

It would not have been so bad if she had been dancing herself, or even conversing with someone interesting. But there was a dearth of young men tonight, and because she took pains to be either too clever or too bubble-headed for all the middle-aged gentlemen on the look-out for an unpaid housekeeper, she was thrown back on the chaperons (whose gossiping she inhibited) or the other unpart-nered young ladies. Caroline listened to them rattle on, interspersing the odd word, all the while calculating for the ten-thousandth time in her head how soon she could be considered a failure in the marriage stakes and thus reintroduce the subject at home of moving permanently to Penfold Lodge to be a companion to Bertrand's mama.

The set ended. Harry squired Louisa over and went in search of lemonade. Alderman Taylor, thought Caroline, looked decidedly unenamoured by Harry's solicitous care of his daughter, but so long as the young pair did not stand up together for more than two dances he could not complain. The fact that they were always the longest two dances on the card had fortunately escaped him.

68

A ripple of interest suddenly spread through the room. Caroline glanced across and to her amazement saw Lord Rothwell's tall, immaculately clad figure stroll through the door. At the sight of the gratified smile on Alderman Taylor's face, Caroline was glad he had decided not to spurn the invitation, although it was possibly only because he and his fine friend were at a loose end that they had made the journey.

The alderman wasted no time in beckoning Louisa over. In a spirit of pure mischief, Caroline linked her arm in her friend's and accompanied her. There was an undignified stir from the chaperons' bench as a number of ladies felt the need to take a prompt turn about the room.

'Louisa, my dear, here is Lord Rothwell desirous of asking you to stand up for the next dance. I'm sure you have that one free, do you not?'

Louisa's dance card had never yet been anything but full within minutes of her entering a ballroom, but she obeyed her father's implicit instructions and bobbed an amiable curtsey.

Out of politeness, Giles d'Arblay should then have offered to stand up with Caroline, but instead he allowed his eye to be caught by one of the ladies behind her and was seamlessly engulfed in a charming flurry of introductions.

'I beg your pardon,' said Lord Rothwell in a constrained voice. 'My friend has no manners.'

'I assure you I do not regard it,' returned Caroline. She glanced at Alderman Taylor whispering hasty instructions in Louisa's ear and chuckled. 'Was it very flat in Newmarket tonight?'

'By no means,' said his lordship austerely. 'But it is a fine evening and as I had already had occasion to mark the elegant exterior architecture in the town, we took a fancy to see these rooms. They are as handsome as report indicates.'

'Spoken like a gentleman. The set is forming, my lord. I had best see if Louisa's erstwhile partner would like me as a consolation prize.'

He did, but with such a bad grace that Caroline was obliged to spend most of the half-hour flattering him into a better humour, with the result that their steps were less than polished. She was all the more astonished when Lord Rothwell solicited her hand for the cotillion.

'Are you sure? The cotillion is the supper dance, you know.'

His mouth twitched at her frankness.

'Precisely. I am paying you back in your own coin. Making use of you, as you used me the other day.'

Caroline felt an unpleasant stab of conscience. 'My lord?'

'Better I take *you* into supper than any of the other insipid females I see lined up waiting to toad-eat me.'

She should have known his manners had not taken such a nice turn without an ulterior motive and she supposed she had deserved his unflattering elucidation. Still, she liked to dance and it was an undoubted pleasure to do so with a partner as accomplished as Lord Rothwell. When he steered her towards Harry and Louisa at the supper tables, however, Caroline determined that the favour was now used up. He would not fix his interest *there* if she could help it. She quizzed him throughout the repast on the luminaries who commonly graced the town during the racing weeks. As she had expected, he was both knowledgeable and sarcastic about his fellows. What was more to the point was that although Caroline herself found his comments amusing, Louisa — who had little interest in the London *ton* — came to the conclusion that Lord Alexander Rothwell was rather a dull dog long before the end of the meal.

* * *

Caroline shot a rapid glance at the White Hart next morning as she and Solange trotted back in the early dawn, but all the windows were close-curtained and no Lord Rothwell gazed out at her. Still abed with any luck. Fatigued beyond measure after being polite to the Bury St Edmunds luminaries for a whole evening. 'So why did he come?' she asked Solange, perplexed. 'For that matter, why is he still in Suffolk when everything about him says London? His clothes, his manner, his friends ... ' She grimaced, thinking of Mr d'Arblay's rather cold-blooded charm, and felt Solange pick up her mood. She made haste to reassure her. 'Apart from you, darling, you're just beautiful. I don't believe he's here simply to see you win a race, even so.'

A dog barked in the yard of the Star, causing the horse to shy across the cobbles. 'Silly girl,' chided Caroline. 'And you five times its size.'

Solange whinnied as if to say size had nothing to do with it.

In the stall, Caroline put Lord Rothwell out of her mind as she spent a while rubbing the mare down. One of Bertrand's tenets had been that the bond between rider and horse was the strongest there is. This had been Solange's first time out of Penfold Lodge; Caroline had to reassure her that she'd been fast and strong and clever and had done spectacularly well. Oh, to have time to linger for as long as she wished with her. But it couldn't be done. One last pat and then, with a look at the lightening sky, she swung herself into Fancy's saddle.

★   ★   ★

There. Alex had been almost sure it was Fortune's mystery rider he'd seen going up to the heath on the bay colt as he opened his curtain. After a frustrating couple of days finding excuses to visit other training yards and seeing neither hide nor hair of him, Alex had hastily made ready after that glimpse — and had been rewarded by the sight of the lad trotting the horse back to Penfold Lodge.

At last. He pulled his cap low and edged along the street behind the colt, his outline disguised by the bulk of the oldest coat in his wardrobe. He'd wait on the corner opposite the stables, then follow the lad to see where he went next. With any luck, he'd soon be free of his obligation to Sally Jersey and could go back to London and civilization.

An excellent plan, but infuriatingly thwarted.

As the archway remained empty, Alex concluded this must be the one day the wretched
boy worked at Penfold Lodge all morning. He
cursed long and hard. He couldn't wait here
any longer, the town was livening up and he'd
already attracted one or two curious glances.
Nor could he stroll into the stables legiti-
mately as Solange's owner, not when he had
such odd clothes on. He'd go back to the
White Hart, change, then return.

Which he did. And found only a yard full
of stable-hands, eating porridge out of a
common tureen and politely astonished that
one of the gentry should be abroad so early.
He thought the whole street could probably
hear his teeth grinding as he strode back.

★　★　★

'I don't know what you were worried about.
Life here is just one dissipation after another,'
said Giles, pouring himself a second cup of
coffee.

Alex threw him a fulminating look. Despite
a robust breakfast, he was still in a thoroughly
bad temper. 'Do elucidate,' he said.

'You cannot possibly have forgotten that we
are invited to Mrs Fortune's At Home today?'

'Giles, we are not! We cannot be. I was
assiduous in not attracting one of that

74

damned woman's invitations!'

'Dear, dear. You should have warned me. Knowing time was likely to be hanging on our hands, I accepted for both of us.'

'Accepted? For poor company and bad wine? Are you mad? Whatever possessed you?'

'She has a deuced pretty daughter.'

'Now I know you are all about in your head. That was last season. And however pleasing a young woman is to the eye, if she has an encroaching mother, it is as much as one's life is worth to pursue the acquaintance.'

'Hence your monopoly of the goldsmith's chit at the Assembly Rooms, I suppose? No vulgar mama to bring you up to scratch.'

'I would hardly describe it as a monopoly. You stood up with her yourself when they called the extra dance at the end.'

'But I had to bribe the fiddle player to stay on for another half-hour — you simply lordshipped your way into displacing some poor yokel for the privilege.'

'And was well-served by being wearied to death. A beauty she may be, but Miss Taylor has precious little conversation.'

'Lord, Alex, there's no rule says you have to *listen* to 'em.'

Which was presumably why his friend had

not realized Louisa Taylor was infatuated with Harry Fortune. Alex decided against enlightening him. A fruitless pursuit might at least stop Giles plaguing *him* out of his life while he was forced to reside in Newmarket.

It gave him a morbid satisfaction when Mrs Fortune's At Home proved exactly as he had prophesied. The room itself was not quite in the newest fashion, overly gilded, and chilly to boot. Giles, naturally, charmed his way into the circle of ladies by the fire. Alex, after nodding glacially and giving his hostess no encouragement when she presented him to Caroline's empty-headed younger sister — who wasn't even out for goodness sake! — decided with no enthusiasm whatsoever that his duty lay in the direction of Fortune Senior and his cronies. The man was a gentleman trainer, after all. Alex would never have a better opportunity to get into conversation with him. And then to steer that conversation towards the race course.

★   ★   ★

Hoping her hospitality to Papa's colleagues' daughters would prevent Mama from finding yet another elderly widower for her to make herself agreeable to, Caroline watched Lord Rothwell out of the corner of her eye as she kept up a flow of inconsequential chatter. He was doing it again! Why did he come to these gatherings, only to be bored? That he was bored she knew full well, even though he was listening to her father with every appearance of interest. He had a tiny little trick of twitching his shoulders inside his coat as if he were longing to be off, but was constrained by politeness to stay. It was a puzzle.

Nothing Caroline had seen of Lord Alexander Rothwell before the assembly inclined her to the belief that he put manners before his own comfort. And yet it was a full forty minutes before he eased himself away. By that time, Caroline had been twice round the circle of young ladies and chaperons, had detached her agreeably flustered sister Selina from Giles d'Arblay and had managed, under the guise of offering him tea and cake, to fit in a very informative chat with the manager of the bank where the racing account resided. Now she crossed to Lord Rothwell as he sought to make his escape. It was ill done in her, no doubt, but he piqued her curiosity considerably.

'Would you care for tea, my lord? Or coffee? I can fetch it over so you do not need to run the gamut of the tray.'

'No,' he said, with more force than politeness. 'I can think of nothing I would like less than tea at this moment.'

Goodness, he really had been bored. How intriguing. 'I am sure that's not true,' said Caroline.

'I do not wish for tea,' he repeated through set lips.

'That I comprehended. I only meant there must be many things you would like less than tea. Worms, for instance. I used to have *such* a penchant for worms when I was younger, but whenever I was summoned to Mama's sitting room and brought a handful to show her and her guests, they were not at all appreciative. Eventually she stopped sending for me. Honoria was far more tractable.'

The corner of his mouth relaxed. 'Miss Caro, you are a hoyden.'

The pit of her stomach did a tumbler's flip. 'Did I give you permission to address me thus?' she asked, feeling her face heat.

Horror flashed across his face as he realized his unguarded familiarity. 'I beg your pardon. I cannot imagine how I came to . . . I fear I must have been conversing too freely with your brother.'

Caroline pushed down the unwelcome flutterings in her breast. 'It is of no import. As a penance, if you are determined to go, may I request you take your friend with you? His conversation is a little too polished for us country-reared girls.'

A tiny frown. 'You do not like Giles?'

'I am sure he is all the crack. It is simply that we are, on the whole, not used to London manners.'

Her companion glanced across at the very moment Selina raised her eyes to Mr d'Arblay's laughing profile. Her heightened colour filled in what Caroline had left unsaid. 'It seems I must apologize again,' he said. He crossed the room and within a very few minutes he and his friend had left.

'My dear,' said her mother in a voice full of meaning, 'here is Mr Anstruther wanting tea. Would you fetch him a cup and keep him company a while?'

Caroline turned. Mr Anstruther was florid, barely literate and fifty-five if he was a day. 'Certainly,' she said, and when they were settled on the bench, confided, 'I am reading Mr Pope's *The Dunciad* at the moment. Now do give me your opinion of the verses. I long for a nice deep discussion about them . . . '

★   ★   ★

'A most amusing afternoon. Did you learn anything?' asked Giles as they strolled away from Fortune House in the direction of the High Street. He tipped his hat to a comely nursemaid shepherding a line of children. The nursemaid blushed and giggled.

Alex was still smarting from Caroline Fortune's reproof. 'I learnt that you are not safe outside the confines of your own circle.'

Giles smoothed down the sleeves of his coat. 'Nonsense. I tell every lady I meet that my home is a ruined castle with insufficient income to make it habitable. If they still insist on throwing themselves at me, it is their own lookout.'

'The average very young lady imagines ruined castles are romantic, and that all you need to live on is love. It is unkind of you to trifle with their emotions, Giles.'

'Ho! I don't notice you worrying overmuch about breaking would-be amours' hearts when you dish out your famous setdowns.'

'*Their* affections are brought on by a perusal of Debrett's Peerage: I do not believe I have ever raised a lady's expectations myself.'

'Then how do you claim to know so much about their sensibilities?'

Alex halted incredulously. 'Good God, Giles, is it possible you have forgotten my sister's appalling escapade last autumn?'

Giles looked back, puzzled. Then his face cleared. 'Oh, that. But it came off all right. Lizzy's safely married to Marshall and t'other fellow vanished from society overnight.'

'And scandal only averted due to Sally Jersey happening on Lizzy in the George at Stamford and claiming she was with her the whole time!' He resumed his progress towards the White Hart. 'Which is why I am kicking my heels here. Do you suppose if I penned her a description of a race-meeting, she would give up expecting me to pinpoint anything shady? Quite apart from the crowds and the jostle around the betting posts, it is rank impossible to keep tabs on which rider is talking to which ruffian.'

'Exactly what I have been saying! And you're missing all the fun by doing so. Easier by far to reckon up who's collecting winnings next day.'

Alex eyed his friend's ingenuous expression. 'Which would be Harry Fortune, I take it?' he said drily.

'Did I say so?'

'As it happens, I *could* bear to know more about one of his riders and where else he works. I thought I had him this morning but he gave me the slip.'

'Is that why you were so ill-tempered at breakfast? I thought it was the dreadful supper last night. Nothing simpler. Get one of the grooms to tail him.'

'As I said before, I have no wish for anyone

else to know our business. One loose word in the wrong ears and it will all be for naught.'

Giles shrugged. 'Your obligation, your decision. I prefer to make life easy.'

'This *is* easy. I shall simply get to Penfold Lodge earlier still tomorrow. See which direction he arrives from and work backwards from there if I lose him again.'

Giles looked frankly astonished. 'Good Lord, Alex, I had no notion that life with a conscience entailed such sacrifices. I shall think of you on your vigil whilst I am cosily tucked up in bed.'

★ ★ ★

Friday. Caroline came awake in the near-darkness and listened to the patter of rain on her window. She had to shin very carefully indeed down the wet ivy, and then skirt around the paddocks so as not to leave betraying tracks in the grass. It was as well she was being circumspect. As she approached the back of the Penfold Lodge stable-block, her eyes took in an out-of-place shadow. There seemed to be something mounded against the wall. How peculiar. What could it be? As she crept forward warily, the mound stirred, making her heart race with alarm. The shadow took on form and shape: it was a man, slumped and doubled over, his clothes when she touched him gingerly soaked completely through with rain. It must be one of the hands, she supposed, passed out with too much liquor. Flood would have something to say about that! Yet, still she hesitated. Something was not quite right. The sodden jacket had felt as if it was made from superfine, not working-man's cloth. And though Caroline was in no doubt that Harry had had his share of sleeping off excessive libations in ditches and other out-of-the-way places, there was enough definition in the shadows to see that this man had straight, dark hair, not close-curled red.

Then who was he? Caroline crouched and took a firmer grip to lift him clear of the rough stone wall. As she twisted him to peer at his face, her fingers met a thick stickiness. Blood! She recoiled instinctively. The man groaned. Caroline dropped him in panic and ran for Flood. She heard his head meet the cobbles as she skidded across the slippery yard.

Flood's opinion when told of the injured man in a barely coherent stammer was that if the fellow didn't have concussion before, he certainly would have now and all to the good if so. 'If he's not one of ours, it'll serve to keep him quiet until we get him to the roadside,' he said. 'Rogues falling out, I don't doubt — and we don't want that sort found on our land.'

Caroline heartily concurred. She grasped the shoulders of the man's jacket ready to drag him towards the archway. The sudden motion, however, caused him to heave; she only just managed to turn his head away from her clothing before he cast up his accounts. 'Devil take me for a lummox,' he slurred. Caroline gave a small cry, her heart careering wildly, and dropped him again.

'That's it,' approved Flood as the unfortunate chap's head once more found the cobbles. 'Keep the skulking varmint under.'

'He isn't a skulking varmint,' hissed Caroline in alarm, all her nerves jumping from this new discovery. 'It is Lord Rothwell! I recognized his voice. We cannot leave *him* in the gutter.' No wonder the cloth of his jacket had been so fine. But what was he doing here?

Flood whistled, his face troubled in the shadows. 'Happen you're right, lass. Robbery, I suppose. Best put him in an empty stall. I'll go for the doctor and you just keep tapping his head against the ground until I get back.'

'Flood!'

But the felled man was heaving again and it was as much as they could do to haul him inside once he had finished. The effort certainly exhausted his lordship. He lay sprawled and comatose on the ground, only the rasp of his breath indicating that he still lived.

'I suppose it is at least dry in here,' muttered Caroline worriedly as Flood left. She gnawed her lip and sank to the floor of the stable to wait. She was horribly nervous, her pulse rate far higher than normal, but the familiar, musky scent in here comforted her as it had done her whole life. Flood had doused the lamp and she heard the horses moving in the darkness. She settled a little, wishing with all her heart that she was on one of them, riding towards the heath rather than waiting here next to an unconscious, badly injured gentleman.

Whatever had Lord Rothwell been doing in their yard? That he had been assaulted — presumably for gain — seemed clear, but why would a common assailant have been here in the first place? Or had he followed his victim and dragged him up from the road after coshing him? What would be the point? It was nonsensical. Caroline's brain, usually sharp and analytical, was in danger of overheating with so many questions. Lord Rothwell stirred, his head shifting restlessly on the hard-packed ground.

Instantly the timbre of Caroline's fears

took on a new direction. Dirt in the wound could be fatal. She knew that from Bertrand. Where was Flood? Why weren't any of the stable-hands awake yet? Taking a deep breath, she inched sideways and eased Lord Rothwell's head into her lap, the better to steady it. His skin was clammy and his clothes were wet through. She ought to at least ease his soaking shirt away from his skin and slide her own muffler around his neck and down next to his chest if she could. As she essayed this tricky task, she wondered anew why he had not been wearing a greatcoat against the rain. Had he perhaps run mad? He had seemed sane enough the previous day. She could just make out an ugly area of deeper shadow on his temple. If she had only thought for two seconds, she could have sent Flood for water first so she could clean the gash. Except, of course, she wouldn't have been able to see.

Then Lord Rothwell spoke, and Caroline — remembering with a start that she was dressed in male clothing — was glad it was dark. 'Nanny?' he said querulously.

'Hush,' said Caroline. 'Hush and wait for the doctor.'

'It was no one's fault,' he said. 'The bridge just broke. It was no one's fault.'

Caroline's heart skittered harder than ever. Dear heaven, he was reverting to childhood!

86

What ever damage had she done dropping him so many times? 'Yes, it was an accident,' she said hastily. 'Do lie still, my lord.'

She saw his eyes fly open in alarm. 'My lord? Is Papa here?'

'No, no, he's gone,' she said, even more hastily. 'Lie still, Alexander. Go to sleep. Wait for the doctor.'

'Nice Nanny,' he said, and pushed himself further against her belly and her thigh.

A strange sensation surged through Caroline's body. She could hear her heart pounding and had to force herself to breathe deeply and calmly. 'Nice Alexander,' she replied.

Incongruously, he giggled. 'You always say that.' Then he sighed and she knew he'd fallen asleep.

Caroline continued to take long breaths. How had she known what to say? Had she pulled the right response from his thoughts, the same way she often knew what was troubling a horse? She stifled a near-hysterical laugh, thinking Lord Rothwell in his right mind would be highly offended at being compared to a horse. And then she wondered at herself again. Because tucking her scarf around his neck and cradling him like this in the darkness, it was already quite difficult to think of him as Lord Rothwell. He was Alexander who had loved his nurse and who'd got into childhood scrapes and who had never let anyone else take the blame. An honourable child.

'Nanny?' he murmured again. His arm wrapped around her leg.

She stroked his hair. There was grit in it where he'd fallen. She finger-combed it, teasing out the dirt. 'I'm here, Alexander. Go to sleep now. You're safe.'

★ ★ ★

Alex drifted in and out of a hellish, pain-filled limbo. The bridge across the Long Meadow lode. They'd been told not to use it. They knew it was unsafe. But Giles had dared him, laughing, running across and back himself over the swollen water to prove there was no danger. It was simply the adults making their usual fuss about nothing. Alex had always envied Giles his quicksilver lightness and his grace. Taller and heavier, he could hear the pounding of his boots on the wooden planks as he used brute force to try and match his friend's speed. And heard the crack of wood splintering. And felt the blow as his temple caught the rail. He knew again the icy shock of water surging inside his collar and up his sleeves. He panicked at the weight of his sodden clothes as he tried to struggle free.

'Hush,' said a soft voice. 'Stop fretting. You're safe. Rest now.'

Nanny, thought Alex, fastening on to this one detail. Lovely, comfortable Nanny. His neck was warm where he rested on her. He pulled her hand under his cheek and went to sleep.

5

By the time the doctor arrived, everybody was up and the sky was getting light. Caroline's lap was numb and soaked through with the damp from Lord Rothwell's clothes. She was anxious about him waking and seeing her like this, even more anxious about him *not* waking, and could most definitely have done without a recital of all the nasty head wounds the stable-hands had ever encountered. They were worse than a parcel of chaperons for looking on the black side.

Dr Peck had known her all her life. He evinced no surprise on seeing her at this hour, in this place, dressed as a lad, with a sopping wet, unconscious man's head in her lap. He nodded to Harry then examined Lord Rothwell. 'Dear me. Considerable loss of blood and several abrasions to the skull. Nasty. Going to take very careful nursing.'

Caroline's stomach turned over, thinking how many of those bumps on the head had been due to her. Oh, please let him pull through this. Don't let her have him on her conscience. 'Will we need a cart to get him to the White Hart, then?' she asked.

'The White Hart?' said the doctor, looking up from his patient in surprise. 'No, no. With care and a length of canvas and four of your stoutest grooms we should be able to get him indoors without further damage, but any greater distance I won't answer for.'

Caroline hoped, she really hoped, that she did not turn as pale as she felt at these words. They would have to look after him here? *She* would have to look after him here? But what if he never recovered? She eased Alexander's head onto one of the men's coats and stood up, wincing at her cramped muscles. She rubbed her forehead, thinking aloud. 'I must get out of these clothes. Give me ten minutes start, Harry, and then send word to Fortune House for me to help Mrs Penfold urgently with the nursing.' She looked at the men. 'You'll need the canvas horse sling. Ask one of the maids for a clean sheet to put on it, and request the back parlour to be made ready for an injured nobleman. You can carry Lord Rothwell into there through the long windows from the terrace.'

★ ★ ★

Scroope, the butler, was so put out by a message from Mrs Penfold requesting Caroline's presence on an indefinite errand of mercy before he'd even got his coat on, that he failed to put up any of the objections he would have fabricated given enough time. Caroline seized the moment and was gone without delay, leaving instructions for her clothes to be packed and sent on.

Dr Peck and the grooms had only just started across the Penfold Lodge lawn, transporting their sling with exaggerated care. He rolled his eyes at her. 'Sort out those fools inside, will you?'

Caroline flew indoors with the result that in a very short space of time a bed had been brought down from upstairs, a maid was making it up, there was a clear path to it from the terrace door, and the rest of the furniture was standing in a surprised manner around the walls.

'Capital,' grunted the doctor. 'Easy, now. Miss Caro, would you . . . ?'

But Caroline was already there, cradling Lord Rothwell's unquiet head as the four sweating grooms suspended the sling over the mattress. Harry positioned himself at his lordship's feet.

'Away,' said the doctor. The sling was gently removed and the three of them lowered the injured man to the bed. They took a collective breath. 'And now,' said the doctor, 'hot water, towels and a clean nightshirt and perhaps I can get to work on him.'

★ ★ ★

This time when Alex awoke, he still felt fuzzy, woolly-headed and ill, but a great deal more comfortable. The room was shaded. He tried to turn his head, but was instantly nauseous. 'What . . . ?'

A firm, cool hand on his brow stopped him moving. 'You are at Penfold Lodge,' said a voice. 'You were found outside the stables and my brother had you brought indoors. The doctor says you are to remain as still as possible, *not* get agitated and only to drink barley water.'

'The devil he does,' muttered Alex weakly.

'He also says you are far from out of the wood and if we do not have you in a delirious fever by nightfall then he does not know his own calling.'

'You . . . ' He swallowed painfully. 'You are a very singular nurse.'

'It has always served Harry to know the truth. And if you *do* become fevered, you won't remember I told you, so it won't matter either way.'

This was too difficult to work out. 'I should like a drink, if you please.'

'Very well, but you are not to move. Open your lips and take this straw. Now sip very gently or you will . . . there, what did I tell you?'

A cloth dabbed the liquid away from where he had spluttered it out as he'd coughed. The incautious movement made his head feel as if it was on fire.

'Once your body has learnt what it can and cannot do, you will prosper much better. Now sip a *little*, and run it around your mouth before you swallow.'

Alex subsided, unutterably weak, unable to summon the strength to do anything but obey. It went against the grain to admit her method worked. He felt his grasp on reality slipping. One of these days, Miss Caroline would learn a good deal about her shortcomings as a bossy, managing female, but until then . . . He slept.

★ ★ ★

It was well into the afternoon before Mr d'Arblay, marvellously spruce and scented, arrived to enquire about his friend. Caroline lay down her book as he was announced. At last! She had sent a message to the White Hart hours ago!

'By God, what a fearsome bandage,' he

94

said, glancing at the occupant of the bed. 'I'll lay you odds it doesn't stay on above a day. Alex has never been one for sick-rooms, not even when we were boys. He'll want to be up and about as soon as may be.'

Caroline was still far from sanguine about Lord Rothwell's recovery. She regarded the visitor's airy confidence with extreme disfavour. 'Then according to the doctor, he will do himself a great deal of damage,' she said repressively.

'I don't fancy being the one to tell him,' said Giles, laughing. He eyed the drawing-room furniture with amusement. 'You have been much put out. I am sure my friend will be appropriately grateful. This is a fine terrace you have here.' He turned the handle of the long glass door.

'Mr d'Arblay! Pray do not let the cold air in.'

'No need to worry about that. Alex doesn't hold with a fusty atmosphere.'

Caroline's lips thinned. One could get remarkably tired of Mr d'Arblay remarkably quickly. 'I shall take care to remember,' she said. 'For the moment, however, Lord Rothwell is sleeping and so does not have a say in the matter. Shall I send word to you at the White Hart when there is a change? I daresay as soon as he is conscious he will be glad of your company.'

'Champing at the bit to be off, more like.' Giles cast another glance at the window. 'Aye, do that. Is Fortune at the stables? I'll have a word with him about — '

'My brother has gone to lodge information regarding the attack. He is anxious to discover how such an assault came to take place on his property.'

There was an infinitesimal moment of silence. 'Of course. An anxious time for us all. Although, of course, there are ruffians everywhere you turn in this town. One of the hazards of Newmarket, don't you think? No matter, I expect I'll run across Fortune at Crockford's later. Well now, you won't want to leave your patient, so I'll see myself out.'

'I would not dream of any such thing,' said Caroline, ringing for the butler with a good deal of suppressed violence. One of the hazards of Newmarket indeed. Who did this cocksure dandy think he was? 'Hibbert will show you out. We are not in quite such disarray as to ignore the common courtesies of life.'

Giles d'Arblay made a smiling bow and left.

Caroline regarded the closing door with narrowed eyes. 'A strange friend you have, my lord,' she said to the sleeping man, 'to put his own comfort and his curiosity about this house before you and your condition. I would at least have expected a question on what you were doing here so early in the morning, even if his belief in your resilience precludes an enquiry of the doctor's prognosis.'

Which proved in the event to be accurate. As the shadows lengthened, Lord Rothwell did indeed become feverish. Caroline mopped his face, set her jaw and changed his sweat-soaked bandage, and then persuaded him to take some of the cooling draught Dr Peck had prescribed. He tossed from side to side, talking in restless mutters and saying repeatedly that he had to overtake Lizzy.

'Where is she?' he cried out, suddenly sitting bolt upright and seizing Caroline's wrist. 'I must get her back or there will be a scandal!' He was clammy with perspiration, staring straight ahead with unseeing eyes, and astoundingly strong for one so ill.

Caroline felt her heart thump and her own brow grow damp with perspiration. Where was the nurse Dr Peck had promised? She would have called for a footman except for not knowing what effect a shout at such close quarters would have on Alexander's mental state. While she hesitated, he put up his other hand to tear off the bandage. 'I must find her before nightfall. It is all my fault. I should not have left the house. I should not have believed her when she said she had the headache. Let me go! Why do you keep me here?'

'She is safe,' said Caroline in desperation, hauling down on his arm and not having the smallest idea who he was talking about. 'She is at home. You will see her for yourself tomorrow.'

'Tomorrow will be too late! She will be at Gretna!'

He started to struggle again and Caroline bore down on him with her body. It took all the strength built up from a lifetime of horse-riding to prevent him from rising. Why had she not insisted on someone else standing watch with her? 'Lizzy is safe, my lord,' she panted. 'Now do lie down.'

'Was I in time, then?' he said in a puzzled voice. 'Did I find her?'

'Yes, yes, you were in time. Lie down, Alexander.'

He fell back all at once, taking her tumbling with him. Heat came off his body in waves. 'Rosetta?' he murmured.

Caroline would have agreed to being the old queen herself, so concerned was she at his behaviour and his burning temperature. 'That's right,' she said and pushed herself upright.

Or tried to. All of a sudden, she was very glad indeed that there was no one else in the room. One of Alexander's arms had come round her and the other was at the neckline of her bodice. 'Too many ribbons,' he said drowsily. 'Such a tease, always. I am glad you are back.'

Caroline's heart leapt into her mouth. 'Shh, Alexander, you are not well.'

'Well enough for this,' he slurred.

For a sick man, his hand was appallingly determined. Caroline swallowed down her panic. 'Lie still while I get you a drink,' she said. 'You need to recruit your strength.'

He gave the wickedest chuckle she had ever heard in her life. It sent a quivering stab right into her belly. 'You are all the elixir I need,' he said and pulled her mouth to meet his.

Caroline went completely rigid. No one had ever kissed her like this. Alexander's lips were hot and dry and papery, but still they covered hers with a seigneurial urgency. Her mouth opened in protest, and instantly his tongue was inside, trying to twine with hers. It happened so fast that Caroline was barely aware of a tingling rush in her body and of not knowing how to respond before he was releasing her, rolling suddenly boneless against his pillows.

'Thirsty,' he muttered. 'I'm thirsty, Nanny.'

Oh, thank goodness. Caroline scrambled off the bed faster than the last Craven Stakes' winner had passed the post. Alexander drank most of the barley water she held for him before falling into a shallow doze.

Behind her, the door opened. Mrs Penfold came in, followed by a footman with a tray of tea. Normality and an overwhelming sense of the everyday flooded the room. 'I daresay you'll be glad of this,' said Mrs Penfold, directing the footman to light the candles.

'Oh wonderful,' said Caroline, falling on the refreshment with real gratitude. With light, bread and butter and Mrs Penfold's presence, the alarming episode with Alexander retreated to a manageable distance. 'I would have called a maid and joined you but I did not like to leave him.' She lowered her voice, eyeing the footman. 'He has been a little indiscreet in his delirium.'

'Ah.' Even knowing her all her life, Caroline was never quite sure what was going on behind Mrs Penfold's placid façade. 'Men will be men, of course.'

'No . . . ' Caroline felt her cheeks scorch, but made herself sound calm. 'He is anxious about some sort of scandal.'

'Then we will wait dinner until Dr Peck's nurse arrives,' said Mrs Penfold. 'Nurses are trained to be circumspect.'

It was just as well. The fever increased its hold overnight. Alexander babbled about

'Lizzy' again and not being able to find his way to her, along with the breaking bridge and other youthful mishaps magnified out of all proportion.

'The poor gentleman,' said the nurse, a stout, practical lady of middle years. 'It always takes the wiry, nervous ones the worst. He'll be the silent type normally, will he?'

Caroline hadn't noticed Lord Rothwell as being particularly uncommunicative, but there was no sense in alienating the nurse by telling her so.

'Ridiculous,' said Alexander, clearly. The nurse turned, ready to be affronted, but he was tossing from side to side again. 'A mare's nest,' he continued. 'Nothing wrong here.'

It could be worse, thought Caroline, trying to prevent him flinging himself off the bed. He could have been talking to Rosetta again.

'Jersey's horse,' he muttered. 'Fortune making too much. That boy. That rider. Never there. Never anywhere. Find out.'

Shock slammed into Caroline's belly, ice cold and indigestible. Was that why he had been in the yard? He was *spying* on them?

⋆   ⋆   ⋆

Alex opened his eyes languidly, aware of a haze of headache consonant with a convivial

101

night. Light was just touching the room. His eyes focused on an unfamiliar cornice. 'Where the devil am I?' he said, baffled. He winced as he turned his head — it must have been a *really* convivial night, which made it rather disturbing that he couldn't remember any of it — and was arrested by the sight of a young woman, fully dressed, thank the Lord, curled up in a wing chair next to his bed. Except that this wasn't his bed and he had never seen this room in his life before. What the devil was going on?

The girl stirred. Her brown hair had come loose from its knot and lay in an untidy curtain across her face. She pushed it back as she straightened up, opening sleep-filled, honey-brown eyes.

'You're awake.' Her voice was wary, yet familiar.

Ah, that was it. He was still dreaming. That's why none of this made sense. 'I don't think I can be,' he said with relief. 'Because if I was, I would know how I came to be here. And I don't.'

She let out a long breath. 'And rational. You have no idea how thankful I am.'

In a floating, dreamy daze, Alex continued to regard her, waiting for his brain to supply her name. 'Caro,' he said at last. 'Miss Caroline Fortune.'

'Correct. Do you know who *you* are?'

He closed his eyes, pleased with himself. 'Don't be ridiculous. Of course I do.'

* ★ ★ ★

Caroline was still looking at Alexander when the nurse came back with more barley water. 'He spoke,' she said to the older woman. 'He knew my name.'

'Well, that's a blessing. He might not remember what happened, mind. They often don't when they've had a bang on the head like that.' She laid a professional hand against his uninjured temple. 'He'll sleep for a couple of hours now. You could do with a lie-down too, miss, if you don't mind my saying so. You've been up three days straight with him. And him no relation.'

'He is important to my brother's future as a trainer.'

The nurse nodded, inured to the necessities of life. 'Then I hope for your sake he's the sort to remember a favour. Run along now, then you'll be fresh later.'

But Caroline had cat-napped sufficiently and in any case had her own method of renewing her strength. She took a bowl of porridge, thick with cream and honey, out to the stables, sitting on a hay bale to eat it whilst Flood groomed Solange.

'That's all to the good,' he said, when she told him Lord Rothwell was mending at last. 'The sooner we get milord home and out of our way, the better I'll be pleased.'

'And I,' said Caroline. She hastily pushed aside the memory of that kiss. Even three days old and with him plainly not aware what he was doing at the time, it had the power to unnerve her if she thought too long about it. 'From something he said at the beginning of his fever, I believe he may have been spying on us.'

'Spying? Nay, Miss Caro, what is there to spy on? You're not mixing him up with that varmint groom of his?'

'No, this was something about Harry making too much money. He wasn't comprehensible for the most part.' And she had been so shocked — so outraged — especially after what had gone before, that some of his words had passed her by.

'Jealous, belike, at your touch with the wagers. More pressing is the problem we've still got with this lass.'

Caroline's attention sharpened. 'With Solange? What sort of problem?'

'Has Mr Harry not told you?'

'I've barely seen him. I've been too busy nursing Lord Rothwell.'

'Ah. Well, she won't go out with any of the men. She'll let 'em groom her and lead her to the paddocks and walk her round and saddle her up. But as soon as even the lightest tries to swing a leg across her back, she's off like a banshee.'

Caroline spooned up the last mouthful of porridge and then moved over to lean her forehead into Solange's neck. 'Silly girl,' she said. 'But now your master's fever has broken, I'll start taking you out again. Get you used to some weight on your saddle.' She made her way slowly around each of the horses in the stable, petting and murmuring to each one. 'Oh, I have missed this,' she said to Flood.

'Aye. They've missed you too. Back to normal now, though.'

'It'll be awkward until Lord Rothwell is fit to go home.' She frowned. 'And we still don't yet know who attacked him or why. There's not been any word from the magistrates? Harry hasn't said anything? You've not seen anyone hanging about?'

'There soon wouldn't have been, if I had!'

'Be as well to keep an eye out, all the same.'

'Be sure of that! I've told all the lads.' He rubbed his mouth. 'We did have that fine friend of milord's here on Friday. After Mr Harry he was.'

'Friday? But I told him Harry wasn't here.'

'Aye, we told him too. We told him again on Saturday.'

'There is nothing here to see,' said Caroline in bewilderment. Oh, this made no sense. What could he be after? What could either of them be after?

'I did think,' said Flood, apparently at random, 'that I'd take Rufus and the young 'un up to the heath myself for their races today.'

Caroline was jolted anew. Was it Monday already? Then this was the First Spring Meeting week. She'd lost track. She hoped Harry had worked out some sensible bets. Flood was looking at her sideways, waiting for her reaction. She made herself focus. Racing. The grooms' enclosure. Gossip. 'That is a very sound idea,' she said. 'Fancy will be much steadier in those crowds with you to reassure him.' She grinned, feeling much more herself all of a sudden. 'And it's always nice to keep abreast of the news around the course.'

★　★　★

Alex came awake to the sound of voices. One of them, for some reason, seemed to belong to Caroline Fortune. How peculiar. It was too

106

much of an effort to open his eyes so he rested where he was, sorting through the words until they made sense.

'A week?' he heard her say in dismay. 'A week or more before he can be moved? But I told you he spoke to me and knew me. And his skin is a better colour, for all he is haggard from the fever.'

A man's voice now. 'Aye, but his brain has been bounced about in that skull of his and needs to stay still for fear other damage may have been done. You'd not have him half-witted for want of the proper care, Miss Caro?'

There was a pause. 'I suppose not,' said the girl ungraciously. 'What is this proper care, then? What must I do?'

'Why, keep him quiet, tempt him to eat, make sure he drinks plenty of the lemon barley. Encourage him to sleep as much as possible and do not let him become agitated in any respect. That is most important.'

'He has *been* agitated! What was all that delirium if not agitation?'

Delirium? What delirium?

Through the sudden hammering in his chest, Alex heard the man — who must, he supposed, be a doctor — suck in a breath between his teeth. 'We can only hope the fever-dreams have not done him any lasting harm. I will look in again tonight.'

Alex put up a leaden hand and felt his head. To his astonishment, there was a bandage around it. And if Caroline Fortune was here, he must either be at Fortune House or Penfold Lodge. Stranger and stranger. What had the doctor said? Fever and delirium? Yes, now he thought back, memories of nightmarish, formless dreams crowded his mind. He shuddered and forced them away. He knew them of old and had no wish to revisit them. More to the point — had he talked in his fever? What had he said? To whom? That was almost more worrying than why he was here in the first place. It occurred to him that the room was quiet again. He opened his eyes, straight onto the sight of Caroline glaring at him from a wing chair.

'Ouch,' he said.

'Good morning, my lord.' The fierce look was gone so fast it must have been a trick of the light.

He moved and made an unpleasant discovery. 'I hurt. What am I doing here?'

'You were found sprawled in our stable yard with your head bleeding. It seemed likely that you would recover faster indoors than if you were left outside in the wet.'

Later he would appreciate the sarcasm. For now, he looked at her in blank incredulity.

'Someone attacked me?'

'That is the conclusion the doctor drew. Your greatcoat had been pulled off and thrown aside. We found your notecase on the ground near the road and have restored it to your jacket.' She nodded to a covered rail in the corner of the room. 'I am afraid there was no money in it.'

Memory flooded back. He had let down his guard. Of all the stupid things to do! He had been triumphant that he had at last got to the stable before anyone inside was stirring. This time, he'd thought, he would finally get a good look at that damned mystery rider. And then . . . 'I don't remember anything,' he said.

This drew a slanting look from her. 'Not even why you should be at Penfold Lodge before dawn in the pouring rain?'

'I went for a walk. I was unable to sleep,' he invented. He put a hand to his chin and grimaced. 'Something I seem to have remedied since. Good God, I must look like a bear.' Had he distracted her? It was difficult to tell. Certainly he couldn't think straight enough to answer any more of her questions right now.

'What odd things men worry about,' she commented. 'Your valet is just the same. He descended on us in a welter of valises and finicky mannerisms as soon as I informed the White Hart of your accident and has been itching to shave you these three days. Such a fuss as he has been making. I wonder you can bear to have him in your employment.'

'My valet is here? Then call him at once!' said Alex. Hot towels and a keen razor and he would be himself again in no time. 'Three days? I cannot believe it.'

Caroline Fortune rose. 'You were found on Friday morning. It is now Monday. My arithmetic is generally sound. Are you in earnest about being shaved? It seems nonsensical to me. You should know that you have been very ill indeed. As well as the loss of blood, you were soaked right through with rain. Mr d'Arblay dismissed the suggestion, but I have been wondering since the fever started if we should not have informed your family?'

'On no account!' he said forcefully. Or at least, he meant to say it forcefully. It came out sounding more horrified than anything else. He tried to laugh it off. 'Just for a bump on the head and a bit of a chill? My mother would take up residence with ten sorts of servant and an army of apothecaries before the sand had dried your ink.'

She met his eyes, her own stricken. He was jolted. What the devil had he said to upset her? Women really were unaccountable. 'That tells me I *should* have sent a letter,' she said in distress. 'Your poor mama. I will do it directly.'

'You will do no such thing. Believe me, the house would not be your own.'

'It is *not* my own house. And Mrs Penfold is the very last person to begrudge a mother's right to care for her son.'

Heaven preserve him from stubborn women. He made another stab at a forceful tone. 'Miss Fortune, my bones may be temporarily made of water and my head may ache like the devil, but I am twenty-nine years old and I do *not* require coddling and fussing over and wrapping in cotton wool. I will write myself when I am recovered.' Which would be as long as he could credibly string it out. The doctor's conversation made sense now. That assailant had wrought better than he knew. Thanks to this injury Alex would have at least a week's further residence at Penfold Lodge. He intended to use it to get some answers.

6

'It is a great nuisance,' said Caroline to Mrs Penfold, injustice burning strongly in her breast. She dipped her pen in the inkwell, frowning at the notepaper as she considered how best to combine truth with a judicious alarm. 'I had no notion Lord Rothwell would have to remain here so long.'

Their unwelcome guest had returned to consciousness with a vengeance. Caroline had very soon given over worrying that those knocks on the head might have done lasting harm. Now she was wishing she had dropped him a little harder. He was presently asleep, having exhausted himself first by insisting on being shaved and then by refusing sensible invalid fare with unwarranted ferocity. Caroline had lost patience with him and had left the day nurse to deal with his bad temper, retiring instead to the morning room to write to his mama. After his outcry against the idea earlier, she had high hopes of the Duchess of Abervale arriving with the next mail coach, riding roughshod over the doctor's objections, and sweeping her troublesome son back to the White Hart amidst a phalanx of the best nursing care money could buy.

'It is inconvenient not being able to use that room,' agreed Mrs Penfold, her knitting needles clicking, 'but it is very pleasant having you in the house, even though I have seen little of you.'

Caroline looked up from her carefully heart-wringing letter, startled. 'Thank you. For myself, as you know, I have always felt at home here. I could wish Mama would agree to me coming to you permanently.'

'She sees no profit in it,' said Mrs Penfold, in a matter-of-fact tone. 'It would be different if Penfold Lodge were mine to leave, but all I have is the right to reside here. She is doing the best thing by her lights. A jointure which reverts back to the estate upon my decease, no matter how handsome, can be of no benefit to you.'

Caroline bent her head to her composition. She hated it, this knowledge that everything came down to money. That without it a female was condemned to live off others' bounty. That with it she was a target for every charming spendthrift or impecunious younger son. Intensely practical, Caroline was well aware that the interest on her late godmother's thousand pounds in funds was insufficient to live on. That was why she doing her utmost to build up the racing account which she, Bertrand and Harry had shared. Youthful ideals were long gone. She had been so sickened by the singleness of purpose exhibited in the marriage mart last spring that she was determined to be as independent as possible by the time she was of sufficient age to leave her parents' roof. That she might be branded as eccentric did not bother her. Yes, she liked dancing and books and intelligent conversation, but she could get by without them. All she really wanted to do — all she had ever wanted to do — was to look after horses, just as she had planned with Bertrand. Life would have been so different had he . . .

But at this point in her musings, abetted by a sad sniff from Mrs Penfold, the pair of them were saved from melancholy by the announcement of visitors.

'Alderman Taylor,' said Caroline in strong surprise. She rose to greet him and to kiss Louisa. 'This is an unlooked-for pleasure.'

'Took a fancy to go to the race meeting,' he said jovially. 'And as Louisa was disappointed to miss you on Saturday, we settled that she should visit here while I am up at the heath.'

Secure in the knowledge that Harry would also be on the heath all day, reflected Caroline. Still, it was a kind thought and she was just about to tell the alderman so when he continued, 'And if, as is daresay the case, you have fatigued yourself in caring for your invalid, Louisa can spell you awhile and give you some respite. She is of just the right temperament to sit by his lordship's bedside with the nurse, and amuse him should he wake.'

At this, Caroline had to bite the insides of her cheeks very hard indeed not to burst out laughing. 'How kind,' she managed, not daring to look at her friend.

Dear single-minded Alderman Taylor. It was a strategy worthy of her own mama. Indeed, now she came to think of it, she was amazed Selina had not been dispatched to Penfold Lodge too, to bear her sister company now the worst of the nursing was over. It was only a matter of time, she felt sure, and all the more reason for Lord Rothwell to be removed to his own apartments as soon as possible.

'Poor Papa,' said Louisa, when her father had departed for his afternoon of uncharacteristic dissipation. 'He almost had my trunk packed for a week's stay before he remembered that Harry lives here also.'

'I hope you do not expect to see him. We have horses running today.'

'Are any of them likely to win? When Papa sees with his own eyes that Harry is a success it will make him look more kindly on him.'

'Rufus should certainly prevail over *his* field. And Fancy has a good chance to take the sweepstake for untried colts. It is not a big purse, but your father might not regard that.'

'Why enter him then? I thought you were trying to build up your capital.'

Caroline regarded her friend fondly. 'To get him accustomed to the noise and bustle of a race day. There are not so many opportunities for two-year-olds that we can be choosy. We also want to get him used to winning, so it is better to enter during one of the spring meetings because there are fewer good horses this early in the year. Maiden's turn comes later in the week.'

Noise and bustle. Caroline suddenly thought of Solange. The grey mare would hate a race meeting. How were they to accustom her to it? The crowds, the noise, the bustle. The men. The whole experience would unsettle her so thoroughly that she would be fit for nothing by the time her race was called. 'However,' she continued, pushing away the thought to worry about later, 'you did not come here to talk of horses, and dear Mrs Penfold must be tried to the limit by Harry and me discussing them all the time. Would you perhaps like us to show you over the house? I really don't advise following your father's suggestion and sitting with Lord Rothwell. He is a shockingly impatient patient.'

'That will be because you keep arguing with him,' said Louisa, with the cheerful licence of long friendship. 'Mr d'Arblay told me Lord Rothwell dislikes it excessively when people disagree with him. What he prefers, Mr d'Arblay said, is to talk of his estate in Surrey. How many acres it is and how much it produces in rents, that sort of thing.'

Caroline grinned. 'In that case, the word Surrey shall never pass my lips and I will make a point of holding a contrary opinion to his on every conceivable subject. That should drive him back to his own well-ordered household with all speed. Thank you, Louisa, I am much obliged to you.'

★　★　★

Alexander stirred at the sound of female laughter in the passage. For a moment he was disorientated, thinking himself in London, with his sister and her friends making merry in the next room. Then a nurse appeared by his bedside, bearing a large bottle that instinct told him would hold a quite indescribable medicine. There was no one else here. 'I think not,' he said, and closed his eyes, unreasonably ruffled.

He dozed, roused to the ignominy of needing his valet's help to the commode, and dozed again. By the time he awoke properly, he felt stiff and irritable. A lamp had been kindled and Caroline Fortune was in the wing chair frowning over a page of figures. 'Oh, you're awake,' she said, tucking the paper away into her reticule. 'How do you feel?'

He looked at her resentfully. He had been neglected for hours and was hungry enough to eat an entire side of cow. He was convinced that if he had been offered proper food earlier, he would not now need her aid in raising himself to a sitting position. 'I would be better for some solid food,' he growled. 'And I mean solid. Not that pap I was presented with before.'

'Oh, certainly. We cannot afford to waste any more broth by having you throw it at footmen's heads.'

Alex refused to have a chit of a girl make him feel guilty. 'If I'd wanted broth I would have asked for it. Where have you been all day?'

She raised her eyebrows. 'Entertaining a friend. Edifying as your conversation is, my lord, I prefer her conscious discourse to your unconscious mutterings.'

'It was you who told me I should rest,' Alex pointed out. Very forcefully as he recalled. He had been quite surprised. 'And you have not been with your friend all day, for I detect at least one visit to the stables. How is my horse?'

'Making progress, I believe.' Caroline glanced thoughtfully at the drawn curtains. 'How do you know I went to the stables, pray?'

'Your gown is shockingly creased and there is a straw in your hair. Do you never take care of your appearance?'

'Only when I am obliged to. Are you intending to be disagreeable all evening? Because I was going to sit with you while you ate and relay the grooms' gossip from the race meeting, but I won't if all you are going to do is find fault.'

Alex modified his tactics. Aggravating as Caroline Fortune was, this room would be completely devoid of life if he drove her out of it. 'If you can procure me something fit to eat and something more palatable than barley water to drink, there is no knowing how agreeable I can be.'

From the look Caroline and the nurse exchanged, Alex suspected he would be lucky to get a sip of ale, much less a decent mouthful of wine. Women were appalling tyrants when they had you helpless.

However, much to his surprise, there was a glass of burgundy with the meal. To his discomfiture, he could not finish it. Nor could he do justice to the plate of food that was set before him.

'Only to be expected,' pronounced the doctor, who was making his evening visit. 'Very unsuitable fare at this stage.'

'*Most* people losing blood through a blow to the head and being delirious for three days find a nice bowl of nourishing broth serves to recover their strength to start with,' murmured Caroline.

'It does not surprise me that Mrs Fortune has had difficulty finding you a husband,' snapped Alex.

Dr Peck chuckled. 'Oh she's found plenty. The wonder is that none of 'em come up to scratch, eh Miss Caro?'

'Indeed it is very strange.'

'But I'm glad of it, for I made a tidy sum on your Fancy today. Rufus too.'

Alex was startled out of his bad temper. The doctor attended the races?

To his discomfiture, Caroline instantly picked up on his surprise. He had forgotten how quick she was. 'Racing is not only the sport of the nobility, my lord. Or have you never spotted the throngs of ordinary folk near every finishing post?'

'I hope I am not *that* high in the instep.' But her eyes held just a suggestion of a jeer and he felt it prudent to change the subject. 'Which is Fancy? The bay colt?'

'You have a good memory. Yes, he won by two lengths from Grafton's roan. Quite an upset apparently. Flood tells me the duke was far from pleased.'

The talk turned to the other races, but within half-an-hour, Alex found his eyelids becoming heavy. He did wake again briefly, out of a dream of galloping hoofs and a splintering of wood, but a steady hand mopped his brow and fed him a drink of something cool, and a soft voice said, 'Hush now, what did I tell you? Sleep, Alexander.' So he did.

★　★　★

It was an odd thing, thought Caroline, wringing out the cloth, that while she found it a simple matter to trade badinage with Lord Rothwell during the day, as soon as night fell and he slipped into this uneasy, sweating doze, he was Alexander again and she did not seem able to leave him to the competent ministrations of the nurse.

He was *so* silly, eating and drinking unwisely, but Harry had always been the same. It was Caroline's experience that the only way to prove to men that you knew what you were talking about, was to let them find it out for themselves.

Fortunately, Alexander's agitation passed without any of the alarm for the onlookers that had attended his previous nightmares. Sighing in his sleep, he turned his head, trapping Caroline's hand under his cheek. She snorted to herself, thinking of the fuss he had made this morning over his appearance. If he only knew it, he was far more comely with the shadow of new growth on his face than he was as the correctly dressed, clean-shaven Lord Rothwell that the rest of the world saw.

She withdrew her hand as gently as possible, feeling the faint rasp of bristles against her skin. And froze as his mouth pressed a sleepy kiss to her fingers. A tremor passed right through her body. Holding her breath, she eased her hand free. She moved back to the chair telling herself she wasn't shaken at all. And she only had a passing thought as to who Rosetta might be.

*　*　*

Tuesday morning. Caroline managed to get Maiden out for a dawn gallop on the heath and felt much better for it. She considered taking Solange up afterwards, but with race meetings all week there would be too many people abroad. Too many gentlemen in the town, too many ostlers and grooms crowding the yards. Riding Maiden was one thing — there were any number of chestnut fillies about, even with the white star on her forehead — but Solange was far too distinctive and, it seemed, too notorious, for an observer to miss. And once Solange was sighted, her rider might come under scrutiny. It wasn't worth the risk.

Over their normal kitchen breakfast, which was so much more pleasant now that she didn't have to hurry back to her Fortune House bedchamber as soon as she'd bolted down enough to satisfy her hunger, she settled with Harry how much they should be on who today, then she washed, changed, visited Mrs Penfold's room and finally went to see how Alexander fared. She found him sitting up with his hair brushed, a dressing gown tucked around him and a mulish look upon his face.

'Good morning, my lord. Do I take it that cook's suggestion of nicely poached eggs and a dish of tea does not find favour with you?'

'Nobody drinks tea at this time in the morning,' he growled.

'Do they not, my lord? I always do.' Caroline nodded to the footman to bring the table over. She poured out two cups and set his lordship's breakfast on a tray on his knees. 'I daresay you would like to see the newspaper. Mrs Penfold has both *The Times* and the *Gazette* delivered, so you may choose. Or, if you are still a little fuzzled, I can read some of the articles to you.'

'I am perfectly capable of reading the newspaper!' he snapped. He picked up his knife and fork and dug savagely into one of the eggs. 'I fail to see why a trifling indisposition should immediately suggest that one has turned feeble-minded overnight!'

This was said with a malevolent glance at the valet and the nurse. Caroline struggled to keep her laughter in check and instead folded open *The Times*, asking his opinion on this new idea of Mr Owen's to create small communities for the unemployed people in the north of the country.

By the time she took out his empty breakfast tray, England's most pressing problems had been solved and various politicians' reputations were in shreds. Caroline had been agreeably surprised by the way Lord Rothwell did not always take the landowner's line. He recognized that there was inequality in the countryside as well as in the towns. Despite herself, her opinion of him had risen by several notches during their discussion. She left him tutting over the newspapers and slipped out to the stables. She had coaxed Solange up to the paddock and was wondering whether to try a side-saddle on her, when she heard the clatter of a carriage stopping in the road. It would be Mama without a doubt. Caroline made a face at the groom and sped with all haste to the side door. It would not do for her to be found absconding from what she had given out as a duty.

It was not Mama; it was an altogether grander equipage. Caroline had barely enough time to skid into the Yellow Saloon before Hibbert was announcing, 'Lady Jersey,' to a startled Mrs Penfold.

'I was at Cheveley with the Duke and Duchess of Rutland last night and heard about poor Lord Rothwell,' said this grand dame, sweeping in. 'Such a dreadful thing to happen. I resolved to pay him a visit without delay.'

It was now well past midday, but neither Caroline nor Mrs Penfold quibbled with her statement. 'Won't you sit down and take some refreshment, ma'am?' said Caroline. 'I know his lordship had formed the intention of getting up for a short while. I shall ascertain whether he is receiving visitors yet.'

'Oh, we do not stand on ceremony, such old friends as we are. I feel sure he will see me.'

'Good God, you can't let Sally Jersey in here,' said Alexander when Caroline acquainted him with his visitor's name. 'If once she sees me laid up in bed, I will be at death's door to half the country by nightfall. She isn't known as Silence for nothing. Tell her I will join you as soon as my fool valet makes me decent.'

This plan did not strike Caroline at all favourably. He was so ridiculously particular in his notions that he would exhaust himself by getting fully dressed and likely put his recovery back a full week. And she would have to amuse the doyenne of London society while he did so! 'What nonsense,' she said roundly. 'You will look perfectly correct attired in your dressing-gown with a silk scarf around your neck. You can sit in the wing chair next to the fire with a rug tucked over your lap for decency and we shall pull the screens across to hide the bed.'

She whisked out before he had time to argue. She would far rather annoy him than antagonize Lady Jersey. Much as she deplored the system, she had two sisters waiting their chance at a London season — a Lady Patroness of Almack's could make or break their prospects.

★ ★ ★

'Dear Alex,' said Lady Jersey in a throbbing voice. 'To put yourself in such danger! For me!'

After transferring from the bed to the chair, Alex felt by no means as steady as he'd expected and Sally in one of her theatrical moods was all he needed. 'Lady Jersey, naturally I am your devoted servant at all times,' he said, flicking his eyes warningly towards Caroline who was conferring with the nurse, 'but on this occasion I was simply clearing my head with a walk when I believe myself to have been set upon.'

She gave a knowing smile and patted his hand. 'Well, well, I hope to see you up and about soon. Now then, would you like to hear the latest *on-dits*?'

Alex acquiesced — she would tell him anyway and it was easier to listen than to bear his part in the conversation.

' . . . and then what do I find when I arrive from London yesterday but that everyone was rolled up because some wretched colt of Grafton's only came second in a race. My dear, you could have *painted* the room with Giles's language when he told me. Of course, if I had been there, I flatter myself that I should have known which one to back.' Sally turned suddenly to Caroline. 'Do you not consider it quite infamous that it is not the done thing for ladies to attend the Newmarket races?'

'Indeed, ma'am.' Alex was amused to see that Caroline was not in the least discomposed at being addressed in such a peremptory fashion. He could wish that she had taken the time to put on a rather more flattering dress, but she did not seem to regard her appearance as any way deficient. 'I have frequently found it most unfair not being able to watch first-hand what my brother describes to me,' she said, totally unconcerned. 'I feel I should apologize to your friends though, for it was our horse that won the two-year-old sweepstakes yesterday. Would you care to inspect him? I daresay Lord Rothwell will excuse you.'

What was the minx up to now? Alex suffered Sally to kiss his cheek and wish him a swift recovery, then once the door was closed behind them made his way at a frustratingly slow pace to the long terrace window. Across the lawn, he could see the back of the stables. He watched Caroline accompany Lady Jersey to the nearest paddock where both the bay colt and the chestnut filly frisked up to them. Sally patted their necks, Caroline gesticulated, they conversed some more and then the ladies turned. Alex let the curtain fall and allowed the disapproving nurse to help him back to bed.

'I thought your brother only allowed his owners up to the stable,' he said when Caroline reappeared in the room a quarter of an hour later. To his annoyance he had fallen into a doze waiting for her, so his tone was nothing like as sarcastic as he'd intended.

She gave him a droll look. 'He makes an occasional exception when guided by his sister. Lean forward whilst I adjust your pillows. You cannot be comfortable like that.'

'But you dislike society,' he said, obeying before he realized she was ordering him about again. 'You told me so this morning when you said the country would be in a far better state if all the money spent on court dresses was given to almshouses and schools instead. Why make an exception for Sally Jersey?'

'You do not tell me all of your schemes, my lord — I fail to see why I should tell you all of mine. How foolish of you to have got back into bed in your dressing gown. How will you sleep with it tangled into a lump in the small of your back? Let me help you take it off.'

'I don't need to sleep,' he said, leaning against her as she reached around to tug at the far sleeve.

'Naturally not. I am sure you are far more conversant with the care of your particular kind of injury than is Dr Peck. So there was no reason for me to draw Lady Jersey out of your orbit lest you do something ungentlemanlike and yawn in front of her.'

'None at all.' But Alex's eyes were closing and he wasn't really attending. As she supported him, rearranged him, fluffed his pillows and guided him down again, he made the drowsy discovery that although she didn't have the ripeness of figure he preferred in his light-of-loves, Caroline Fortune was nevertheless pleasantly rounded where it counted. It meant nothing, of course, but after the ridiculously fatiguing morning he had had, it was far easier to dwell on that than on her words.

7

'Is he all right?' Caroline asked the nurse in alarm. 'He lolled against me, then fell asleep.'

'Wore out,' said the nurse with a professional sniff. 'And I don't wonder, what with getting up in a hurry and then her ladyship chattering on like that. It was a fair treat to see you head her off, miss.'

'I fear she thinks me an oddity. But her husband owns a considerable string of racehorses and if I have but planted a seed in her mind that my brother is very good at bringing young ones on, then she may mention him to Lord Jersey.'

'Aye, it does no good to offend the gentry, when all's said and done.'

Which was true. And it was also true that she'd had an eye to Selina and Eliza's future prospects in London. But principally, thought Caroline, wondering at herself as she made her way once more up to Solange's paddock, it had been to give Alexander some respite. He was not near as strong as he thought himself. He *would* keep trying to do too much.

It was a little risky working with the horses at this time of day, but Caroline reasoned that the few grooms of her father's not up at the heath to watch today's Two Thousand Guineas race wouldn't see anything unusual in her trotting a lone grey mare about the field sidesaddle. Solange almost felt as if she was going to object after so many days without a rider, but on Caroline's keeping up a steady murmur of small talk, consented to the unusual weight distribution.

'I don't know what Flood was talking about,' said Caroline. 'You're not bothered by me on your back at all, are you, even if it isn't as good as astride? Next week we'll be able to get up to the heath and ride properly.'

Solange whickered and started to mince sideways.

'Whatever are you doing?' Then Caroline noticed Rufus on the other side of the paddock rail and laughed. 'So that's the way of it. Well, I don't know — what a terribly forward lady you are. Not that I blame you, for he is a fine-looking stallion, but I think your master might have something to say on the subject.'

'Miss Caro!' yelled one of the stable hands, pelting up from the yard. 'It's your ma for sure this time!'

Instantly, Solange began to rear. Caroline tensed and balanced herself to cling on. But after a split-second when events could have gone either way, the mare's muscles unbunched. She didn't quite drop her head to graze the way Rufus was doing, but Caroline felt sure the big chestnut had had a steadying effect on her. She dismounted very carefully indeed and handed the reins to the stable lad who was white as a sheet and horrified at his own thoughtlessness.

'No harm done,' she said. She patted both horses and hastened indoors, checking herself for stray wisps of straw as she went.

It transpired that one of Mama's bosom bows had seen Lady Jersey's carriage at the door of Penfold Lodge and had lost no time in making her whole acquaintance privy to the information. Mrs Fortune had immediately discovered a need in herself to enquire of her daughter how she went on. Caroline's duty was clear. By the time she left, her mother was in full possession of the minutiae of her ladyship's gown, pelisse, shoes, parasol and hat and only mildly disappointed to find that the state of Lord Rothwell's health precluded the society of any visitors.

'And Lady Jersey will assuredly remember your name when I apply for Selina's voucher next spring,' she finished in satisfaction. 'You have done very well indeed, my dear.' Much as Caroline hoped that this artless observation meant she herself would be permitted to remain behind when the family went to London, she thought it simply pointed to her mother's singleness of purpose where her more marriageable daughters were concerned. Interestingly though, it did appear from Mama's way of talking that she considered Caroline as fixed at Penfold Lodge for the present. Caroline wondered if she could simply forget to go home when Alexander left.

He was still asleep when she looked in later, so she ate with Mrs Penfold, thinking that she would likely have another trying evening with him after the exertions of the day. To her surprise Harry dropped by to change his clothes, in high good humour that they had backed so many winners today. 'Wanderer was only five-to-four on,' he called from his dressing room, 'and Aquilo came second to Wilson's colt in the Hundred Guineas Sweep which was something of a surprise, but the others were good odds indeed. You were right about Manfred. He took the Two Thousand Guineas at four to one! I doubt he'll be fit for anything tomorrow though. Lake's been resting Gazelle. What do you think to him instead?'

Even while she was rejoicing in their success with the betting, Caroline was worrying about her brother. She knew him in this mood. Yes, he might start the evening dining with friends, but then they would go on to Crockford's where he would be unable not to crow about his luck and then all manner of people with far longer pockets than he would try tempting him into making them longer still.

She reached the bottom of the stairs resolved to invent an emergency with one of the horses to keep Harry at home, when by the greatest providence she heard Lord Rothwell's voice issuing testily from behind his door. She could lead two ponies with one yoke if she was clever here.

Accordingly, 'Must you depart straight away?' she said to Harry, as he swung jauntily down the stairs. 'Only Lord Rothwell has been lying in that room positively blue-devilled that he could not get out onto the heath for the big race. It would be a great kindness if you could perhaps take a glass of claret with him and tell him something of what went on today.'

Hating to be constrained himself, and being of a naturally good-hearted disposition, Harry looked much struck by this. 'Well,' he said, 'I daresay the fellows I'm dining with at the Star won't notice half an hour here or there.'

And since Lord Rothwell was indeed interested in the racing and Caroline took care to keep her brother's glass topped up and ensured that Alexander's meal was brought in at exactly the time when Harry was likely to be getting hungry, it appeared to him to be his own decision that he should abandon his friends to their own devices and join Lord Rothwell to eat. It was equally reasonable that they should play a hand of piquet afterwards. And it was sober judgement, not the two glasses of excellent brandy which finished off the evening, that made Harry decide to seek his bed rather than venture out to carouse at Crockford's after all.

'Nicely done,' said Lord Rothwell, sleepily conversational, when she slipped back to check that the night nurse had all she needed.

Caroline turned. It *had* been nicely done, and done with the best of intentions too, but his lordship's amusement made her defensive. 'Thank you. It seemed to me you both enjoyed your evening which was, I confess, my intention.'

He yawned. 'You are infernally managing, are you not?'

She raised her eyebrows as she pulled his covers straight and turned down the lamp. 'You would rather have teased your headache by reading, perhaps? Or been irritated by my inability to remember trumps?'

A further yawn shook him. 'I will admit your brother to have been not as unintelligent tonight as I had imagined. Dammit, why am I so confoundedly weak? I did not drink one-tenth the wine he did.'

'Possibly it is something to do with having been extremely ill. Go to sleep, my lord. You may be as bored as you like tomorrow.'

His eyes closed. Caroline turned down the lamp still further. 'G'night,' he slurred.

Caroline glanced at the nurse, making herself comfortable on the other side of the room with no sign of having heard. 'Good night, Alexander,' she murmured.

He may have fallen asleep rapidly, but bad dreams hit him within the hour.

'Was I wrong to serve the wine?' asked Caroline, holding him down on one side of the bed while the nurse stood ready on the other. 'But how could I not, when Harry was drinking it also?'

'It's like the doctor said, miss, he's got to work the cranks out of his skull. He'd have got himself into a worse state if we'd kept him from it entirely.'

'Oh do hush, Alexander,' said Caroline, dabbing his brow with cool water. 'You will wake the whole household and that will never do.'

'Thirsty,' he croaked.

'*That'll* be the wine,' said the nurse. She held a glass of barley water to his lips as Caroline propped him up.

He drank greedily, then turned his head and nestled into Caroline's shoulder.

'Are you sure you are quite comfortable?' she asked with a touch of irony. But squinting down at his closed eyes and his dark hair tumbled across the bandage, she was swept by such a wave of unexpected tenderness that it startled her into nearly dropping him. This would never do. She felt ridiculously flustered. She eased him to the pillow, hoping the nurse had seen nothing untoward.

'You've got the right way with him, miss, that's for sure.'

'I think it is simply that my voice reminds him of his old nanny.'

The nurse chuckled. 'Aye, that'd do it. Wonderful childlike these grand gentlemen get when they're in the mopes.'

Which observation was no reason at all to depress Caroline's spirits.

★   ★   ★

In the morning, there was no sign that Lord Rothwell had ever been anything but an irascible twenty-nine years of age. This was all to the good. It pushed any wayward imaginings firmly to the realms of fantasy where they belonged.

'If I want to get up today, then I will,' he repeated.

Caroline drew a sorely tried breath. 'I am not arguing with you, my lord, I am merely suggesting that you put off rising until after you have breakfasted. Cook has made an omelette in the Spanish fashion which is far better eaten hot than cold, as I am sure you are aware.'

'An omelette?' His level tone was ominous.

'It is a very good omelette, for I had one myself earlier. And if you would consent to look at the tray you might observe some slices of ham as well.'

'And a pot of tea. Did I not make my feelings about tea in the morning plain?'

Caroline drew a chair up to the table that had been placed by the bed. 'The tea is for me. I can spare you a cup if you are thirsty?'

Alexander glowered and gestured to the patiently waiting footman. 'Very well, put it down. I can see shaving water and fresh linen will not be forthcoming until I bow to this despot.'

Arguing must give him an appetite, thought Caroline as he made short work of the tray's contents. She was amused to see that he drank the tea she poured him without comment too. A few more good, nourishing meals and he would be well on the way to recovery and off their hands for good. And not before time too.

'How much earlier?' he said suddenly.

'I beg your pardon?'

'You said you ate earlier. It is not my experience that ladies in general eat heartily at this hour of the day.'

Oh, so the omelette was allowed to be 'hearty' now, was it? All the same, she had very nearly slipped up there. 'It is possible that your experience is incomplete, my lord. This is a training stable and there is much to be done on a race day. I would be a poor sister not to bear my brother company while he ate.'

He looked at her for a long moment, then let the subject rest.

* * *

'Dr Peck says Lord Rothwell is so much better that he no longer needs a nurse during the day,' reported Caroline jubilantly.

Mrs Penfold looked up from her knitting. 'That is good news for the poor man. What of the nightmares?'

Caroline hesitated. 'I did not mention those in front of Lord Rothwell, for I thought

140

it very likely that he would contradict me and say he never had a dream in his life. I spoke to the doctor privately about them instead. He does not believe from my account that Lord Rothwell will do himself any harm during the dreams, but thinks a night-nurse might be a wise precaution for the time being. He says very often in these cases, as the patient becomes more active during the day, the less likely his mind is to wander at night. I can see I shall have to introduce Lord Rothwell to the billiard room.'

'Is that advisable so soon after leaving his bed?'

Caroline grinned. 'I was jesting. I wonder if there is any correspondence at the White Hart that he needs to answer. There should be by now, such a man of affairs as he professes himself to be. If so, it would keep him nicely occupied once he has finished being cross with the newspapers. May I send one of the footmen to enquire?'

There was indeed a small pile of post, and Caroline took great pleasure in bringing it to Alexander's attention. She calculated that the combination of business letters to write and a luncheon of meat, pickles and the mildest ale the butler could find should have their guest dozing in no time, leaving her free to work with Solange some more.

Sadly, she had overlooked the power of the local gabblemongers. She had scarce been on the mare's back an hour before the stable-lad called up that there were visitors arriving.

'Good girl,' praised Caroline as her mount merely twitched her ears in annoyance at the shout, 'but I fear our exercise is over for the day.'

She was proved correct. As she remarked drily to Mrs Penfold, they had never been so popular. If it hadn't been for the loss of the riding time, it would have been quite amusing waiting for the various visitors to lead up to a casual reference to Penfold Lodge's illustrious guest. In each case Caroline said he was still under the doctor's care and it was a shocking thing that an assault like that should have taken place in a respectable part of Newmarket. This turned the conversation very neatly, but she did not discover that any other attacks of the same kind had occurred recently.

As if their own visitors were not enough, they also had to contend with Mr d'Arblay calling in straight from the finish of the day's racing, just as Caroline had persuaded Alexander back into his bed. There was by now quite a nip in the air and remembering Giles's thoughtless fidgeting with the terrace door on a previous visit, she called a footman to move the screens across the window.

'Whatever are you doing?' said Alexander testily.

Telling him she was preventing his friend from compounding his injuries by adding a chill to them did not seem a politic answer. 'Masking the nurse's table, my lord. You will not wish the evidence of your enfeeblement on view to your friends.'

'Good God, as if Giles will even notice! It will be nice to have some company that doesn't cosset me beyond bearing, I can tell you.'

He had the drawn look of one who had been up for too long, but if Caroline suggested as much he would likely blast her clear across the room. After showing Mr d'Arblay in, she hovered in the passage, not liking to go too far out of earshot in case she was required.

'I'd have thought you'd have that bandage off by now,' she heard Giles say by way of a greeting.

'Tomorrow, I'm told,' came the reply.

'And still abed! I never thought to see that. Getting feeble in your dotage?'

'For your information I have been up all day and am only just returned here. Under duress, I might add.'

Caroline snorted. Men were so boastful.

She moved down the passage to avoid eavesdropping further, but Mr d'Arblay's voice was tiresomely penetrating.

' . . . shocking bad luck yesterday,' he was saying. 'The only good horse on the whole damn heath was Wilson's colt. Lord, Alex, do you really need all these medicines?'

'No, of course I don't. I wish you would desist from roaming around the room, Giles. It's enough to make one dizzy.'

'Today wasn't much better. Of course we all went for Manfred or Sylvanus for the Newmarket Stakes after yesterday's showing, and the blasted nags were nowhere in sight at the finish!'

'Who took it then? Gazelle?'

'Yes. How the devil did you guess that?'

'Do you never study form, Giles?'

Caroline grinned to herself. Study form indeed. Alexander had got that straight from talking to Harry last night.

'Heigh ho, thank God it's a fuller programme tomorrow. Shall I put something on the One Thousand Guineas for you?'

'Do sit down, Giles. And thank you, but no. I have lost quite as much as I want to the Newmarket roughs.'

'Pshaw. Small change.'

'If you consider the contents of my pocketbook small change, no wonder you are always sailing close to the wind. Do you dine at Cheveley tonight?'

'Yes. What o'clock is it? I'd better be off if I'm to make myself ready.'

Caroline snorted again. An extremely short visit. She wondered Mr d'Arblay had bothered to call at all. She went towards the entrance hall, meaning to see him firmly off the premises, but was arrested by the sound of his voice.

'Sure you don't want a flutter? Trictrac's supposed to be a dead cert. Oh, by the by, I've been looking about for you, but I haven't seen anything smoky. Not unless you count your precious host collecting indecently large rolls of soft this morning from the bookmakers.'

'Giles, we have had this before. He is a trainer. And an owner in a small way. What is it Bunbury always says? That if it wasn't for the betting, no racehorse owner could afford to keep a string at all?'

'Ha! Seems damned unlikely that his untried colt should run the legs off Grafton's the other day with all that pedigree behind it. Lost me a pretty packet, I can tell you.'

'Your losing bets are always the unlikeliest of occurrences. Leave it.'

Caroline retained just enough presence of mind to whisk up the passage as the bell sounded for the butler. She was so angry she found it difficult to give Mr d'Arblay even the coldest of nods as he bid her a cheerful farewell.

'I knew Alex wouldn't let himself be hedged around with nurses and suchlike for long,' he said as he straightened his hat in the mirror.

'No indeed,' she said. 'He is so improved that I daresay he will be back at the White Hart with you in short order.'

Mr d' Arblay looked a little startled. 'Do you think so?'

'Oh, certainly.'

The shorter the better as far as she was concerned.

★ ★ ★

It wasn't until after Lord Rothwell had dropped off to sleep that a messenger arrived with the news that the night-nurse was very sorry, but she'd been called to a confinement.

Caroline was not best pleased. Lord Rothwell may not share his friend's conviction that Harry must have fixed Fancy's sweepstake, but she did not feel very friendly towards him nevertheless. She had been prepared to talk him out of any dream terrors, but she didn't want him falling asleep

146

on her shoulder again and she would have much preferred to spend the rest of the night in her own bed for once rather than the wing chair.

'I'll sit meself in the passage, Miss Caro,' said the footman obligingly. 'I'll soon hear if you need me.'

'Thank you,' said Caroline, capitulating with a sigh. She fetched her book, moved the chair so she would not keep catching glimpses of Alexander whenever she looked up, and prepared to wait.

She was still waiting some hours later. Or rather, she was curled up in the chair fast asleep when a noise woke her. She blinked, disoriented. Certainly she had heard a thud, as if Alexander had flung an arm out of bed preparatory to his usual tossing and turning, and that was the first direction she looked. But he was sleeping soundly. Besides, the noise had come from quite a different part of the room. Caroline stood up, puzzled, stretching cramped muscles as she traced back her waking memory. Not from the passage, it must have been something outside. Curious, she crossed the room in her stocking feet and pulled back the curtain. And screamed as a masked face leered through the glass at her.

The masked man turned and ran straight away across the lawn, disappearing through the archway leading to the road.

'I'm here, Miss Caro,' yelled the footman in a sleep-befuddled voice. He wrenched the door open wider and stumbled into the aperture.

'Intruder,' she gasped. 'On the terrace. He ran towards the town. If you hurry you might catch him.' The footman swore and staggered off.

'What the devil is going on?' said Alexander, sitting up in the semi-darkness. 'Who's there? What o'clock is it?'

'There was a man,' said Caroline, her voice shaky. 'Outside the terrace door. He — he had a mask on.'

Alexander rubbed his eyes. 'Sit down before you fall,' he commanded. 'What moonshine is this?'

Caroline regarded him with indignation, but as her legs were indeed about to fold up on her, she tottered to the edge of his bed. 'It is *not* moonshine. A noise woke me and it wasn't you so I opened the curtain and ... and ... ' To her horror she almost retched. She held it down. 'I am never ill,' she said fiercely. 'Never!'

A warm arm came securely around her shoulders. 'Easy. I believe you.'

'So I should think,' she muttered. His arm both helped and worried her. And she would be a lot happier once she had persuaded her stomach to behave.

'I *meant* I believe you are never ill. I'm reserving judgement on the housebreaker.'

Furious, Caroline tried to wriggle free, but he held her more firmly. Warmth seeped into her, dispelling both the incipient hysteria and the unruly behaviour of last night's supper. 'Better now?' he asked after a moment, his voice holding a suggestion of a laugh.

Caroline was better. She was also, if possible, even crosser. *She* was supposed to manipulate *him*, not the other way around.

'He got away, Miss Caro,' called the footman, puffing back up the passage.

Instantly, Alexander let her go and Caroline discovered she could stand very well after all.

'I heard him running, like,' continued the man, appearing in the doorway holding a hand to his side, 'but he must've dodged down between the inns.'

'It can't be helped. You did very well. The house is still secure which is what counts.'

'And he is unlikely to try again,' said Alexander. 'I daresay you gave him as much of a fright as he gave you.' He glanced meditatively at her. 'I believe a hot drink might be of service.'

'You're not wrong, sir,' said the footman

with enthusiasm. 'There'll be some warmth in the kitchen range still. I could mix a nice bumper or . . . ' His voice trailed off as he looked at Caroline. 'Or perhaps a pan of cocoa.'

'Cocoa,' said Caroline.

'Both,' said Alexander at the same moment. The footman hurried out.

'Now sit down again,' said Alexander, 'and tell me properly what happened.'

'I did tell you. I was woken by a noise and — '

'I said properly. What, for example, were you doing in this room?'

'Oh, well, the nurse had to go to a confinement.'

'The nurse? Dr Peck was not of the opinion that I needed a nurse any more. There was no nurse here when I went to sleep.'

If Caroline had ever given into the urge to howl in her life, she would have howled now. First the face at the window, then Alexander's arm around her shoulder, now she had to tell him he'd been having nightmares. He would hate it, hate this evidence of weakness. 'You do not need a nurse during the day,' she began falteringly, 'but at night you . . . that is, when you sleep you . . . '

His temper snapped. 'Caroline, sit down here and tell me why the devil you were in my room overnight, completely unchaperoned.'

She had been about to resume her seat on the bed. Now she shot up as if there were live coals on the coverlet. Compromised! That was *another* complication she hadn't thought about. A firm hand on her shoulder pressed her down again. '*Will* you be easy.'

'You are still having nightmares,' she said, too rattled to be anything but blunt. 'And the door was ajar and Thomas just outside so I was *not* unchaperoned.'

'Your parents may take a different view! Good God, I simply don't believe it! Of all the ill-considered, idiotic schemes — '

'They will not know! Have no fear, my lord, no one in this house is likely to acquaint them with the particulars. There is not the least danger of you being constrained to make me an offer.'

She felt a jolt of distaste from him. He did not like her to speak his thoughts out loud. 'Has my valet perhaps left the house?' he said icily. 'Should he not have been the one to occupy that chair? He has been doing remarkably little else to earn his wages recently.'

A valet who had recourse to the sal volatile at the sight of a pinprick and who wore himself out just pressing a neck-cloth to perfection? Caroline gritted her teeth. 'You do not understand. When you are in the grip of the nightmares, you grow extremely anxious — disturbed, even — and could easily injure yourself.'

His face grew grimmer. 'And you — a slip of a girl — can cope with that better than a full-grown man, can you?'

'I can cope with it better than your valet, certainly.'

He was surprised into a crack of laughter. 'He *is* very good at what he does.'

'He would have to be,' said Caroline. She took a cautious breath, hoping she had diverted him.

'But that still doesn't explain why *you*, and not a burly footman for instance, should be the one to restrain me.' He said this with measured revulsion, as if the thought of not being in control of himself was repellent.

Caroline moistened her lips. 'Because my voice soothes you. I don't know why, my lord. It just does.'

He frowned at her. She had the impression he was casting back through fevered memories. She hoped they weren't the ones associated with Rosetta. 'Say my name,' he said in an odd voice.

'Lord Rothwell.'

He shook his head impatiently. 'Say my name.'

She looked at him. 'Alexander.'

There was a moment of utter stillness. A

nearly burnt log settled in the fireplace with a soft whump. Alexander sat back, shifting uncomfortably.

Caroline slid to her feet. 'Your pillows are awry. Lean forward and I will straighten them for you.'

'Thank you.' He held himself stiffly until she had plumped them up. Then, 'Did I dream tonight?'

His manner was casual, but Caroline was not fooled. 'No,' she said. 'Dr Peck said you might not, the more active you became. It encourages me to hope that you really are recovering.'

'Then there is no need for you to stay once you have had your cocoa.'

'No, my lord.'

More cinders fell through the grate. Caroline crossed the room to put on another log.

'What . . . what do I seem anxious about?'

Again it was said off-handedly. Caroline kept her face turned towards the fire. 'Oh, you are not coherent for the most part.'

'Caroline, please answer me.'

She walked slowly back to the bed. 'That is twice tonight you have used my name.'

'Please tell me,' he repeated. On the coverlet his hands were clenched.

'I think you must already know.' He was

hurting; she could *feel* him hurting. She sat down on the bed again and took one fist between her palms. This was no time for maidenly affectation. 'When you dream, you are overwhelmingly anxious to reach someone called Lizzy before nightfall.'

He let out a sharp breath. From the way his fingers jerked, she knew she had understood his apprehension aright. This was the secret he did not want the world to know about, and no wonder. An elopement, if such it had been, was a scandal that no family would want spread about. 'No one has heard you except for me and the nurse,' she continued quietly. '*I* do not pry, and she has a score or more years of discretion behind her.'

There was another long silence. 'Why did you not tell me?'

'That you were still having nightmares after the fever had passed? Because I did not want any daytime anxiety to interfere with your recovery! I wish for you to get better and resume your normal life.' *Away from here. Away from me.*

Footsteps in the passage heralded the imminent arrival of hot drinks. Caroline retreated to the wing chair.

'Go to bed,' said Alexander with finality once she had finished her cocoa. 'I shall not dream tonight.'

8

Dawn streaked thinly through a gap in the brocade curtains. The fire was down to rosy ash. Alex lay in the unaccustomed silence of his room and contemplated the events of the night.

It seemed he'd added his sister's thwarted elopement to his repertoire. That in itself was hardly surprising. He'd been out of his mind with worry that day — knowing he was to blame for not making his point more forcefully, knowing he'd been found wanting, all the leads sending him wrong, and time marching relentlessly on. Small wonder his unconscious mind kept reliving the agony. The astonishing thing was that he ever had a night's respite.

He felt his hands ball into fists. He loathed the idea of nightmares he couldn't control, but he had sweated them out before with no ill effects. What was far worse was Caroline now being conversant with his weaknesses, his lowest moments. And taking it upon herself not to inform him what was happening. Damned chit of a girl, thinking she knew best yet again. She seemed

155

honourable enough, but just let him catch one hint of pity in her eyes and he'd . . . he'd . . .

He took a calming breath. This wasn't solving anything. He would cultivate composure, become more active during the day, and the dreams would go away. That was the way it worked. He slid from the bed, testing the strength in his legs. He was infernally weak still. But he made it to the window in less time than it had taken yesterday and pulled the curtain aside.

Nothing. Nothing to show that there had ever been a face pressed up against the panes. Just a terrace, a lawn with a shrubbery and ornamental bridge, and the stable block over on the right leading to paddocks where horses and grooms were already at work. All perfectly innocent.

But, impossible as it seemed, something smoky must be afoot at Penfold Lodge. Last week he had been very efficiently put out of the way before he could, presumably, stumble on some compromising occurrence, and this week there had once again been an interloper in the grounds.

Who? And why? And who had they come to see?

He focused on the back of the stable block where a stripling was bent low, patting a horse's neck before dismounting and leading it inside. That lad again. Was he part of the mystery? It was infuriating to be on the spot yet constrained by his injury not to take part in the routine of the house.

Frustration gave him the answer. He must make an attempt to alter the circumstances. In the first instance he needed to expand his boundaries. He was never going to learn anything if he kept to this room. He would start by breakfasting with the family.

★ ★ ★

Lord Rothwell's declaration, delivered by the maid who had crept into his room to make up the fire, caused not a little consternation in the kitchen.

'Eat with the family?' repeated Caroline, a forkful of ham suspended halfway to her mouth.

'Yes, miss. Ooh, he did give me a fright. I had no notion he was awake.'

'He has no call to be awake this time of day,' said Caroline crossly. 'Tell me again what he said.'

'To fetch his man to him, so's he could get up and shaved and dressed and have breakfast with the family. He said as how he didn't want to inconvenience the household any more than he need.'

'He will inconvenience us more! None of us has 'eaten breakfast with the family' since Lady Penfold died. What a confounded nuisance. You'd better set some water on to boil, but don't you call that fuss-pot valet of his before I'm back down. That's all we need, him finicking about the kitchen.' Caroline pelted up to her room to scramble into a dress. It was her own fault for not changing as soon as she got in from the horses, but the porridge had been bubbling hot and she'd been hungry and . . . It wasn't a mistake she'd be making again this week, that's for sure. She wondered what was really behind Lord Rothwell's decision. He did not strike her as a man who habitually considered his hosts' servants. Despite her vow to be more than ever rigorously uninterested in their house guest, Caroline nevertheless found her movements slowing as she thought of him. Would he be Lord Rothwell or Alexander this morning?

★ ★ ★

When Alex was shown into the breakfast parlour, he discovered it to be empty. He sat in solitary state as the footman helped him to bacon, kidneys, potato and eggs.

158

'Good morning,' said Caroline, entering the room a little later. 'I am glad to see the alarms of the night have not interfered with your progress.' She smiled at the footman. 'Tea please, John. And toast.'

Tea and toast. Ha! As he'd thought, yesterday's line about her eating an omelette had all been a hum to persuade *him* to eat. Just another instance of her high-handedness. 'I wish I could say the same for you,' he commented. 'I seem to recall you mentioning that in general you made a very hearty breakfast.'

Having expressed himself with what he considered to be a nice irony, he was a little put out when she pulled the marmalade towards her and chuckled. 'I did. Some two hours ago. I can particularly recommend the bacon today.'

She was, without doubt, a most irritating young woman. Now he looked more closely, he noticed that she had dust and straw on her gown again and her hair was almost certainly not as it had left her maid's hands. It exasperated him that she didn't seem to mind. No wonder she had not had any success in attracting offers. Not that that seemed to bother her either. 'I was hoping to speak to your brother,' he said abruptly.

'Oh, you should have said. Harry has gone

out. I daresay he will be back before the racing starts. Or perhaps not. Maiden runs today. He will be trying to get good odds on her.'

Alex began to think he had got himself up for nothing. An enquiry about the newspapers elicited the information that they were upstairs with Mrs Penfold, but that he should have them as soon as she had finished.

'It is her one luxury, not being obliged to rise for breakfast any more. Lady Penfold used to get up fearfully early, you see, and liked the whole household to eat with her when she had finished going around the stables.'

'I can see why you got on so well with her,' said Alex, somewhat acerbically.

'Indeed, we had a lot in common. Did I mention that she was my godmother?'

'Yes. She left you the chestnut stallion. I realize now that it was not so bizarre a bequest as I first thought.'

Caroline gave a peal of laughter. 'You *are* out of sorts. Never mind, my lord, the doctor will be here later and I daresay will pronounce you fit enough to return to your rooms where the newspapers are all your own, the chef delivers what you want to eat when you want it and no nocturnal prowlers disturb your sleep.'

At this, Alex experienced a profound jolt. He had been sparring with Caroline as he might with Giles, or with his sister, forgetting that she was in a sense on the other side of the fence. He could not tell her that whatever the privations, he was by no means ready to leave this house.

★ ★ ★

'Not go back yet?' said Caroline, dismayed.

'A couple more days,' said Dr Peck. 'He is weak still, and more worried about his nightmares than he would have you believe. I am firmly of the opinion that a quiet, orderly house will be better for his full recovery than a noisy coaching inn.'

Oh would it! Unable to vent her feelings on the object of her ire, Caroline expressed herself at great length in a letter to Louisa instead. *However*, she wrote at the end, *I am determined to work with Solange as soon as he retires to rest. She is responding very well and it would be a crime to interrupt the training now. Oh, and I have just thought of a famous notion! If Lord R chances to be awake and sitting with us later (as I fear may very well be the case, for his indisposition seems to have robbed him of the ability to amuse himself) and we have an influx of callers as we did yesterday, I shall ask Hibbert to show them in without giving him the opportunity to escape. That should convince him fairly speedily of the need to return to his own well-trained servants, do you not think?*

It was clear that Lord Rothwell had not considered this hazard of life in a female establishment. If she hadn't been so determined to give him a distaste for continuing to convalesce here, Caroline might almost have felt sorry for him as the fourth set of callers in as many half-hours remembered the existence of her and Mrs Penfold and were ushered into the Yellow Saloon.

'Do you seriously enjoy the inanities and time-wasting nothings that were paraded in this room today?' he asked with some incredulity, once all the visitors had finally departed.

'No, of course not,' replied Caroline. 'No one could who was not entirely pea-brained.'

'Then why put up with it?'

'Because not all of us are infernally rude. One cannot be forever saying one is not at home. Besides, apart from Mrs Penfold's particular friends, they did not come to visit us at all.'

She saw the unpalatable truth hit him. 'They came because I was here?' he said indignantly.

'Well, neither Mrs Penfold nor I have a title and an estate in Surrey,' On the mantelpiece, the clock ticked on. Flood should be on the way back with Maiden by now. Caroline wanted to be in the stables to meet them and find out how the race had gone. She bestowed a kindly smile on Lord Rothwell. 'I believe we might now tell Hibbert we are not at home. The doctor mentioned that you should not put in a whole day without resting if you wish to continue your encouraging progress. Will you eat dinner with us later, or would you prefer to take it in your room?'

As soon as he had opted to eat with them and asked for his valet to be called, Caroline sped out to the stable. The grin on the face of the stable-hand who most often cared for Maiden was all the answer she needed.

'She won by a length and had plenty more in reserve, Miss Caro, only the rider said there was no need to show her hand a'cos the others were tiring. She'll take the Novice Stakes next month for sure.'

'Oh, I do hope so.' Caroline reached up and buried her face in the filly's neck, inhaling the lovely scent of warm horse. 'You clever, clever girl. Extra feed tonight for you.'

'Some weren't so happy,' said Flood quietly as the groom led Maiden into the stable. 'One or two mutterings about how lucky Mr Harry

163

was getting, and how it weren't natural for a new trainer to be winning so often.'

Caroline looked at him, worried. 'Influential people?' she asked.

'Depends on your outlook. Did seem as though most of the muttering came from groups Jem Jessop had just left.'

'Jessop? On the heath when his master is laid up here?'

Flood shrugged. 'While the cat's away, Miss Caro. I did notice one thing . . . '

'Yes?'

'He was hanging around the ring when Mr Harry bet on Neva to take the One Thousand Guineas. Then he slips off. Then, lo and behold, his lordship's fine friend arrives and puts money on Neva himself.'

'Well! How two-faced can you get!' Caroline was incensed. After Mr d'Arblay had sniped away about Harry yesterday — to blatantly use him like that! Like Flood, she was in no doubt at all that the events he'd relayed were connected. 'At least he should be in a better mood tonight if he calls,' she said crossly. Then looked at her head groom in sudden doubt. 'Neva did win, I take it?'

Flood chuckled. 'That she did, lass. You were spot on again.' He ran over the other winners but for once Caroline's attention wasn't fully on the recital. Was there really such bad feeling about Harry on the racecourse? Surely the small wins they were enjoying ought to add to his prestige amongst the other trainers, not diminish it. Of course, it would help if their father would only be proud of his son for once and take his part. Oh, bother it, why were people so complicated? No wonder she preferred horses.

* * *

From his window, Alex watched Caroline stretch up and hug the chestnut filly. The horse must have won. He wondered if Giles had overcome his prejudice and put money on her. He was startled at how natural and spontaneous Caroline looked, compared, though he hadn't realized it at the time, with the polite artificiality she had displayed towards the visitors in the saloon. Did all women act a part in front of others? Which her was it who coaxed him to eat? Or traded quips with him? Not that it mattered, of course.

She was talking to the head groom now, and even from this distance Alex saw her countenance change. Some sort of unwelcome news for sure. At length she made her way back, still looking thoughtful, and passed out of his field of vision. Now, how was he to find out what had taken the bounce out of her usual sprightly step?

★ ★ ★

'Does your brother not dine here tonight?'

Caroline didn't look perturbed at the question, so whatever had bothered her earlier, it wasn't Harry Fortune. 'He rarely does during a racing week.' She finished her soup and helped herself to a large portion of the chicken in caper sauce. Alex had come to the rueful conclusion that her statement about substantial breakfasts had been no less than the truth. She was the least fussy young lady he had ever shared a dinner table with. 'By the by, I am glad to hear you let Jessop go,' she commented.

He frowned. 'I haven't.'

'Have you not? We thought you must have done, because Flood saw him on the heath today.'

'I daresay Giles took him.'

'Oh, of course. Though why he would be at the betting post and not in the grooms' enclosure is a little puzzling.'

'Running an errand probably.' Alex carved his own chicken thoughtfully. 'I have never asked you what specifically you have against Jessop.'

'Save that he has been turned off in short order from his last three positions, that he lies, that he keeps dubious company and that he is unnecessarily hard on the animals in his care, nothing. How did you come to employ him, my lord? I own I was surprised once I had seen you with our foals.'

A very odd warmth took Alex by surprise. That had almost sounded like a compliment. 'He was sent by the livery office when one of my men left.'

'I am astonished he was on their books, considering his character must be well known in the town.'

Alex grunted cynically. 'A commission on a hire is a commission on a hire. I did not specify the nature of the groom required, so they may not have sent me their best man. When I am returned to fitness I will watch him. If I am not satisfied, he will be dismissed, I promise you.'

A smile lit her face. 'Thank you, my lord.'

What curious things pleased her, he thought, finding himself smiling back. He was just about to ask whether she had any other news from today's racing when an imperative knocking sounded at the front door.

'Whoever is that at this time of day?' Wondered Mrs Penfold aloud.

Caroline's hand went to her breast. 'I hope

it is not about Harry.'

Ha! She was worried! So pleased was Alex at rumbling her that he completely failed to mask his horror as the dining room door was flung open to disclose —

'Alex, darling!' cried his mother, shedding furs and scarves as she burst in. 'Oh, why didn't you *tell* me? Thank heavens you are all right!' A slim, expensive whirlwind, she flew around the table and threw her arms about him while he was still only half-risen from the chair.

'The Duchess of Abervale,' announced Hibbert unnecessarily.

Embarrassment hit Alex like a solid wall. With an immense effort, he dredged up a measure of his usual *sang-froid*. Over the top of his mother's regrettably askew bonnet, he met Caroline's startled eyes. Good. Now she would see what became of unnecessary interference. 'This has to be your doing,' he said. 'I can spot your touch five furlongs off.'

His mother pulled back, her bright gaze seeming to take him in all at once. 'And very grateful I am,' she said. 'I cannot conceive why it is that my children never deem it necessary to tell me of their misadventures until after the event.'

'Can you not, Mama?' said Alex drily. 'Pray let me make known to you my exceedingly good-natured hostess, Mrs Penfold — and your rather too zealous correspondent, Miss Caroline Fortune.'

'Better zealous and right, than dilatory and regretful,' said Caroline, recovering. 'I am delighted to meet you, your grace.'

Confound the girl, she was only just not laughing at his discomfiture. 'You won't be, when you see the contents of the coach,' he warned. 'Did you satisfy yourself with just the one carriage, Mama, or does your retinue follow you in another halfdozen?'

His parent gave the enchanting smile that had won over disrupted households the length and breadth of England. 'You see how it is, Mrs Penfold? A mother is never appreciated. And I would not dream of landing myself here without a word, you bad boy. I am staying at Cheveley, of course, and going on to see Lizzy in a day or so. She is increasing — *such* a blessing it did not happen any earlier, do you not think? — and although she writes that she is in the best of health, I do feel I ought to check for myself how she is keeping.'

'Naturally, you do, Mama. And very wise of you. One cannot be too careful at such a time. If I were you I would press onwards without delay.'

But the butler was already laying another

place and a footman was divesting her of her hat and remaining furs. Alex had no doubt at all that a third man was stationed outside to direct further conveyances to the Duke of Rutland's estate and that the Abervale coachman, groom and outriders were even now being drawn tankards of ale from the barrel in the kitchen.

'Oh good,' said Caroline with satisfaction. 'I was worried that Lord Rothwell's distressing lack of manners was a result of his illness, but as your grace does not appear concerned, I must conclude that it is habitual and that he is indeed recovered.'

The duchess beamed at her. 'The dear boy. His bark is far worse than his bite, you know. Is this for me? How delicious, I do adore a nice white soup. How very kind of the cook to send it back up. Pray tender my thanks. Alex, my love, is not that injury to your temple in the same place where you hit it all those years ago falling into the river? So *ill* you were then, I was quite prostrate with worry.'

Alex surrendered. He applied himself to his plate and signalled to the footman to refill his glass in defiance of Caroline's frown. He knew from experience that his mother would now talk her way through every one of his childhood ailments as if she herself, and not his old nanny, had had the nursing of him.

With any luck the recital would take her until the end of the meal and slake her parental impulses once and for all. He continued to eat, trying to shut out the litany. In this he was unexpectedly aided by Mrs Penfold. His hostess, more animated than he had hitherto known her, seemed convinced she had encountered a kindred spirit and was sharing with the duchess all the misadventures that had blighted her only son Bertrand's formative years.

Alex glanced at Caroline, thinking to point out with a wry look that she thoroughly deserved what she had started. He was pulled up short at the stricken expression on her face.

★   ★   ★

' . . . and so there was an end to it. I don't complain because I was blessed while I had him, but it is a hard thing, your grace, to know that you will never hear your son's joyful laugh again, and never rock your own grandchildren to sleep. Not even a daughter-in-law for company and consolation because with Caro being so young at the time nothing had been formally agreed. But we are hoping her mama will give up on her marriage prospects soon, which I daresay she will because of her not having any money apart from the betting, though of course Adeline doesn't know about that. Besides, Caro's sisters are easier and prettier and have more style to them. Caro can then live here.'

As Mrs Penfold's words pattered gently into the conversation, Caroline told herself she had often been this mortified before and that one day it would cease to hurt. And because it was Bertrand's mama talking and Caroline had loved her son, she continued to eat as though the matter-of-fact truths meant nothing. She didn't even know why she should feel she was dying inside until the Duchess of Abervale met her eyes. With that swift, compassionate look Caroline realized she had wanted this warm, lively, completely-unlike-her-son woman to esteem her despite her lack of assets or standing in the world. How ridiculous. She wouldn't even see her grace again once she had whisked Alexander away.

She glanced at him now as his mother simultaneously ate and brought him up to date on the Abervale news without in the least excluding her other listeners. He had a half-smile on his face, but she noticed he was holding himself stiffly, as if he was tired.

'Shall we move into the drawing room?' she said once everyone had finished. 'Do you accompany us, my lord, or are you going to sit here in solitude a moment and pretend that you are not forbidden port?'

Her grace rose at once. 'You are going to think me very rude, I daresay, but I believe I should be running away. John Coachman will want to get the horses settled for the night, and if there is one thing I have found to be paramount in this life, it is that it is of no more use to cross your coachman than it is to cross your gardener. But I shall be back tomorrow, so will bid you all a good night until then. Miss Caro — if you do not mind me addressing you so familiarly — I wonder if you could show me where I may make myself tidy? One does not want to arrive looking a complete scarecrow, you know.'

But once apart from the others, Alexander's mama gave herself only a cursory glance in the mirror before taking Caroline's hands and saying, 'Now tell me — how bad was he? My boy? Did he have nightmares?'

There was a tiny, held-in pain at the back of her eyes. Almost for the first time, Caroline was at a loss as to how to answer. Absurdly, she found herself not wanting to expose Alexander's weakness. 'He . . . he was very ill indeed, as I wrote to you, and yes, he was feverish, but he is improved considerably. If he was but back on his own estate, busy with his own concerns, I feel sure his recovery would be complete in short order.'

The duchess turned back to the glass, but she didn't seem to be seeing her reflection. 'The time the bridge broke under him he nearly died,' she said, her voice shaking a little. 'You will know about that, for he relives it every time he has a fever and I perceive you have been doing the bulk of the nursing. I am sure you have witnessed what he foolishly sees as his other failings too. He makes so light of them on the surface, but they *tear* at him fit to break your heart. Pray how did you get him through them? He is so very strong when in the grip of his terrors.'

Caroline blinked at this unnerving woman. 'I . . . I talked to him, your grace.'

The duchess blinked back. 'You *talked* to him?'

'Yes.'

'Just talked?'

'Yes. And soothed him, I suppose, whenever he seemed likely to do himself an injury. I did have to hold him down on occasion. To begin with. Not lately.'

'Good heavens. And he heeded you?'

'Well — yes. Mostly.'

Alexander's mother was still for a moment, then gave a small, bird-like nod. 'I would like to see the doctor for myself tomorrow. Can you arrange that for me? And then you must introduce me to your horses. Goodnight my dear. I am more grateful to you than I can say.' And to Caroline's utter astonishment she kissed her on the cheek before sailing out of the room.

9

'Miss Caro — his lordship's having them dreams again!' Caroline was awake and pulling a shawl around her nightgown before Thomas had finished speaking, almost as if her sleeping body had been waiting for just this summons. She hurried down the stairs to where Alexander was tossing from side to side in the bed.

'Hush,' she said. 'Hush, you need to rest.'

'Go then,' he muttered, 'go and be damned to you.'

This wasn't the bridge. Nor was it his sister. Caroline dipped a handkerchief in water to cool his brow, afraid that he would split open the healing cut. 'My lord, you must calm yourself.' This was what came of extra wine at dinner.

He put up his hand and bore down on her wrist. 'Go! Cease torturing me!'

'Are you all right, miss?' called Thomas, hovering anxiously in the doorway.

'Is that him?' growled Alexander. 'I will make him more *interesting* than me for you. I'll riddle him with holes, damn his hide.'

His emotion burnt how she must act into

Caroline's mind. She flapped her free hand at Thomas to tell him to go right away. If she had guessed correctly, the last thing Alexander needed in this particular nightmare was a male voice intruding into his scarred memories. Was it Rosetta who had spurned him? Or a more legitimate love? Whoever it was, she had hurt him badly and the hurt had to be eased. Caroline sat on the edge of the bed. 'I have changed my mind,' she said softly. 'I was wrong. Forgive me, Alexander. I will stay, if you wish it.'

He stopped threshing. His grip lessened. 'Stay?'

Caroline stroked his cheek, feeling the faint roughness against her fingers. 'Yes, I will stay. Go to sleep, my lord. I will be here.'

She was not prepared for his hand to release her wrist and move to her breast as surely as if his eyes were open and the lamp lit. She almost forgot to breathe when he cupped the roundness through the stout cotton of her nightgown. Not stout enough, she realized in further shock as his thumb stroked backwards and forwards across her nipple. 'Lie down, sweetheart,' he said drowsily.

Caroline could barely concentrate, so awash was she with this strange, sweet sensation. She knew, in a hazy, urgent way, that she should move away, that she should leave. She was alone in a gentleman's bedroom wearing nothing but a nightgown. And even if that gentleman was asleep, his hands were very much awake. But . . . but . . . His thumb stroked her again. Pleasure shot through her, branching up to her throat and down to her loins. Dear God, this was wonderful. She twisted to look behind her; the doorway remained mercifully empty of footmen. Praying with everything she knew for it to remain so, she eased herself to lie on the covers next to Alexander.

He turned onto his side with a great sigh, his hand slipping to her other breast. 'Need you,' he murmured, so low she hardly heard him. 'Don't go.'

Her heart hammered. She couldn't have moved if she'd tried. 'Why would I want to leave?' she whispered.

His breath was warm on her face. This time Caroline parted her lips as he kissed her. His hand slid over her breast, her waist, her hip. In that moment, Caroline truly grew up. She understood why her beautiful sister had accepted such an undistinguished suitor. She understood why Harry must have Louisa. She understood why lovers risked scandal and social ostracism in order to elope. She understood why some widows never remarried.

Alexander made a contented sound in his throat. In a very few moments his chest was rising and falling with the regular breathing of a man deeply asleep. Caroline remained where she was, her limbs as heavy and boneless as water, searching his face, committing it to memory in the dim light. It was, she thought shakily, a quite remarkably awkward time to fall in love.

★　★　★

All through the dawn horse work, Caroline concentrated on burying her secret deep inside her. She couldn't let it out. She daren't. It would be so *mortifying* if Alexander ever suspected she felt this way. But it would be all right. She would only have to be circumspect a short while longer. Now that his mother had arrived in Newmarket he would be leaving. The duchess might even effect his removal today. The sole occasions when Caroline would meet him from here on would be if he came to see Solange before the race.

The race. Focus on the race. That was better. More productive than retracing his sleeping features and wishing that the world was different. Much more like real life.

So, the race. It was a scant two weeks away:

179

a private match over the eight furlongs of the Rowley Mile against a hotch-potch of untried horses volunteered by their owners on the night of Harry's fateful wager. Having ridden her sufficiently to judge her strengths, Caroline wasn't worried about Solange's speed or stamina over that distance. However she was mightily concerned about the effect of the crowd. They had gradually built up the noise level in the stables without any ill effect, but in an unfamiliar situation anything might happen. The obvious solution would be to take her up to the racecourse and mingle with the race-goers to accustom her, but first they had to get her used to a male rider.

And this was the really awkward part: Solange still refused to let anyone but Caroline on her back.

'Enough,' called Harry as she cantered around the furthest paddock revolving the problem. 'Look at the sky.'

Caroline dropped the grey mare's pace straight away. She had been so deep in her thoughts she hadn't noticed the passage of time. She hunched low, just in case any of her father's hands should recognize her. 'Sorry,' she said.

Harry shrugged. 'Not like you, that's all. Something on your mind?'

'No, no. Only how to get this horse used to

a crowd in the next thirteen days. We'll have to get her up to the heath on a race day. Have *you* tried riding her?'

'Oh yes. She dumped me on the ground last weekend before I'd so much as bid her good morning.'

'She might not if I were to hold her head and talk to her while you mount?'

'Worth a try. We'll do it later. For now you need to de-lad yourself.'

Caroline caught her breath. 'Especially if that wretched valet of . . . of Lord Rothwell's is up betimes and wanting water and hot towels and I don't know what. Let's get going, Solange, quick trot back.' It was a good thing Alexander would be leaving them today. She needed to keep all her wits about her, not have half of them languishing over something that could never be.

★ ★ ★

Alex woke from the best night's sleep he'd had for a long time, to see light dancing on the ceiling of his room and his valet with a bowl of warm water ready. The man's expression made his feelings about rising at such an uncivilized hour abundantly clear. Alex ignored them.

Not only was the breakfast parlour empty,

it did not look as though there was any danger of it being used in the next several hours. Alex hesitated, then followed his nose and his instinct. Not since childhood — when his appetite had outstripped his ability to wait for the schoolroom breakfast — had he visited domestic quarters. The aroma as he pushed open the door took him right back to those days. Bacon fat, new bread, broth . . . Did all kitchens smell the same?

There had been a hum of voices. As he entered, silence fell — absolute and complete.

'And just what,' said Caroline Fortune from her place at the scrubbed table, 'do you think you are doing here?'

He pulled out a stool next to her. 'You are always telling me to eat.'

'Has your bell ceased to work? Has your valet lost the power of speech?'

Across the table, Harry Fortune grinned affably. 'Morning, Rothwell. Don't mind Caro — she likes to have the distinctions preserved.'

'This is a *working* breakfast,' she told him, frost in every syllable.

'I have no intention of interfering. Pray continue.' He caught the quick flash of a look pass between them. 'I take it your brother is telling you how yesterday's horses performed, ready for your report to your cousin. You

182

must have a prodigious memory, since you do not appear to be taking notes.'

'Thank you, my lord. I have often been complimented on it.'

She was admirably cool under fire, he'd give her that. He accepted the plate of ham and eggs that was put in front of him no wiser as to what this wretched pair were up to. Unless . . . 'I was meaning to ask,' he said idly, 'what did Mrs Penfold mean yesterday when she said you had no money, apart from the betting?'

Caroline and Harry exchanged a much longer look this time. Harry shrugged, as if leaving it to her.

'It is not something I would want spread abroad,' she said slowly.

Alex glanced around the busy kitchen. She trusted the servants, but not him? He was ridiculously hurt. 'I believe I am as discreet as you are.' His comment came out rather stiffer than he'd intended.

She looked at him for a long moment. It was astonishing. Never before had he had this crushing sense of being weighed up, not even when meeting with the influential men who were the power behind his chosen political party. 'Bertrand loved horses,' she said at last. 'He was fascinated with bloodlines. He used to study who had won what and under which conditions so he could breed the perfect racehorse. Harry, of course, was always up on the heath watching the races and the training. I suppose I was amazingly precocious, but it seemed perfectly clear to me that if I put their knowledge together, I could predict who should win each race. I didn't have any money to bet with, being so young and being a girl, but Bertrand did. It didn't always work, but we learnt as we went on and we built up a reasonable sum. We were going to purchase a stable — the three of us. This was when Bertrand's papa and grandpapa were alive, you understand. Penfold Lodge was simply a gentleman's residence then, not a racing yard. We . . . we had good times. Then, when Bertrand was bought his colours, he wanted Harry and me to carry on, but I was *still* a girl and much too young to have money lodged in a bank, so we all wrote a paper and signed it to say that Harry should have control over the account until Bertrand came back, and that if Bertrand didn't come back, then his third was to be mine too, but Harry should administer it until I was of age.'

Alex was stunned. The work of the kitchen went on around him but he didn't hear so much as the hiss of the fat or the rhythmic thump of kneading dough. He couldn't believe it. Of all the cork-brained schemes!

'And now I manage Penfold Lodge for our cousin,' said Harry, 'so instead of saving for an establishment of our own, we are building up our string.'

'Lady Penfold knew about it,' said Caroline. 'I think it helped her get over Bertrand's death. We had to explain, because otherwise she would have wondered what was behind the legacy.'

'People may bequeath their own assets as they like,' said Alex, still trying to grasp the idea of this self-possessed girl weighing odds and laying bets. 'I, for instance, made out my will some years ago leaving my estate to Giles, even though he is not family.'

'But he is your close friend, your mother's godson. He told us when you were ill that he had grown up with you. No one would think such a bequest strange. Bertrand was nine years my senior and *I am a girl*. I would not have been allowed to use any of the money if it had been done formally. Papa would have either refused it, or put it into trust where it wouldn't earn a fraction of what it does now.'

She sounded so reasonable about it. She truly believed she was acting in the most sensible way. In an appalled rush, Alex thought of all the men he knew whose lives had been ruined by betting. 'And he would be right,' he said with emphasis. Good God, did this girl know nothing? 'More horses lose than win. Many more.'

'Of course they do. But if one only wagers what one can afford to lose, the winnings are a bonus.' Caroline pushed away her plate. 'You asked; I have told you — and I wouldn't have done that had I not known that you were an honourable man. That is an end to it, if you please.'

He frowned. Much as he hated to admit it, these antics were indeed nothing to do with him. But she had left so much unsaid. There were so many points she could have expanded on. 'Is that why you do not wish to marry?' he asked, picking on one thing at random. 'Because having a husband would put a stop to the excitement of betting?'

Caroline snorted. 'There is little excitement when I do not know the results until Harry tells me next day! The money is simply a means to an end.'

'What end?'

'To be independent. Not to have to marry. Would you wish to be shackled for life to someone you dislike, merely to have a home? No, of course you wouldn't. Nor do you have to. Men have the option of remaining single and making their own way in the world. Women don't.'

Now what nonsense was she talking? 'It is

the job of men to provide,' he said impatiently.

'It need not be,' she fired back. 'That is what I am saying. If women were given the chance, they could look after their own affairs just as well as gentlemen do. Lady Penfold was my godmother. I loved her dearly and I love Penfold Lodge just as much as she did. If she had left this house to me, I would not have to petition my parents to live here. If she had left it to her son's widow, then Mrs Penfold could make me her heir. But she believed in blood and the male line, so instead left it to a great-nephew she hardly knew — though indeed we like him well enough. Please understand me, I am not criticizing her judgement, for it was simply the way she was, the tenets with which she had been brought up. But you must see that it is hard.'

Confound it! His statement about bequeathing property was about to come back and bite him. 'She was wiser about the world than you,' he said brusquely. 'If this house were yours, you would have more suitors than you knew what to do with. And all of them after your assets rather than you.'

Caroline turned as pale as he had ever seen her. 'Then I should doubtless count my blessings,' she said, and left the room.

There was a silence in the kitchen.

Disapproval came off the servants in waves. Harry looked across the table with raised eyebrows. 'Well, and I don't say you aren't right, but if I'd put it like that, she'd have boxed my ears.'

Why? What had he said? Alex revisited his words — and felt himself grow aghast. He might champion plain speech, but his unintentional implication that Caroline had no charms of her own had been unforgivably rude. He rose. 'Good God, I must explain! I didn't mean . . . could someone please send for . . . ?' He got a grip on himself. 'Could someone please *ask* Miss Fortune to grant me a few minutes' conversation?'

'She'll be with the horses,' said Harry, rising to his feet. 'I'll give you my arm up there.'

★ ★ ★

Caroline stood with her face buried in Rufus's neck. 'So stupid,' she said to his warm, chestnut hide. 'I am just so stupid. I know I have no attractions. I have always known it. It should not hurt that he thinks so too.' She took a juddering breath, trying to keep the raw, ripped part of her soul in place. 'And he has no idea I love him, so why should he think to mind his words? He has done me a favour. I know now — even if I did not before — that there will never be any hope.' She sniffed mightily and took a step back. 'I will shake this off. I will be calm, and normal, and shake this off.'

'Caroline,' called Alexander's voice behind her.

Oh no. Please let him not have heard her. 'You should not be outside,' she said without turning round. 'Go back to the house.'

His voice came closer. 'Caroline, please forgive me. I did not mean my words to sound the way they did.'

'It is of no consequence. It is only what I might have said myself.' *Do please go away. I have no wish for you to see me with red eyes and tear-stained cheeks.*

'Listen. Please listen. I must explain what was behind my most ill-considered remark. My sister Lizzy was courted for her money. She had her head turned and was persuaded to think herself in love with a penniless wastrel. I only meant that you might find yourself in the same position. I intended no slur. Would you like my handkerchief?'

Caroline held out her hand blindly. 'Thank you.' She dipped the linen in the horse trough and pressed it to her burning face before blowing her nose thoroughly. 'You may be easy, my lord, I am not likely to imagine

189

myself in love on the strength of a few pretty phrases.' No indeed, two kisses and an unconscious caress had done the job nicely. There had been no necessity for words at all.

Rufus blew on her hair and ambled away to graze, appearing to think his task was over. Traitor.

'Not even if they were in praise of your horse?' Alexander's voice was very near now. 'Fortune-hunters are deuced clever.'

Caroline laughed shakily. 'Ah, there I confess I might be more easily swayed.' She glanced at him, very quickly and sideways in case there was any pity in his eyes. 'But as I have no fortune, it hardly matters. Would you like to see Solange, now you are up here?'

'Certainly. I would be most interested to — Good God, you have put her in with other horses.'

He stumbled as he took an incautious step. Caroline was there in an instant to take his weight on her arm. 'You should not have followed me. You are by no means steady enough. Here, girl.' She held out her free hand to Solange.

She felt Alexander move to stop her. 'You are mad! She'll have your fingers off before you can . . . Well, stap me.'

Caroline felt only slight conceit as the grey mare nuzzled her palm. 'I did say she was progressing, if you remember. But you need not stroke her if you think she may yet hold you in dislike.'

'I am astonished,' he said frankly, but she was glad to see he extended his hand to Solange's neck as readily as she had herself. 'And also pleased. She bolted with me for no reason. I had thought she would have to be destroyed.'

'Bolted? Yet you sent her to my brother for a bet?'

He reddened. 'We were neither of us ourselves that night. How has this transformation been achieved?'

Hmph. If he thought she was going to give their secrets away, he was far and away out. 'At Penfold Lodge we work *with* the animals, not against them. Tell me, has she ever been bred from?'

'How the devil would I know?'

Caroline stared. 'Because she is your horse.'

'I had her from Giles. Ask him.'

Caroline stood perfectly still. Solange had previously belonged to Giles d'Arblay who, for some reason, bore no love for her brother. And the wager had been urged on them by 'one of Lord Rothwell's friends'. Was it possible Giles had effected the bet? To strip Harry of a thousand pounds? But that would be ridiculous. Wouldn't it? 'No matter,' she said. 'Some mares' natures become less challenging once they have foaled, that is all.'

'And some mares bite their offsprings' heads off.'

Caroline laughed. 'Not she. And I do think she is interested in Rufus.'

'I don't believe this. Are you petitioning for a stud fee? You are the most unnatural young lady I have ever met. I daresay you could recite your precious chestnut's bloodlines too.'

'I could. And I am not that unnatural, for Lady Penfold was quite as knowledgeable as I am.'

He smiled down at her, making her bones behave oddly. 'Trust me, you are unique. And now I will complete your satisfaction by admitting you to be entirely in the right about my strength and ask you to very nobly help me back to the house.'

Caroline masked the quiver that ran through her. 'You should not have come out in the first place. There was no need.'

'I beg your pardon, but there was every need. And while I am in a conciliatory humour, you may also be right about the ability of some ladies to manage their own affairs. I shall have to think about that. But now I own I should like to rest.'

If she were of a romantic disposition, she would treasure this, thought Caroline, as they traversed the path back to the house together. As it was she was too concerned with the pallor of his face to enjoy the feel of his forearm along hers. She was too worried about the shallowness of his breath to appreciate its warmth stirring her hair. Or so she told herself. 'I will call your valet to attend you,' she said, once she had helped him to the wing chair in his room.

'Wait,' he said, his hand reaching to hold hers for an instant. 'I was cavalier, thoughtless and dogmatic earlier on. Thank you for being so generous.'

'I daresay I shall think of a boon to offset it,' she said lightly, and disengaged her fingers. His touch was dangerous.

10

As soon as Caroline left the room, Alex rose and moved to the window. He was a little ashamed at having deceived her, but it would excuse his remaining here longer if he were thought not as fit as he actually was. For a moment, his legs seemed disinclined to obey him, but he put the trifling annoyance aside as he saw Caroline — as he had expected — return to the stable block. He leant against the window frame watching her wide, knowledgeable gestures as she conversed with her brother and the head groom.

Women managing their own affairs . . . Yes, he could see her running a small household: weighing up whether she could afford a parlourmaid, knowing when the butcher was robbing her. But why would she want to do that on a slender income when she could have the same freedom inside a marriage? A husband would expect his wife to order all the daily business of a house. It was the way of the world — men paid and women arranged. Where was the difference?

Would you wish to be shackled for life to someone you dislike?

It was as if she had spoken inside the room. With a jolt, Alex bethought himself of other things that a man expected of his wife. And he thought of some of the gentlemen of his acquaintance. And he looked again at Caroline.

His ruminations were cut short by the entry of his valet, fussily appalled at the state of milord's boots and milord's coat and milord's neckcloth.

It was fortunate the man couldn't see the state of milord's handkerchief. Sobered, Alex allowed himself to be steered back to the chair by the fire, remembering Caroline's stiff, upright back against the warm chestnut of the horse and the way she had resolutely worked through her chagrin. She was younger than his sister (*only in years*, as Harry Fortune would say), but what a difference in temperament. All the difference between an indulged youngest child and the plain one in the middle of a string.

Except that she wasn't so very plain when she knew what she was talking about. There was quite a challenging sparkle in those honey-brown eyes. And when she laughed she wasn't plain at all. And as for her voice — here Alex discovered with mild surprise that his valet had got him out of his coat and both boots without him noticing — Caroline Fortune's voice was simply beautiful.

★ ★ ★

Alex suspected it was not an accident that his mother's call later that morning coincided with that of the doctor. Caroline's guileless face confirmed it. He was pleased to see she had changed out of her dusty gown into a clean one which became her better. He was *not* pleased when his offer to accompany her and his mother to the paddocks was vetoed. From the window he watched their progress with deep misgiving.

It was ridiculous. He was twenty-nine years old; he was the master of his own estate; he would soon be a Member of Parliament, God-willing, and it did not make a jot of difference whether Mama found out he was still having nightmares or not. All the same, it did ease his mind that they appeared to be laughing. Caroline had evidently fallen under his mother's spell and remained chuckling when they returned, attended by her equally charmed brother, ready to partake of a nuncheon before Harry went up to the heath for the last day of the week's races. Fortune pulled out a chair for her grace to sit on, Alex did the same for Caroline. She met his eyes with a startled *thank you*.

'My pleasure,' he said uncomfortably. Had he been that graceless recently? 'I hope my

196

mother has not been bullying you into divulging any racing tips?'

'No indeed,' said Caroline. She gave a mischievous smile. 'I have been far too well employed hearing all your shameful boyhood anecdotes for that.'

He raised his eyebrows, ready to be amused. 'Surely not. I have always been led to believe I was a model child.'

'Model children generally slide down bannister rails directly into the arms of royal princesses, do they?'

'Ah, well, that was not my fault. Giles bet me we could not get down the grand staircase and back up again between the time the carriage stopped outside and the time the visitors entered the house.'

She twinkled at him. 'And what of the occasion when your cook's famous orange syllabubs disappeared *en route* from the kitchen to a very important dinner?'

'An error of judgement on the part of my parents. They should have included us children amongst the dinner guests.'

After Mrs Penfold had discoursed in her turn about her late son's propensity for falling out of apple trees when scrumping (Alex was getting just a little tired of Bertrand's exploits) and Harry recalled how his mother's prize Grecian statue was found to be cradling

a maid's feather duster in a *most* inappropriate manner one memorable Twelfth Night,
the duchess cleared her throat.

'Well now, Alex,' she said, 'have you any
messages for Lizzy when I go on to her
tomorrow?'

Caroline spluttered over her wine. Alex
glanced at her curiously before saying, 'Only
my love, as always, and my commiserations to
her husband. I daresay they will be far more
appreciative of your maternal concern than I.'

'I don't suppose they will for an instant,'
said his mama candidly, 'and I would have
you know that I am not *completely* happy
about you either. It is only knowing I am
leaving you in Miss Caro's capable hands that
enables me to travel on with equanimity at
all. But I find I have perfect faith in her ability
to curb any tendencies you may develop in
the next sennight as regards night-time strolls
alongside bands of dangerous ruffians.'

Caroline was staring at her grace with dismay.
'But, ma'am, surely I heard you agree with Dr
Peck that his lordship would benefit of all
things from a stay in the bosom of his family?'

'The doctor is a good man, my dear, but I
assure you if I were to take Alex with me to
visit Lizzy, we should have at least two
murders on our hands before the week was
out. I will collect him on my way back

through. His father was expressing the sentiment only yesterday that he had quite forgot what our second son looked like. And I may say, Alex, that I have had words with Lady Jersey. I was surprised to find her at Cheveley rather than in Town, though it seems she has been flitting back and forth. Such nonsense that woman does talk.'

Mama *always* did this. Made ambiguous pronouncements in public so it was impossible to argue. In order to answer at all, Alex had to pick his way through a bog of double meanings. 'I shall, of course, be delighted to visit you and Papa, but I believe I will do it in my own good time. And I consider it very kind in Sally Jersey to call as soon as she knew I was laid up. She did not tire me at all.' He turned to his hostess with a smile borrowed from Giles at his most charming. 'Mrs Penfold, it appears my mother and the doctor between them insist on my trespassing a while longer on your hospitality. I can only apologize for the imposition, and trust I may not disturb your household arrangements too much.'

★   ★   ★

'Another week entire! Harry, that means he will be here when we take Solange to the heath to practise!'

199

Harry shrugged. 'Just because he was up betimes this morning, does not mean he will always be. You are usually out and back by cock's crow anyway.'

Caroline felt herself seethe with frustration. 'Exactly! What if he takes it upon himself to have nightmares when I am on the training ground? And how are we to accustom Solange to a male rider with him watching every move?'

'We use the far paddock.'

'Oh yes, the one backing on to our father's land.'

'Don't fuss, Caro. I need get up to the heath now. Daresay you'll have thought of the solution before I get back.'

I must not scream at my brother. Caroline repeated this several times to herself as she watched Harry leave the house with a jaunty, unconcerned step. Alexander and his mother were conversing privately in his room so — remembering his taunt that morning — she fetched her ledgers and sat in the parlour with Mrs Penfold to write her weekly report to her cousin.

'I declare,' said her grace, sweeping in not long after, 'there is no dealing with you in this mood, Alex. I only said I must see what I could do, not that I *would* make any such arrangements. Do you go and bother poor

Miss Caro, whilst I have a comfortable coze with Mrs Penfold.'

'You had best *not* bother me,' warned Caroline, as Alexander joined her at the table. 'If I have to start sanding out errors, I will not vouch for the evenness of my temper. You had much better play cribbage against yourself instead. The board is in the drawer.'

'I could read out the figures for you.'

'Only if you want your recuperative period extended by my breaking this ledger over your head.'

His lips twitched. 'Now I come to think of it, cribbage is an excellent way of passing the time.'

'I am glad we are in accord, my lord.'

He became absorbed in his game straight away. Caroline, perversely, found it difficult to settle to the rest of her letter. Alexander's right hand kept moving in and out of her field of vision. It was the one that had caressed her. The firm, straight fingers fascinated her and she could not help willing it on when it started to draw ahead of the left hand on points. She made a conscious effort and finished her report at last.

'Is it private?' asked Alexander. 'May I read it?'

'Yes it is private, and no you may not read it! What a thing to ask! Do you allow your friends to peruse accounts from your own steward?'

He smiled, not at all offended. 'I beg your pardon. I was merely interested in the workings of a very small establishment. Will you play cribbage against me instead?'

'I will play against your left hand, my lord. Your right is too good.' Caroline spoke before she thought — and then had to duck her head as she cleared away her work for fear he would see the wash of colour in her cheeks. Dear Lord, she would have to conquer this ridiculous sensibility, or she would never be able to talk to him normally again.

Eventually the duchess left, saying she would call on her way out of town on the morrow. Caroline, in debt to the tune of several thousand points, left Alexander to rest, and hastened to the stable block. But there was no news of how the day had gone, so she simply rode Solange around the paddock side-saddle, talking to her the while, then brought her inside.

★　★　★

No alarms. No disturbances. Caroline told herself she was pleased Alexander had passed an uneventful night. Harry had been home to dine, nobody had eaten too much or taken more wine than was good for them. The conversation had been informed and amusing. Would that this state of affairs lasted the week.

★   ★   ★

Alex was perusing the newspaper next day when Giles called. 'Ah,' he said. 'I deduce the racing has finished.'

'Eh? Of course it has finished. It's Saturday. Mind, I'm not surprised your wits have gone begging, living in this dead-and-alive house. You had much better remove back to the White Hart.'

Alex looked at his friend in surprise. 'I thought we agreed Penfold Lodge was a perfect base for investigations.'

'Yes, but Sally has lost interest in her little business and to be frank, Alex, the landlord's getting a touch restive, wanting something on account.'

'Tell him to send the bill to my steward. You have not forgotten, Giles, that *I* have an interest in this 'little business' too? Someone hit me over the head! I find I have a strange hankering to know why.'

'Oh, there's nothing in that. Always a rum set of coves around Newmarket. Why, someone at Crockford's only the other night was saying he'd disturbed a housebreaker or some such at his window. Fellow got away, of course, but it just shows you.'

'Which night? Who was it talking?'

'Burn it, I don't know.' Giles took his usual restless turn about the room. 'Lord, it's slow here. I don't know how you can stand it. And that Friday-faced chit looking at you as if you were wearing the wrong coat or something all the time.'

Alex had to control a small rush of most unexpected anger. 'Do you mean Miss Caroline Fortune? I daresay she thinks you might lead me into some scheme that would set back my recovery. I am told there is a billiard room — shall we have a game?'

'You will have to loan me the wherewithal to pay you if I lose,' said Giles. 'I dropped most of mine at faro last night.'

Alex rang for a footman to ask where the billiard room might be found, but as they crossed the hall, the front door was opened to admit Alderman Taylor and his daughter.

'Then again,' murmured Giles, 'after spending the week largely in the company of gentlemen, I suddenly feel a great urge for a spot of feminine frippery. I think we might join the ladies, don't you?' He moved forward with polite effusions, giving Alex no chance to disagree.

In the saloon, Alex saw a tiny smile play around Caroline's lips as she took in the visitors. 'A lovely day for a drive, Alderman,' she said. 'So kind of you to bring Louisa to visit me again.'

Alex turned his head away hastily. The wretched girl was *dangerous* in company. It took him an instant to compose himself in order answer the alderman's civil questions about his health.

Giles, he noticed, had pulled up a hard chair next to the sofa where Miss Taylor was seated by her friend.

'I am glad to meet you again also, Mr d'Arblay,' continued Alderman Taylor. 'I thought you danced in a very distinguished manner at our assembly the other week. Almost, may I say, as distinguished as Lord Rothwell here.'

'You are most kind, but I have always known that my friend is a far better dancer than I am,' said Alex, and saw the tightness leave Giles's smile.

'Indeed, how could one not be, when one has such a charming partner?' said Giles, inclining his head to Miss Taylor.

Alex was fairly sure he had not imagined the faint snort coming from Caroline's direction, especially when she asked a commonplace question about the state of the lanes on their journey today, which turned the conversation nicely.

However, though Giles seemed content to play a waiting game, Miss Taylor's father was not distracted for long. After moving the discussion on lanes bodily to Surrey and praising the roads indiscriminately around that area where Alex's estate happened to be, he turned to Giles with a question. 'Talking of landowners' obligations, it says in the *Gentleman's Magazine* that your family hall was 'once fine, but now sadly neglected'. Surely that cannot be so, can it?'

'Alas, my esteemed father is not always as good at investments as he imagines,' said Giles easily. 'It is a great sadness to me, for I have many happy boyhood memories of the estate, but I am convinced it will come about yet.'

The alderman shook his head. 'Ah, that's the way of it, is it? It is always a mistake for men without a head for business to manage their own affairs. I am for ever saying so, am I not, Louisa?'

His daughter smiled lovingly at him. 'You are, Papa. You say that it is better for a man to do what he can do well, than to make a bad fist of something he can never be.'

Just for a moment, Alex caught Caroline's eye which was brimful with amusement.

Again he found it a struggle to keep his expression under control. He had no doubt that by the time Miss Taylor was wed to Harry Fortune, her poor father would be under the impression he had made the match himself.

Across the room, Giles praised the alderman's perspicacity with his usual panache. Just as the visit lengthened beyond the polite norm, the alderman arose. Alex was unsurprised when Giles affected astonishment at the passage of time and elected to take his leave also.

On the sofa, Caroline relaxed infinitesimally. Alex, exchanging a few words with Giles before he went, wondered what she had been concerned about. Then the door to the saloon opened, Harry Fortune breezed in, and Miss Taylor — who had been beautiful before — positively glowed.

All through the laughing flurry of I-beg-your-pardon and We-were-just-leaving and Sorry-to-have-missed-you, Alex was aware of Giles's brittle smile. Following the party into the hall, Alex saw him win the honour of handing Miss Taylor up into the carriage. He also saw that though her lips thanked his friend, and her hand remained in his a little too long, her eyes were on Fortune. Giles turned and strode towards the town without a backward glance.

Alex winced, knowing from experience

that, rather than admit Louisa's affections were already engaged, Giles would put her lack of attention down to his own lack of fortune. Often, of course, this was the case and as he had always done, Alex could not help but feel sympathetic. Very early on in life he had noticed the different way adults treated his elder brother — the heir to the Abervale titles and lands — and him — with only his mother's comparatively small estate to look forward to — and he had become disillusioned and disgusted with society in consequence. Even less favoured was Giles, the late-born third son of a neighbouring baronet with no prospects at all. But whereas Alex became colder and more scornful of the world as a result of his perspicacity, Giles tried that bit harder to please. It was always he who charmed extra sweetmeats out of the kitchen, always he who could get away with explaining why shirts were stained and knickerbockers torn after a day's adventuring in the woods.

What worked on cooks and nursery maids had little effect on schoolmasters until Giles learnt the knack of simulating interest in those opinionated gentlemen, and uncomplainingly ran the most boring of errands for them. Then school, too, became an easy ride. The fathers of the town damsels were rather more difficult to charm, but fortunately Giles established that avoidance-of-scandal money was about the one thing his parent *would* spare from his own gaming purse.

Already cynical, Alex became even more so on entering society, discovering that amongst gently born young ladies, professions of love went hand-in-hand with attention to one's rents. For Giles, the revelation came as a particularly hard-to-swallow pill. The heiresses he favoured turned markedly less affectionate on hearing about his father selling ever more parcels of land and his eldest brother's increasing progeny. He had even begun to talk of giving thought to a profession until the happy day when his godfather suffered an apoplexy in the arms of his mistress, leaving Giles a ruined castle for glamour and three snug farms for rent. It would have been even better if the income from those farms ever managed to last the quarter.

So yes, Alex understood that Giles felt life had dealt him an unfair hand, but he needn't go on griping about it. Maybe it was disloyal in Alex, but really, compared to Harry Fortune, who was now asking civilly whether he would care for a game of billiards, Giles seemed a touch — thin.

* ★ ★ ★

Caroline waited until she heard the reassuring click of ivory balls behind the door, then hurried upstairs to don a riding coat. Provided Harry did his part, she would be able to take Solange right around Newmarket with no one being any the wiser. The traffic in the town was lighter by far than it would be on a race day, but still sufficiently busy to test the mare's nerve. Flood insisted on walking alongside her. It was of no use Caroline reminding him that she had already ridden Solange to the heath and back without incident. He simply replied that what worked in the very early morning was of no account on a bustling afternoon and who was head groom in this establishment anyway? So they walked sedately along the High Street, turning before they reached the White Hart, 'just in case some inquisitive little ferret isn't up to his horrible eyes in a gambling den' as Flood put it, and then circled down around St Mary's and came back.

There was no doubt that Solange wasn't happy, but with Caroline talking to her and Flood's solid presence at her head, she acquitted herself without more than a few eye-rolls and then one long whinny when a butcher's boy came pelting out of his master's shop after a thief.

'Enough for one day?' asked Caroline, when the Penfold Lodge arch came into sight.

'I'd say so, Miss Caro. A nice rub down and a bucket of mash and she'll be right as a trivet.'

Caroline slipped into the billiard room to watch the last game. She noticed Alexander smile as he glanced at her gown. She looked down to see a thatch of straw clinging to the hem. She bent to pick it off, hoping her flush would be attributed to her change in position rather than warmth because he found her habit of slipping up to the stables endearing. Love, when you were deceiving the unconscious object of your affections, was a tremendously complicated affair.

'What do you do tomorrow, my lord?' she said, following a certain plan of her own that had its roots in the Duchess of Abervale's various confidences. 'Are you sufficiently recovered as to attend church with us? The neighbourhood would be delighted if so. There has been much regret and mortification felt that you should be attacked so basely in our particular area. I daresay you will be inundated with enquiries as to your health.'

Alexander set his cue in the rack beside Harry's. 'How gratifying. But alas I believe it would be sheer foolishness to sit for that length of time in a draughty church and risk a set-back.' He opened the door for her to precede him out of the room. 'You must lend me your Bible that I may spend a profitable hour quietly perusing it whilst you are out.'

'Certainly,' she replied. 'If you like, I shall also repeat you the text of the sermon over dinner.'

He looked thoughtfully at her. 'I think,' he said, 'that my immortal soul will survive without.'

'It is your decision, my lord.' Caroline made a mock-grieving sigh and was rewarded by the sight of another smile on his lips.

Again, the night passed without incident.

★ ★ ★

As Caroline had half-suspected would be the case, Giles d'Arblay was not at All Saints to give thanks for the past week any more than his friend. In the churchyard after the service, she found her sister Selina mourning the fact.

'He is prodigious handsome,' sighed Selina.

'And prodigious exigent,' said Caroline drily.

'He told me I had eyes like stars,' said Selina.

'Well, I have never yet seen cornflower-blue stars, so I would not know. And furthermore

212

he knows you are not out, so it was very wrong of him to be whispering nonsense to you. When was this?'

'He called on Papa last week to look at one of the horses, and then stepped inside to take tea with us.'

'Indeed. And had he poetic words for any other part of your anatomy?'

Selina looked at her sister resentfully. 'He said my lips were like an unfolding rose and my ears were like shells, nestling in a bed of spun gold.'

Caroline let out a peal of laughter. 'What moonshine! I wonder he does not try to publish a volume of poor poetry to pay his debts, rather than sponge on his friend.'

Selina and the other young ladies in the group looked taken aback. 'Does he do so indeed?' asked Selina's bosom bow.

'Oh yes. I overheard him asking Lord Rothwell to lend him money only yesterday. And when her grace the duchess called to ascertain the extent of her son's injuries, she told me — ' Caroline broke off as if she had only just realized she was being indiscreet. 'You won't pass this on, will you?'

'Oh, no,' they all fervently assured her.

'Because it was told to me in confidence.'

'We won't say a word.' Half-a-dozen pairs of eyes were fixed on her imploringly.

'Well,' said Caroline, dropping her voice, 'she told me that every time they make a stay in a place, Lord Rothwell not only picks up the tab for both of them, but frequently finds himself applied to by tradesmen whom his friend has given his name to as standing surety for his purchases!'

The young ladies looked suitably appalled. In a town where not a few of them lived within sight of the shop, this breach of fiscal etiquette shocked them almost as much as the duchess's insights into Giles's morality would have done.

Caroline gave her arm to her brother and sauntered back to Penfold Lodge justly pleased with her morning's work. Giles d'Arblay was not going to cause havoc in *her* town if she could avoid it!

* * *

Alex had also been busy. As soon as the church party disappeared from view, he had taken his stick and walked carefully up to the paddock. He leant on the rail, watching the yearlings. As he'd expected, it wasn't long before Flood was leaning beside him.

'Morning, milord. Was you wishful of something?'

'Merely enjoying a breath of fresh air

without a pack of women watching my every step.'

The head groom grunted.

'I do not believe I have thanked you, by the way. It was you who found me and went for the doctor, was it not?'

'Aye, I went for the doctor, right enough. Bleeding like a stuck pig, you were.'

Alex winced, this being rather more information than he required. 'You didn't see anyone who might have done it?'

'No, milord. I'd have strung 'em up if I had and apologized to the magistrate later. Summat like that happening on our land — makes my blood boil.'

'A friend of mine tells me there have been other incidents of attempted housebreaking in Newmarket recently.'

'I couldn't say, milord. I've not heard of any such thing myself.'

There was a small silence. Alex nodded at the foals frolicking in the sunshine. 'I have been wondering why you keep so many youngsters? Penfold Lodge cannot make a profit from them when all they do is eat and grow.'

Flood gave a rumble of laughter. 'Ah, that's Mr Harry's specialty. He's a dab hand at bringing on a young horse. Train 'em gentle, tickle the public with the two-year-old races, mop up as a three year old and sell 'em on for a good price.'

'That's very sound,' said Alex, startled.

Flood rumbled harder. 'Aye, it would be if it weren't for Miss Caro. Such a soft heart on her, she's got. Can't bear the thought of the beasts going to a hard trainer so won't let him sell unless they're off to Robert Robson or the like.'

'And there I was thinking she was the brains of the outfit,' said Alex softly.

There was a long silence.

'Was there anything else, milord?' said Flood.

'I might take a look at Solange.'

Flood paced alongside him.

'Who's going to be riding her in the race?'

Flood looked properly shocked. 'That's Mr Harry's business, not mine.'

Which was a blatant lie if ever he'd heard one. 'Yes, of course. I do beg your pardon.' Then, 'Was Miss Fortune really going to marry Bertrand Penfold?'

'Oh, aye,' said the groom readily. 'They'd have made a match all right. It would've suited her a lot better than all that jaunting to London last year. Never saw so much of a change in anyone as when she came back when her ladyship fell ill.'

Alex felt a sharp jolt. 'She was altered? In what way?'

Flood ruminated, watching Solange cropping the grass nearest to Rufus's paddock. 'Smaller,' he said eventually.

'Smaller?'

'Aye, like she needed the air of this place, and the horses around her to fill her back out again.'

In the distance, they heard the peal of church bells.

'Reckon they'll be back soon,' said Flood. 'Give you good morning, milord.'

Alex made his way reflectively back to the house. He was no nearer finding out who had attacked him, but for some muddled reason, that no longer felt his primary concern.

11

Caroline was creeping past Alexander's room to fetch a drink when she heard him cry out towards midnight. She was in and hushing him before the footman outside had so much as stirred from his slumber.

It was vastly different now, cradling his head against her shoulder. Blood thrummed uncomfortably in her veins. Her hands shook against his nightshirt. She was completely and absolutely convinced that she shouldn't be here. She was also completely and absolutely convinced that she wouldn't be leaving until he was safely quiet again.

'Why?' he murmured. 'Why? Why?'

'Why what, Alexander?'

His brow wrinkled, as if placing her voice. 'C'me here,' he said.

Heart in mouth, watching the doorway, Caroline lay on the bed next to him. His arm came across and held her close. 'Don't go,' he breathed. 'Stay. Don't go.' He buried his face in her hair, but did nothing else except hold her tight.

Caroline fitted herself to the line of his body without thought. Even with him under the blankets and her on top of them, this was so much the right place to be and so much what she wanted to do. In the clear light of day she would be plain, insignificant Caroline Fortune again and he would be the son of a duke, but right now he needed her and she was here. There was a strange, heartbreaking pleasure in taking by night what could never be hers in the morning.

He fell asleep again almost straight away. Caroline listened to his regular breathing and felt his arm relax. She should go. This was madness. She must leave now, before she succumbed to the comfort of lying beside him. In a few hours she would be dressing as a lad and riding his horse across Newmarket Heath. And he must not know because ladies had no place in the masculine world of racing and there would be a scandal and he would never look at her again. Not that he looked at her anyway.

Why did you not depart with your mama? she cried silently. *Why did you not exit my life yesterday? Every day you are here makes this harder.*

He stirred, almost as if he had heard her. Her heart in pieces, she eased herself free and fled, her hair escaping from its braid and sticking to the tracks of tears on her face.

★ ★ ★

In his dream, Alex knew something was missing. He searched formless towns and asked faceless people. Heat beat at his body and rain soaked his face. Dimly, his conscious mind recognized this phase. He put out an immense effort and woke up, his cheek rough and sore from being scrubbed against his sweat-soaked pillow. He lay in the dimness with silence around him. Good. He had got himself out of the nightmare without waking anyone. He was beating the cycle at last. He should feel victorious. Why, then, was there this sense of loss? He sat up wearily and shook his pillow, turning it so that he should lie against the dry side.

Something fell across his face. Something light and soft, there and gone. A moth? A spider? Alex sat very still, letting his eyes become accustomed to the dim light spilling from the lamp in the hallway through his partly open door. He looked down. Across the pale band of sheet slithered a strip of . . . of ribbon. Alex picked it up, feeding the slippery satin length through his fingertips. Unquestionably, this was a woman's. It should be laced into the neck of a gown or threaded into a fall of hair. What was it doing on his pillow? He curled it around his fingers and went back to sleep, waiting for what the morning might bring.

★   ★   ★

By daylight, the ribbon proved to be a deep cherry colour. Alex stared at it, flummoxed. Rosetta used to have narrow, feminine ribbons in pinks, blues and greens to tie her peignoirs. She had lain on her couch, teasing him with promises, until he had undone every last bow to reach the delights within. Both Rosetta and the peignoirs had been expensive; Alex had foolishly assumed he was buying exclusivity. It had been a shocking blow to his pride when he found he was not. The memory had been raw ever since.

But now, staring at the plain cherry ribbon twined in and out of his fingers, Alex felt the old pain fall away and a strange, half-entranced tugging take its place. Rosetta's perfect, painted face, her flawless body and delicate, scalloped surroundings dissolved to nothing. What was accomplished mock-innocence when you had a sturdy, honest red ribbon in your bed? And unless the maids were in the habit of flitting in and out of his room at night, there was only one person it could belong to. Alex found the idea strangely invigorating.

'Good morning,' he said, strolling into the kitchen. The various servants bobbed, bowed or, in the case of Cook, inclined their heads magisterially at him. Fortune grinned. Caroline looked resigned.

'Could you not sleep again, my lord?' she said. 'I am sure if you had rung your bell, a soothing posset could have been brought to you.'

Alex smiled. Her hair, he noticed, was braided and pinned in a workaday fashion around her head. Her gown was a particularly distressing shade of blue. 'Do you ever wear red?' he enquired.

'Red?' she echoed in disbelief. 'Oh yes, I can see it now. An unmarried young lady, not living under her parents' roof, wearing red as she goes about her daily business. I wonder I have never thought of it for myself.'

Alex laughed. 'You are right, I suppose. I keep forgetting you are so young. But it would become you far better than that colour you have on now.'

'Why, thank you, but as the polite world is not driving four-in-hand up the London road to sit at my feet this morning, you will forgive me if I do not immediately rush upstairs and change.'

A plate of hot rolls arrived on the table, direct from the oven. Alex promptly broke one open. 'It would be a shame if you did, for these smell wonderful.'

The assistant cook bobbed, flustered.

Caroline consumed a roll, dripping with butter, before saying, 'As it happens, this dress used to be Honoria's. It is the curse of having fair-haired, blue-eyed sisters that when something that was supposed to be for them fails to suit, it flatters me even less.'

Alex thought ruefully of the pin-money his own sister frittered away. 'You surely have an allowance? Do you never have lengths of material made up for you alone?'

Caroline buttered another roll and wrinkled her nose. 'Well, I could, I suppose, but I would have to battle Mama for it, and honestly if it was a choice between that and taking a chance on a nine-to-one promising outsider . . . '

★   ★   ★

Red! Caroline flung open the door of her wardrobe and looked at the contents in despair. *Red!* She had a round gown in cream cotton with a dusky pink spot. Was that close enough? She could wear it for dinner, and perhaps thread one of her night-braid ribbons in her hair. Except the ribbon would not stay in place, of course, and then she would look both untidy *and* foolish. Could Mrs Penfold's maid help her to anchor it? But she would wonder why.

This was nonsensical. She collected her writing desk and went downstairs in disgust. She couldn't believe she was even *considering* dressing to please a man who wouldn't give her a second glance once he was gone from this house.

By the greatest good fortune, a stack of letters addressed to Lord Rothwell from his steward arrived just as Caroline was running out of reasons not to spend the morning with him. Alexander looked at them glumly. 'And I was thinking of petitioning for my horse to be brought round from the White Hart that I might have some exercise. It had best be tomorrow, after all.'

Caroline pursed her lips. Did this man never reflect? 'If you are of a mind to ride, you should send to your groom to get the fidgets out of the horse today,' she told him roundly. 'It has been over a week since you were on him. Do you really feel strong enough?'

'Chieftain is of a placid temperament, and I thought I might prevail on your brother to accompany me in case of any difficulty.'

Her brother. Yes, of course.

'Or,' continued Alexander with a ruminative air, 'if he is engaged, perhaps you might join me to make sure I do not overextend myself. My groom would be with us, naturally.' He smiled at her suddenly. '*Not* Jessop.'

Colour flooded Caroline's cheeks. It was a good thing he did not employ that smile often, or half the country would be undone. 'You should certainly have *someone* you will listen to,' she said. 'And, as I feel I owe it to your mama's faith in me, I will be pleased to accompany you. But will your friend Mr d'Arblay not wish to join you if you are to ride out?'

'Lord, no. Giles would find the short amble across the fields which I fear is all I may manage, far too slow for his taste. Also I should prefer to essay this first attempt back in the saddle in the morning when I am strongest. Giles rarely departs his valet's hands until noon.'

This was welcome intelligence. Caroline left Alexander to his letters and scampered quickly up to the paddock to take Solange for a brisk turn or two about the town. It was not that she did not precisely trust the mare's erstwhile owner should he see her on Solange, it was that she simply preferred not to take any risks. Not with the betting-odds *and* not with the animal.

As it happened, she was able to work with Solange that afternoon as well. With the gentlemen of the *ton* returned to London for the week, Mr d'Arblay found himself at such a loss that he called to play billiards with his friend. The billiard room, most fortunately, was at the side of the house facing away from the stable.

When she returned they were still in there. Indeed, Mr d'Arblay stayed so long that Caroline, without in the least wishing to, was obliged to penetrate their masculine fastness to offer him dinner. He was all politeness, regretting that a trifling inconvenience with his digestion precluded him eating at such an early hour. Caroline accepted the fiction with a colourless nod of her head. She dearly hoped it was sheer habit of years that enabled Alexander to still call the man a friend.

★   ★   ★

As Caroline withdrew, Alex reflected he had never in his life had to apologize so much for Giles as he had since they had taken up residence in Newmarket. Later, however, when he touched awkwardly on the matter, Caroline merely smiled and said she was not in the least surprised his friend might find it slow at Penfold Lodge compared with the quality of his normal life.

He eyed her, suspecting irony, and retorted

that it was more likely Giles had heard a rumour that the doctor had forbidden more than one bottle of wine to be opened at any one meal.

'A baseless untruth,' said Caroline serenely.

Untrue or not, it was another comfortable evening. Alex felt himself replete with good food and conversation, and sought his bed without repine at an hour Giles would have stigmatized as indecently early. And surprised himself by sleeping the night through with no dreams, no tumbled, sweat-soaked sheets — and no vagrant ribbons.

★　★　★

It wasn't until he joined Caroline in the stable yard next morning that Alex realized the extraordinary fact that he had not yet seen her on a horse. Now, a rush of pleasure surprised him as he looked at her. She was wearing a dull green riding habit that became both her and Rufus very well, and she sat him upright and graceful. Tan leather boots and matching gloves completed the ensemble. The reins were loose in her hand, proclaiming her unconscious ease in the saddle. Alex was impressed for Rufus was no small horse.

She had evidently taken the time to check Chieftain over before he arrived, for she complimented him on the brown gelding before asking whether he really felt up to a hack.

'I really do,' he assured her. 'It is a fine day and I should like to be allowed to enjoy it without a catechism.'

She blushed and nudged Rufus to a walk. 'I beg your pardon, my lord. It must indeed have been frustrating for you to be kept indoors. I am always out of sorts myself when I am unable to ride for any period of time.'

'Is that why you did not like London?' he asked.

She shot a startled glance at him. 'In part. Honoria is not seen to best advantage on horseback, so Mama did not think it necessary to hire us mounts. But I also found everything so artificial. Watching people at the parties was amusing for a while, until I realized that for many it is a matter of ceaseless work. Always to be seen in the right clothes, in the right places, with the right people. One is forever concerned about making the right connections, attracting the right attention. And then a single unthinking step out of line, one person offended, a careless or cutting remark about you by a person of consequence, can make all the effort count for naught. It sickened me.'

Alex felt a welling up of anger. '*Were you* slighted in some way?'

She laughed. 'No, I had no expectations, so was not concerned enough to be disappointed. But I saw it happen to others. I saw the way people were treated when they were not rich, or beautiful, or well-connected. And then, of course, Lady Penfold fell ill and I was anxious about her so I *could* not make myself appealing. My mother was pleased enough to let me come home.'

He was silent for a moment. 'I am sorry it was not an agreeable experience. I spend most of my time at my club when in town, or latterly at the House, but even so there is a lot to like about the season. Though I too have frequently found balls and parties trying.'

'It *is* hard to be universally affable,' she agreed gravely.

'It is hard when one's political aspirations are continually interrupted because one is being chased by husband-hunters,' he retorted without thinking. 'And when one's sister is behaving in a potentially disastrous manner completely overlooked by one's imbecilic sister-in-law!' Even as those words left his lips he felt himself cringe. 'I beg your pardon. Would you be so forbearing as to instantly forget that last sentence?'

'Forget what? Sorry, my lord, I was not attending.' Caroline picked up her horse's pace a little.

And that had not been well done of him either! What was it about her that always put him in the wrong? 'Caroline,' he said despairingly.

She looked back. 'My lord?'

He took a deep breath. 'I beg your pardon. Properly. It is not that I do not trust you to be discreet. I only meant I should not have spoken so about my brother's wife. May I tell you the whole story? Fill in the pieces you do not know?'

'Why?'

To explain his previous conduct. 'That you may not think me quite so much of a boor as I fear you do at this moment.'

She hesitated, then inclined her head. 'If you wish.'

They moved on again, their horses side-by-side. Alex arranged his words. 'My sister Lizzy is younger than me and very spoiled. She had been out two years without forming an attachment sufficiently strong to make her wish to marry. My parents, you must understand, are very hot on the subject of love within wedlock. Last season my father's health was not good, so Mama stayed at Abervale with him, leaving my brother's wife to chaperon Lizzy. We thought this would be a mere formality, since over the winter she had met Mr Marshall, a most suitable match in every way. An engagement looked set to be announced, but there was some sort of falling out — I still do not know the details — and Lizzy's head was turned by Captain Jarman, an adventurer who came from nowhere into the heart of London society. I tried to see him off and failed. I sent to Mama, but Papa's condition worsened around then and she could not leave him. I repeatedly warned my brother and sister-in-law what was like to occur. I explained the *raison d'être* of fortune-hunters to Lizzy herself. All without success.

'Then the worst happened. It was perhaps a base thing to do, but I had set a watch on my sister. I received intelligence that she had eloped with Jarman. Naturally, I chased after them, but there were false trails all along the Great North Road that sent me wrong and I despaired of ever reaching them before night fell.' He looked at her shamefacedly. 'This part, I think you know full well.'

'I must admit to having some inkling of the sort. What happened?'

'A coincidence far better than I deserved. By a great stroke of fortune, Lady Jersey's carriage threw a trace at Stamford that very night, and on entering the private parlour of the George she found Lizzy and her would-be swain having an acrimonious exchange of views. By the time *I* got there, Sally had taken Lizzy up and was halfway back to London, declaring to the world that my sister had been with her all along.'

'And what of Captain Jarman's remains?' enquired Caroline.

Alex was surprised into a reluctant chuckle. 'Had I laid hands on him, that's all there would have been for sure! Alas, when I finally reached the inn, Giles told me he had searched the environs, but the rascal had escaped. No one has heard of him since.'

Caroline's horse checked for a moment. 'Mr d'Arblay was with you?'

'Ahead of me. I told you I got turned around on the trail.'

'How extraordinarily good of him,' said Caroline slowly. 'It is not many gentlemen who would forego their own comfort to chase after a friend's sister. But I suppose he had known her all her life, and was fond of her.'

Alex was gratified that she was for once seeing his friend in a better light. 'As to that, Lizzy is much younger than us, so was mostly in the nursery. If Giles considered her at all until she grew up I would be surprised. But since she has been out, he has always been happy to stand in as an escort for her, or to make up the numbers in a party.'

'Yes, I see.' Caroline shot an unfathomable

look at him. 'A very useful man to have in one's circle. She regards him as quite another brother I daresay.'

'I have never thought of it, but yes, I believe you are right.'

'And with you delayed, he would doubtless have dispatched her abductor in the same wise had Lady Jersey not arrived so fortuitously and taken charge before he could get there. Yes. Yes, I see it all quite clearly.' She glanced at him with the directness he was coming to expect of her. 'You have not asked me to keep this confidential.'

He held her honey-brown eyes with his own. 'I do not believe I need to.'

She smiled. 'Thank you.'

They talked of other matters until they got back. On dismounting, Alex was chagrined to discover how much even an hour's riding had taken out of him.

Caroline tutted and slipped her arm under his to lend him the appearance of stability from the yard back to the house. 'I do not think you yet realize how ill you were,' she chided. 'There is nothing wrong with getting better slowly.'

This was embarrassing. 'I am not accustomed to being an invalid,' he growled.

She looked up at him with a merry twinkle in her eyes. 'No, really, my lord? I should never have guessed.'

Alex felt himself lurch. Dizziness swirled about him forcing him to stop and catch his breath. For a moment there, he had looked down at her infuriating, half-laughing face and had wanted nothing more than to cover her parted lips with his.

'Alexander?' And now she was alarmed, curse it, putting up her free hand to feel his brow.

'I am well,' he gasped in a harsh voice. 'I am well.' He took a ragged breath, aware of her innocence, of her softness, of the fact that they were standing in full view of an entire stable's worth of her brother's grooms. 'Just get me back to my damned chair and leave me be.'

She smiled, reassured. 'That is more like you.' And she continued to support him to his room, giving orders for tea and a fire and a small, sustaining snack and the newspapers, if Mrs Penfold had finished with them.

Alex let himself be directed, listening to her capable voice, feeling the swell of her bosom against his arm, tallying the difference in their ages. 'I should go back to the White Hart,' he said abruptly.

She glanced at him with a flicker of surprise. 'If you wish it, my lord. Will you inform her grace, or shall I?'

Alex laughed, and sat down, and the world righted itself again. 'I beg your pardon. My thanks for your company on the ride, Miss Fortune, and if it would please you to send my valet to me that I may get out of these boots, I shall shortly join you for a dish of tea and a slice or two of bread and butter.'

She looked at him askance, murmuring, 'I wonder if the doctor is free,' as she left the room.

★　★　★

Caroline reached the sanctuary of her room and sank nervelessly onto the bed with her head in her hands. How she had kept up an appearance of normality then she did not know. When Alexander had stumbled just before entering the house, there had been such an expression of — of *warmth* in his eyes Caroline had almost given in to the temptation to stretch up and kiss him! Her cheeks burned to imagine the outcome of such an action. He would have been horrified. As it was, when he had made that ludicrous suggestion of returning to the inn, every sinew had cried out against it and she had been hard pressed not to emulate them.

She took off her riding habit and put on the gown with the dusky pink spot. She might never have Alexander's heart, but she was blowed if she was going to have any more of his censure about wearing the wrong colours.

Downstairs, all appeared to be normal again. Harry joined them for a nuncheon and talked over Chieftain's points with Alexander. When the post was brought in, Caroline recognized Louisa's writing and eased opened the seal in full expectation of a comfortable gossipy letter.

'Oh dear,' she said aloud, after she had perused the first sentences.

The men looked up. Harry's eyes, also recognizing Louisa's round hand, sharpened with anxiety. 'What is it?' he said. 'Is she ill? Tell me!'

Caroline shook her head. 'No, they are well. So well, in fact, that we are all invited to dine there before the assembly on Friday.'

Harry's lips thinned. 'Even me?' he said with a touch of bitterness.

'Certainly. Louisa writes 'your whole household' with double underlining under the word *whole*.' Caroline glanced at Alexander. 'I daresay, my lord, if you dislike the scheme, we need simply say that your health is not yet robust enough to partake of evening engagements.'

To her surprise, Alexander looked merely resigned. 'I suppose you will make me go both ways in a closed carriage, will you?'

Caroline felt her mouth drop open. 'You intend accepting? Louisa's father will be transported.'

'I shall have my reward some day. I imagine he keeps a good table and it seems hard on Fortune to be deprived an evening of Miss Taylor's company.'

Harry went bright red. 'I will be placed as far from her as the seating arrangements allow. But we should not have received the invitation had you not been staying here. Thank you, sir. If my sister agrees, I would be happy to take you up in my curricle.'

Caroline nibbled her lip as she perused the second half of her friend's letter. She wondered when would be the right time to break it to her table companions that Giles d'Arblay had 'run across' Louisa and her father when 'taking the opportunity to view the wonderful architecture of the Church of St James' on Sunday and had got himself invited to dinner too.

12

Alexander elected to ride the following day also. On their return, Caroline noticed the jockey who usually raced for them in the yard talking to Harry. Over the man's shoulder, Harry gave her the very faintest shake of his head. Caroline's heart sank. Solange had not let him mount up.

Which meant that either they would have to pull out of the race and thus forfeit the wager. Or . . .

Or . . .

Or Caroline herself would have to ride.

'Are you all right?'

Caroline came back to her surroundings with a start. Alexander was looking at her with concern on his face. It was — nice. Unsettling, but nice. She tucked the look away into her store of memories. 'Yes,' she said. 'Yes, I am perfectly well. I have just remembered a number of letters I need to write, that is all.'

It was noticeable that today he was steadier when he dismounted. Nor did he need help walking back to the house. It seemed once Lord Rothwell decided to get better, his body obeyed him. That was all to the good. Caroline need not worry about him when the time came for him to leave.

'Must you write them now?' He had a half-smile on his face.

'Oh, I think so. I do not believe in putting off the inevitable. It only makes the task harder, do you not think?' Harry. She had to talk to Harry.

'You are shaming me into addressing my own business concerns,' he said.

Why did he have to choose *now* to be amiable? Now, when she was about to discuss with her brother and her head groom how best she might deceive him in order to win that wretched wager!

'I . . . I am sure your steward will be most grateful,' she said.

'Once he has picked himself up off the floor from astonishment.'

He was still eyeing her speculatively. Any minute now he would again ask if there was anything wrong. It was with the utmost relief that Caroline saw his valet hovering ostentatiously in the hallway, clothes brush in hand. 'I will see you later, my lord.'

As soon as his door was closed, she sped outside. Harry and Flood were in the stable, both looking glum. 'I am going to have to ride, aren't I?' she said. She was surprised at how steady her voice sounded.

'There might still be time . . . ' but Harry's voice trailed off.

'You can't ride as a lady, Miss Caro,' said Flood bluntly. 'For all it's a private race, they'll not let a lass mount up for it.'

'Mrs Thornton did.'

'In York. Not in Newmarket. And a dozen years ago now and her no better than she should be.'

Caroline moistened her lips. 'Could we . . . could we perhaps explain to Lord Rothwell that . . . '

Both men just looked at her.

'There is money on this race, Caro, not simply the original wager. D'Arblay for one has side bets. One of Grafton's horses was put in for it. One of Rutland's. They are both influential gentlemen.'

'The principals in a race are not responsible for other people's bets.'

'No, lass, but it would generate bad feeling amongst the gentry if Mr Harry were to pull out.'

'And as well as needing their custom, I need to maintain my integrity. You do not have to tell me that there are enough whispers as it is about my 'lucky touch'. I *have* to keep my name as an honourable trainer. It is the only chance I have of winning over Louisa's father.'

Caroline felt a cold lump of fear settle in her chest. 'Then I must ride as a lad.' She faced both the men. 'It is not as if I have never done so before.'

Harry put his head in his hands. 'Caro, that was four years ago.'

'I am not so very much more grown,' said Caroline. Her entire stomach was ice now, but she could not bear that look of misery and defeat on Harry's face. 'I can bind myself flat and grime my face and wear the cap low on my brow and call myself Mr Brown as I did before. I weigh in, ride the race, weigh out and disappear into the crowd. Flood can lead Solange home. She'll be easy enough with him.'

'Provided she is easy at all on the course.'

'We will do trial trips during the race week and mingle with the crowd. Lord Rothwell is getting fitter every day. He will be off with the duchess by next week. I will be able to slip away.'

She was convincing herself as much as her brother. Flood knew it. Caroline saw him step back, his watchful gaze going from face to face, ready to support whatever decision was reached.

'What if he is not?' said Harry. 'What if he remains here?'

Caroline wanted to scream or stamp her

foot at him for seeing only the problems. 'Then we recruit Louisa to make a long call. Lord Rothwell will never know I am not with her and Mrs Penfold. If he chances to remain in the saloon, I shall simply develop a headache and retire to my room. We will contrive, Harry. We have to.'

'You never have the headache.'

'Lord Rothwell does not know that.' In truth, he knew little about her at all. She felt a small pang that he never would.

'Caro, let's try the other men on her again. I cannot ask you to do this. It is dangerous. Dangerous physically and dangerous socially. If you are discovered you will be ruined.'

From somewhere, Caroline found a smile. 'Well, that will at least stop Mama's matchmaking efforts, will it not? Truly, I believe Solange must have once been very badly frightened by a male rider. I don't know how or why, but I do know she trusts me and I think we have enough of a bond to carry it through. But Harry, whether she wins or not, I am going to ask Lord Rothwell if I may buy her from him. I might even ask him this week, before the race.'

Her brother looked at her, very white and strained. 'I swear, Caro, that as long as I live I will never enter into another wager like this one.'

'Sense at last,' said Caroline in a shaky voice. 'And at only twenty-four years of age. Louisa will be thrilled.'

★ ★ ★

From his seat at the table in his room, Alex watched for Caroline to emerge from the stable block. He was puzzled. Surely if she was going to shy away from being in the same room as him, she would have done so yesterday, not today. There had been nothing untoward in their conversation this morning; they had sparred amicably about education and agreed on the relative merits of winter and summer grazing. But as soon as they got back, she could not be rid of him fast enough.

He was confounded to find himself piqued. Giles would no doubt be in whoops that Alex was cross because Miss Caroline Fortune preferred the society of her horse to being in company with *him*.

The ink dried on Alex's pen as he absorbed this unpalatable fact. And here was another: he would not be telling Giles anything about it. He had been avoiding this admission, but these past weeks, Giles had diminished in his estimation as much as Caroline and her brother had increased in it. Indeed, now he came to reflect more honestly, the friendship had been fading on his side for some time.

His eyes focused on movement outside. Caroline was walking down the path to the house at last. She was alone, lost in thought, her arms wrapped about herself and her expression withdrawn.

She was *hurting*. Alex wanted to start from his chair, to stride to her side, to demand to know what was wrong. He wanted to shield her in his arms and hurl damnations against the world. But he didn't do any of those things. Because the knowledge that he wanted to had turned his entrails to liquid metal and held him riveted in his seat. He *loved* her? He loved Caroline Fortune?

★   ★   ★

Giles d'Arblay once again visited in order to play billiards with Alexander. Caroline saddled Solange and took her for a much longer walk around Newmarket.

'You can see how much easier she is becoming,' she said to Harry, who was keeping pace alongside her on his own favoured mount. 'Will you come up to the heath with me tomorrow morning to watch her paces?'

Harry grimaced at the early start this would mean, but nodded. 'You have worked a miracle.'

Caroline frowned. 'I think it is more what I have *unworked*. Harry, did I tell you Lord Rothwell mentioned to me that Solange used to belong to Mr d'Arblay?'

'There's nothing in that. Daresay he only owned her five minutes. Some of the gentry use horses merely as currency for their bets, God rot 'em. I tell you, Caro, If I hadn't been so deuced unhappy over Louisa, I'd have steered clear of Crockford's long ago.'

Would that he had! Caroline chose her next words carefully. 'I have thought, once or twice, that Mr d'Arblay has not looked on you with a very friendly eye. Have you done anything to make him take you in dislike?'

Harry glanced at her in astonishment. 'I hardly know him! He wanted to buy Rufus when we pulled off all those wins last October, but then so did several others. I told 'em all he was not for sale.'

Caroline gnawed her lip. Should she mention that she thought Alexander's friend was trying to fix his interest with Louisa? No. Harry was quite capable of either going into a monumental sulk or calling his rival out. She would keep her own counsel and trust to Louisa's light handling of whatever situation arose on Friday.

★　★　★

Dawn. Alex stood in his window, wrapped in his greatcoat so as not to be noticed by any casual observer. It had come to him during the night that though he had seen Solange being rubbed down and lip daintily at Caroline's hand and not attack her stable companions when in close proximity, he had not yet viewed any actual evidence of her training. In theory this didn't matter, since he stood to win a thousand guineas if she failed to beat the other entrants next week. Absurdly though, he did not want her to lose. He wanted Caroline's brother to make good on his boast. Thus it had become a point of some urgency to see with his own eyes that Harry was turning the uncontrollable mare into a racehorse.

Alex shivered in his greatcoat but remained at the window, the curtain drawn behind him. Up by the stable block he could see Flood directing the grooms. He could see barrows of muck being wheeled towards the dung heap. He could see horses being ridden towards the road in pairs, but he could not see — ah, yes, there they were, coming *up* the side path. Harry Fortune on his roan gelding and next to him, trotting easy as you please, Solange with the lithe stripling on her back, half-obscured by Harry's gesticulating form. They had obviously been taking their exercise as early as possible in order to avoid interested eyes. The two horses disappeared into the stable and Alex moved back into his room with a feeling of a burden having been lightened. He slipped off his coat and returned to bed. Solange would perform, the youngster would ride her, all would be well.

★   ★   ★

The arrival of the Duchess of Abervale that day was just as unexpected — and attended by just as much turmoil — as her first descent on them had been.

'Mama,' said Alexander, rising on her eruption into the saloon. Caroline glanced at him in surprise. Surely that had not been a trace of annoyance in his voice? He had only been describing the Epsom racecourse near his own estate to her after all. 'Could you not, just once, Mama, let us know when we are to have the happiness of your presence?'

'Well, no, dearest, because I have often found that when I do that, people are apt to be off pheasant shooting or some such, so one never gets to see them.'

'Astonishing,' murmured Alexander.

Her grace settled down, attended by several footmen to take away her various wraps. 'You will be pleased to know that Lizzy is very well indeed and she and Mr Marshall are still so much in love that he dropped a hint to me that he should like to have her to himself for as long as possible before the babe is born. So I came away yesterday and am now ensconced at Cheveley. Giles is engaged there for the whole day and offered to escort me over, but I could see he would much rather flirt with Rutland's duchess, so I told him I was going to catechize you on your health. Which I won't, by the way, for I can tell at once that you are quite yourself again. Rutland says I am at liberty to make a stay there until after your horserace, you are all to come to supper tomorrow, and if I can find out any details about your killer mare he will be enduringly grateful.'

'She is not a killer mare,' said Alexander mildly, 'and I am afraid we are bidden to a master goldsmith's house at Bury St Edmunds to dine tomorrow night. And then we must show ourselves at the town assembly.'

'Not the same dinner where Giles's beautiful heiress will be?' cried her grace, clapping her hands together. 'He mentioned her in a very by-the-by manner this morning and I should adore to see her. Now I wonder how I might get myself invited?'

Caroline stared at her with horror. 'I beg your pardon, ma'am, but Louisa has been my particular friend since the day we first attended the same seminary. She and my brother have an understanding that her father knows about full well but has not yet seen fit to bless. I fear if Mr d'Arblay considers her 'his' heiress, he is being disgracefully forward and doomed to disappointment. I beg you will not mention any such phrase in front of Harry for I really don't think he could survive the scandal of calling Mr d'Arblay out.'

Alexander was also looking at his parent askance. 'Mama, you cannot simply go around inviting yourself to dinner with respectable goldsmiths.'

'Can I not, dear? But I wish to more than ever, now. This is not at all well done of Giles, if it is true. But if her father disapproves, I suppose he may not know of Mr Fortune's hopes. Or he may think that all is fair in love and war. That would be quite like him.'

'Yes, Giles does tend to only see his own prospects,' said Alexander in a constrained voice.

Caroline was thinking hard. 'Alderman Taylor would be in transports if the duchess were indeed to grace his table,' she said to Alexander aloud. 'If Harry were to ride over there today to mention that your mama is unexpectedly in Newmarket and had some thoughts of attending the assembly with us, he would certainly be moved to invite her.'

'And he would be enormously grateful to your scapegrace brother for informing him of the situation and for being his messenger,' said Alexander drily.

Caroline beamed at him. 'He would, would he not? Dear ma'am, do you mind being involved in this little subterfuge? Harry and Louisa are so in love.'

Her grace was looking delightfully diverted. 'There. I knew I was right to leave Lizzy and Marshall together. Pray hurry to Mr Fortune and have him wrap the bait any way he chooses.'

Caroline sped outside and was lucky enough to find her brother heading for the house. 'Do go, Harry,' she urged, when she had finished the breathless recital, but not mentioning Mr d'Arblay. 'The alderman would adore being able to drop into conversation that he entertained a duchess at his table before the assembly. And he will feel so kindly towards you for bringing him the news.'

'Best of sisters,' said Harry, giving her an exultant hug. He ran indoors to change his coat, darted in to press a kiss to the duchess's hand, then hied back to the yard without giving them a farewell.

'You will like the alderman when you meet

him, ma'am,' said Caroline. 'He is such an endearing snob, and so fond of Louisa. But he feels he has to be mother and father to her, you see, and simply cannot perceive that Harry would love her and look after her in exactly the way he himself would wish.'

'And you don't think Giles would?' said Alexander. There was still a small wrinkle marring his forehead.

'Oh no, dear,' said the duchess, earning Caroline's undying loyalty. 'Even at his most charming, Giles will never love anyone near so much as his own self.' She looked at her son serenely. 'And I am afraid once the girl's money runs out, he will not love her at all.'

At this, Caroline could feel Alexander's anger. 'You are a little harsh today, Mama.'

'Am I, dear? Ah well, I daresay you know him best. Is he travelling with you tomorrow? Shall I take both of you up in my carriage?'

'In truth, ma'am, we had not yet fixed the details,' said Caroline quickly. 'I shall be accompanying Mrs Penfold, of course, but I am sure if you offer Mr d'Arblay a place in your equipage, he would be delighted to accept.'

'Aye, do that, Mama. I can always come back with you if I cannot stand Fortune's handling of the ribbons for more than one trip.'

'Or if a second fifteen-mile journey in the

night air does not seem a wise move after dinner and dancing,' murmured Caroline.

After his mother had taken her leave and they had seen her carriage depart along the Cheveley road, Alexander caught Caroline's arm when she would have gone upstairs. She beat down the thrill his touch gave her.

'Did you know?' he asked. 'Did you know Giles was going there tomorrow?'

Caroline moistened her lips. 'Louisa wrote that Mr d'Arblay had been looking around the Church of St James when he happened to meet them on Sunday. Anyone who praises his town is always sure of a welcome in the alderman's house.'

Alexander looked at her without expression. 'Thank you,' he said finally.

'For what, my lord?'

'For not saying that Giles probably didn't mention his invitation because he assumed I would not be interested.'

Did that mean the scales were beginning to fall from his eyes regarding his friend? Caroline hoped so. 'He may not even know you are going,' she said diplomatically. 'I daresay Louisa's father merely commended him to come and take pot-luck with them before the assembly. Mr d'Arblay would not know that the alderman's notion of pot luck runs to five courses with two removes and as much company as the table can hold.'

Alexander grinned wryly. 'In that case, I'd give a monkey to see his face when my mother extends *her* invitation tonight.'

⋆　⋆　⋆

'Lord Rothwell,' said Caroline, oddly formal, at dinner. 'I have a favour to ask you.'

Alex had to repress an indulgent smile. She was wearing a dark-pink gown tonight. He suspected from the cut that it had once belonged to Mrs Penfold and been inexpertly taken in, but anything was better on her than insipid blue with those dreadful ruffles. 'If it is within my power,' he said.

'It is about Solange.'

He felt himself go cold. Surely her brother had not put her up to something? He shot a look across the table, but Harry was listening amiably to a rambling story of Mrs Penfold's. 'What of Solange?' he asked.

'I should like to buy her. What is her price, please?'

Alex stared at the composed girl next to him as if she had run mad. 'Forgive me, my hearing seems to be at fault. For a moment there I thought you said you wished to buy Solange.'

'I do.'

'This is not some scheme to void the bet should your brother lose, is it? I am afraid the entry in the book reads ' . . . *will train the grey mare Solange, currently owned by . . . .*''

'No, my lord, though that would have been a very good ruse if we had but thought of it.'

'Minx. Then why?'

An intriguing wash of colour ebbed across her face. 'I have taken a fancy to her,' she said.

A bubble of amusement rose inside him. 'I see. It is not that if she wins, her price would naturally increase, so you think to get her at a bargain rate?'

'There. You have found me out. How unfortunate that you are of such a discerning turn of mind.'

'Caroline, this must be nonsense. Consider, if I take you up on your offer, and she then unseats her rider and tramples him, you will have bought a killer.'

'She won't.'

'I admire your confidence in your brother's training. Have you thought that if she loses, the pair of you will be out by a thousand guineas *and* the price of the horse? And you will never be able to sell her on.'

'I do not wish to sell her on! Indeed I can fairly promise you that I won't.'

'Then why?'

She took a deep breath. 'You will remember how troubled and ungovernable Solange was before. She is *happy* at Penfold Lodge: I want her to stay happy. If you sell her to anyone but me, she will almost certainly be taken elsewhere.'

She cared. He could hear the passion in her voice. Something stirred in him. 'Are you so certain, then, that I will sell her? Why should I not leave her with your brother, to race again at the next meeting?'

Caroline's fingers twisted the fabric of her gown. Alex wanted to lay his hand over them to calm them. 'You know as well as I that Solange is no racehorse. I do believe she will not disgrace us this time, but it would be arrant cruelty to force her into it again.'

'But what other use could she be? A horse that might buck at any time is clearly not a lady's riding mount.'

He knew he was teasing her, which was not the act of a gentleman, but he loved the agility of her mind. She did not disappoint him. 'I believe she will prove an excellent mother,' said Caroline firmly. 'I am thinking of making a book on what colour foal she and Rufus will have first.'

Alex laughed. 'Caroline, I cannot sell you Solange.'

Her face lost its animation, as if she was

absorbing a body blow without wanting the pain to show. His own heart quickened.

'I will give her to you.'

Her lips parted. She regarded him with disbelief. 'Give? Why?'

Because you want her. 'As . . . as an expression of my thanks for the excellent nursing I have received here.'

He saw her assimilate this. Interestingly, it seemed to please her no more than the body blow, but it did not stop her accepting. 'Thank you, my lord. Then I will gladly take her on those terms. Will you write me an owner's paper this evening before you change your mind?'

'I will.' He glanced again across the table. His voice dropped and his tongue took off without him. 'But I should like it very much if you were to thank me with my own name.'

There was a moment of something nearly-there between them. Caroline held his eyes. 'Thank you, Alexander,' she whispered.

★   ★   ★

The deed was done, the transfer of ownership signed and witnessed by Mrs Penfold and the butler. And Caroline felt lower than a worm, crawling between the cobbles of the stable-yard.

There had been that warmth in his eyes again. He had wanted her to call him Alexander. He had *given* her a valuable horse. It felt horribly as though she had tricked him.

Caroline rested her forehead against the cool glass pane as she looked out over the night garden. Up at the stable block, one of the grooms would be on watch. Flood was not taking any more chances with unwanted intruders. On the ground floor, to her left, a bar of oblique light showed that Alexander was also gazing out at the night. The footman outside his door had been dispensed with some days ago. It would be perfectly safe for her to slip down and ask again why he had given her Solange so easily. Safe as far as her reputation went, that is. Not safe at all in terms of her heart. Caroline shut her curtains with a decisive pull and climbed into bed. Alexander was the younger son of a duke and as far above her touch as the moon. One presentiment of danger at a time was all she could manage.

13

Friday. Alex had slept abominably. He had felt himself to be constantly on the point of slipping into nightmare, so had kept waking up instead. He was restless and uneasy, the clouds outside were pressing down, and having decided that he couldn't wait another couple of hours for his valet, and being disinclined to ring for him now and endure the man's frowns and fussiness, he dressed and headed for the stable. Perhaps the early morning routine would soothe him.

In the yard, all was purposefulness and bustle. Stalls were being mucked out, horses were being wrapped with blankets and led into the damp, crepuscular dawn. Fortune was in working garb, talking to a couple of the men. Flood was checking girths and straps. Caroline, however, was nowhere to be seen.

One of the stable-hands noticed him. His eyes darted nervously over Alex's shoulder as he pulled his forelock. Flood saw him too, and trod stolidly across the yard. 'Off you go,' he said, making a shooing motion to the nervous lad. 'Mr Harry don't pay you to stand around up here. Won't you come under cover, milord? Miss Caro would have our eyes if you caught a chill in this nasty drizzle.'

'Thank you. I thought she might be here, as a matter of fact.'

'Oh aye, she's around the place some-where. Probably lending a hand with the men's breakfast. The weather don't make a lot of difference to Miss Caro.'

Out of the corner of his eye, Alex saw the nervous groom take off at a run. He followed Flood into the stable block, already feeling more settled by the company and the sense of work being got on with.

'I couldn't sleep,' he said abruptly. 'I wondered if there was anything I could usefully do?'

Probably there was a directive in the grooms' handbook for Dealing With Recalci-trant Gentry because Flood eyed him measuringly and then set him to polishing leatherwork, much as his father's head man at Abervale would have done. Sitting there, buffing cloth in hand, the scent of horse in his nostrils and busyness all around him, Alex dismissed once and for all the notion that these stables were concerned with anything shady. He bent his head to his work, imbued with calm.

A whinny behind him heralded Solange's

arrival. Alex turned, thinking to have a word with her rider, but it was one of the older men leading her in. She was sweating and hungry from the morning exercise and he marvelled again at how different she was from the rearing, kicking, biting animal they had brought here not three weeks ago. A little later, Caroline appeared, bearing a covered cauldron of porridge. Her hair was beaded with rain.

She met his eyes with surprise, and left the men to help themselves. 'I did not think to see you here, my lord. If you are like to make a habit of it, I had best bring up an extra bowl.'

He smiled. 'There is no need, for all I am being tolerated very nicely this morning. I merely thought employment might suit me better than being unable to sleep. It is the weather, no doubt.'

Her brow furrowed with concern, which gave Alex a quite inordinate sense of well-being. 'Then you must have a mug of porridge,' she said. 'I dare not say so in the kitchen, but on those not conditioned to it, it is guaranteed to induce torpor within the hour.'

He laughed, but found to his surprise that once back in his room where a fire had been lit in his absence and Harry's valet was cheerfully on hand to pull off his boots, he did indeed drop into a dreamless sleep.

★ ★ ★

The rain increased and kept everyone inside for the rest of the morning. Caroline would not have been able to work any more with Solange even if she had dared to after Alexander's shock appearance in the yard whilst they were out on their early run. It really was becoming ever more difficult to keep her activities secret from him.

Towards afternoon the weather cleared, however, and the sky became brighter. 'Thank the Lord for that,' said Harry in relief. 'We shall be able to take the curricle after all instead of squeezing into the carriage.'

'I am sure Mrs Penfold and I are equally pleased that you will not be crowding us and crushing our skirts,' retorted Caroline.

Because of Mrs Penfold's fussing about not being late, the ladies were amongst the earliest arrivals. Mrs Penfold was borne off by Louisa's aunt, but Caroline remained near the door keeping Louisa herself company. Lord Rothwell and Harry naturally gravitated to their side, so all four had a first-hand view of the scene when Alderman Taylor, with swelling chest and beaming visage, was able to welcome the Duchess of Abervale to his house.

Her grace behaved beautifully, bathing everyone in her smiling warmth and praising every gilded touch. Watching her progress from the vestibule to the best spot in the salon leaving a swathe of complacency in her wake, Caroline thought she could very easily learn to love Alexander's mama.

'I had no notion you were recovered enough to junket about,' remarked Mr d'Arblay presently, coming up to where Alexander was suffering his mother to quiz him about the adequacy of the hood on Harry's curricle and the warmth of his travelling rugs.

'No? If you thought me so infirm two days ago, I wonder you did not give me a head-start in our billiards game. I should then not have dropped that pony to you.'

Caroline laughed with everyone else, but continued to watch Mr d'Arblay. To her, at least, he did not appear so well pleased with the company as the alderman's other guests.

He seemed to take the reply in good part. 'Well, and I am glad you are better. You won't miss the Second Spring Meeting next week, and you will find it much more the thing at the White Hart. I daresay it is living so quiet that has made you slow to mend.'

Caroline's eyes connected with those of the duchess, swiftly and urgently. There was a flash of comprehension before her grace tapped Mr d'Arblay's hand with her fan. 'Now, now, Giles, it is all settled that Alex will come to Cheveley with me for the week and we'll go on to Abervale from there. I am sure the White Hart is a very good sort of inn, but a mother never really feels safe unless her brood is gathered around her, you know, especially when one of that brood has recently received a nasty knock on the head.'

Caroline waited for Alex to say this was the first he had heard about his removal from Penfold Lodge, but he was uncharacteristically silent. Doubtless he was too much the gentleman to contradict his mama in public.

When they sat down to table, it was clear that Mr d'Arblay had suffered another blow. The duchess, naturally, had been placed next to her host but it was Alexander who had been awarded the seat by Louisa. From her lowly position making competent conversation with a wool merchant on one hand and a banker's son on the other, Caroline watched Giles outwardly charming the banker's wife, but all the time darting needle-fine glances at Alexander and Harry.

Harry, who should also have been jealous

of Alexander, was on the contrary in high alt. The whole group had seen the alderman lay his hand on Harry's arm earlier and say sincerely that he depended on the young man to make his neighbour at dinner feel comfortable, for she was Louisa's godmother — an old friend — and not at all used to society.

For all the array of dishes, the dinner was brisk; before too long the company were donning cloaks and taking carriages the short distance to the Subscription Rooms. Having observed the slight, occasional twitch to his shoulders during the meal, Caroline was anxious that Alexander might consider his duty done and fail to ask Louisa for the first two dances, but it was evidently not one of his days for defying convention so she was able to breathe again that her friend had not been snubbed.

'Well now,' said the duchess, pausing next to Caroline a little later, 'I have told your alderman that I have not enjoyed myself so much in ages, that I am very much obliged to Mr Harry Fortune for bringing tonight to my attention, and that the arrangements here are far superior to our country assemblies at home. Was that not well done of me?'

'Very well done, ma'am,' said Caroline gratefully. 'And I could not tell you before, but I am so pleased that Lord Rothwell will be going with you to Cheveley instead of back to the White Hart. You know his disposition better than I do of course, but I cannot feel him to be quite as much recovered as he thinks himself.'

'And no nurse likes to see her best endeavours thrown away. Quite so. I could not agree with you more. On which head, by the by, if it so happens that Alex finds himself a trifle over-extended tonight and Mrs Penfold does not care to leave early, I shall be more than happy to take her home in my carriage leaving the Penfold Lodge one available for you.'

That very subject had been exercising Caroline's mind to a considerable extent ever since the outing had been proposed. Alexander would never admit to weakness in company, yet Mrs Penfold looked forward so much to relaying the whole business of the evening to her particular circle of friends that it seemed sad to curtail her gentle pleasure. 'You are very good, ma'am,' said Caroline gratefully.

'Not at all, my dear. But I do have the best interests of my children at heart.'

★ ★ ★

When Alex was finally able to claim Caroline for his two dances, he saw her search his face worriedly. 'Don't say it,' he warned. 'Do not say I should not have come out tonight. If I have the appearance of being fatigued it is merely the effect of several hours' exposure to *duty*. And I may tell you that if Miss Taylor were not your friend, I might not have put up with it so long as I have.'

Caroline's face flushed a delicious pink. 'Thank you, my lord,' she said. 'I know she might chatter a little too much for your taste, but it would have been uncomfortable indeed for Louisa had you not danced with her after being her neighbour at dinner. I am sure you will be rewarded.'

Alex looked down at her quizzically. 'When?' he asked.

He saw the startlement in her eyes. 'In . . . in the fullness of time, naturally,' she stuttered.

'Ah, I was afraid it might not be until then.' He led her to the set, berating himself for letting the teasing question out. He must be more tired than he thought. 'Good God,' he said aloud. 'Giles has beaten your brother to be Miss Taylor's next partner. How remiss of Fortune.'

Caroline gave the candid chuckle he had come to enjoy. 'Not at all. However much you may doubt it, Harry does think ahead when it suits him. He will have put himself down for the supper dance. And look — he is leading your mama into this set. That will be a considerable feather in his cap with the alderman.'

The supper dance. The evening suddenly seemed endless. And Mama making an enchanting exhibition of herself and Giles sniping both at him for being born higher and at Harry Fortune for his careless address. 'I suppose this is not a waltz by any chance?' he said.

Caroline looked shocked. 'Certainly not, or I would be sitting it out. Young ladies are not permitted to waltz.'

'That is a pity. I could have leant on you under the pretence of leading you around the room.'

Now she was alarmed. 'I thought you said you were not fatigued.'

How astonishing to *like* her concern, to solicit it even. 'The thought of having to last out beyond the supper dance has changed my mind.'

The music started. Caroline seemed to match her steps to his without thinking. She ran the tip of her tongue around her lips. He had noticed it was a trick she had when nervous or unsure of herself. 'Your mama did say that if you chanced not to be equal to the whole evening, she would convey Mrs Penfold home leaving the Lodge carriage for you and me.'

Mama had said that? Alex turned to stare at his oblivious parent. 'That was very good of her,' he said slowly. 'But I would not wish to suspend your pleasure by having you leave the assembly early.'

'What pleasure would I have in knowing you were ill? Do not be ridiculous, Alexander. You have been so very sick that if you are like to be unwell again now, we should most certainly leave.'

Alexander. She had called him Alexander. His hand clasped hers as they came together then apart. 'We will see this dance out,' he said, 'and then yes, I own I should like the carriage to be called.' After all, as a dutiful son, who was he to go against his mama's express directions?

★ ★ ★

Alex took his hat off with a sigh of relief and put it on the opposite seat. 'That is better,' he said.

'Do you have a headache?' asked Caroline.

'A little. I daresay it will ease off now we are away from all those chandeliers. The subscription book must be full indeed to afford so much display. Do you wish to remove your bonnet? We have a way to travel.'

She grinned. 'Very much, but if I do, my hair will disgrace me. Mrs Penfold's maid has a most ruthless way with pins. I have endured them all evening so as to appear just a little more poised than normal, but I have to admit to pulling several of the more stabbing ones out before cramming on my bonnet to come home.'

Happiness was stealing up on Alex with every unconventional word Caroline uttered. He could feel it happening and was in no way moved to prevent it. 'I promise I shall not tell a soul,' he said. 'And once we are out of the town gate, there will be no flares to light the interior so I shall not see any thing amiss.'

'My lord, there is a full moon in the sky.' But she untied her bonnet strings and laid it on the seat next to his. Then she grimaced and pulled out another hairpin, putting it carefully in her reticule. A lock of hair promptly fell down.

He touched it, unable to stop himself. 'Do you need any help?' he said, a laugh in his voice.

It was a moment priceless beyond all others. She looked up at him, her face open and shy. 'Are you *very* experienced in these things, Alexander?'

Alex's heart turned over. 'Not *very*,' he said gently. 'But some.'

'Well . . . well that is good. For it is as well that one of us knows what we are doing, don't you think?'

There would never be any beating about the bush with Caroline Fortune. No simpering smiles or coy misunderstandings. Alex felt around her silky hair for the rest of the pins. Strands slithered over his fingers, straight and fine. 'I am not sure I *do* know what I am doing,' he said. 'That's the lot, I think. Do you?'

'Thank you.' She stowed the pins safely. 'And no, I don't know either, but . . . ' She moistened her lips again. 'That is . . . if you are minded to, which I begin to believe you are, I do think I should like you to kiss me when you are awake.'

He felt his scalp creep, destroying the moment of intimacy. Ice puddled in his gut. 'When I am awake? Have I kissed you asleep then?'

They were out of the town now, but the moonlight was strong enough to see she was blushing. 'It is all right. You thought I was someone else.'

'It is *not* all right.' God's tears, he was not safe to be out! What else might he have done to her in his delirium? He was appalled!

In an instant, he felt her shrink into herself, away from his disgusted anger at his lack of control over his nightmares. 'No . . . Caroline . . . I did not mean . . . ' But he had hurt her badly — *again* — so he did the only thing possible to make amends. Quite instinctively he wrapped one arm around her soft, slim body and tipped her chin up with the other hand. It was what he had wanted to do for some time.

★   ★   ★

Alexander was kissing her. Finally he was kissing her for herself and it was just as wonderful as Caroline had hoped it might be. One of his hands was in her hair. She felt it rubbing against the back of her head. It felt so nice that she reached up to tangle her fingers in his dark locks too. She smiled against his lips. How strange that something so simple could add such a dimension of delight. His hair against her palm, his lips nibbling at hers, and then his tongue creating delicate sensations of pleasure as he explored her mouth. Emboldened, awash with wonder, she copied him and felt him hold her more tightly still.

The fifteen-mile journey had never seemed

so short. After the kiss came to a natural end, Caroline nestled against Alexander watching the familiar flat landscape slide slowly past the windows under the silver moon. 'That was lovely,' she said.

He squeezed her shoulders. 'It was.'

There was contentment in his voice, but fatigue too. She smiled, twisting to look up at him. 'I shall not be offended if you wish to sleep.'

A yawn shook him. 'You are a woman to be prized above rubies,' he said, 'for churlish as it seems and wondrous though that was, I do not think I can stay awake.' He eased himself into the corner squabs and tucked her into his side. 'I am content, Caroline,' he murmured.

'And I, Alexander,' she whispered. It was true. They lived in different worlds and nothing could possibly come of this, but just for a moment Alexander had loved her and Caroline felt herself to be the happiest person in England.

★ ★ ★

I am content. The words echoed bitterly around Alex's scull as his valet readied him for bed. He *would* have been content — more than content. Caroline was open and trusting and intelligent, and loyal and fierce and uncompromising, and she stirred a quite astonishing desire in him. But he couldn't forget that he had not apparently confined himself just to raving about Lizzy's flight and his boyhood escapades when he was ill. And if he had done so once, he could easily do so again.

I should like you to kiss me when you are awake. Dear God, his blood ran cold just to think about what he might have done! That he had stopped at kissing her was not far short of a miracle, the way his loins stirred now whenever he looked at her — whenever he thought of her even. How could he live with himself if she trusted him and he hurt her? The bleak truth was that he was not fit to spend time with any woman until the demons that took possession of his sleeping brain were vanquished. It was a good thing indeed that he was leaving Penfold Lodge.

He dozed fitfully, forcing himself awake when he would have slept deeper. He heard the household return, heard Caroline's voice asking Mrs Penfold how she had enjoyed herself, heard her accompanying her upstairs and listening to the older woman's gentle monologue. He heard Harry Fortune's calls of goodnight. He heard the soft footfalls of the servants making the house safe, shutting it down for the night.

He was so, so tired. But every time he shut his eyes, ghastly images of what he might do in his sleep blazed across his brain. Eventually he let out a wild groan and staggered out of bed, lighting a candle to banish the visions. He crossed to the window, pulling aside the curtain to lean against the glass.

He had been there five, maybe ten, minutes — trapped in the dark circle of his blackest thoughts — when the door behind him opened softly.

'What is it, Alexander?'

He turned, unbalanced, his joints stiff with having been standing by the cold panes. She was across the room in an instant, helping him back to the bed where he sat with his head in his hands. 'Go away,' he said in a low voice. 'You should not be here. Go away.'

She stooped and put another log on the banked fire. 'I will when you tell me why you have been standing unmoving in your window instead of recruiting your strength in sleep.'

'Dammit, Caroline, you can manage many things, but you cannot manage this.'

She pulled her shawl more closely about her and sat beside him. 'If you are regretting kissing me, you need not. I am not *expecting* anything, my lord. I know full well I would not fit in your world. So do not think you have compromised me or anything nonsensical like that.'

'I am not regretting kissing you,' said Alex through gritted teeth.

'Good, for I enjoyed it tremendously.'

She had enjoyed it. For a moment he wanted her so much he could barely trust himself to move. 'Caroline, it is so improper for you to be here that I am lost for words. Will you please return to your room.'

'Why do you not get back into bed? Then we shall be nurse and patient again and you may tell me what is bothering you.'

'If I get back into bed, I cannot put my arm around you.' *Dear heaven, where had those words come from?*

He felt a tremor run through her. 'Would you like to?'

His longing for her peaked. He was so tired that all there was left in his head was the truth. 'Yes,' he said, his voice breaking, 'but I can't because I am afraid of what I might do when I fall asleep.'

She chuckled and slipped off the bed. 'Well if that is all, you shall get inside the covers and I will lie down on the outside and then you will do nothing at all because you will be held securely in place.'

Why had she not run away? Was she mad? Didn't she know what men were capable of when their reason was clouded by lust?

'I make the world's most shameful declaration and you laugh at me. What sort of girl are you?'

'A practical one. There, your bedding is straight again. That will be more comfortable.'

'Caroline, please tell me everything I have raved about and everything I have done. Everything.'

'I will once you are in bed. You are chilled to the bone and I would have you get better, not worse.'

Alex couldn't quite believe he was doing as she directed but, oh, it did feel good to be lying down again with his head on the pillow, warmth tucked around him and a firm, soft voice taking charge. 'You will be cold too,' he said.

'Then I will wrap myself in your dressing-gown. See, it is so big that it covers me from head to foot.' Alex felt the edge of the bed dip as she settled herself next to him. 'Now then — when you were ill, you relived chasing after your sister; you relived the time a bridge broke when you were crossing it; you talked about falling from a tree, tipping over your curricle . . . '

Those he had expected. 'And what of when I kissed you?'

He felt her chuckle. 'You thought I was Rosetta. It was very brief, Alexander, and it was only a kiss. You do not need to worry.'

Alex screwed his eyes tight closed in shame and clenched his fists under the covers. 'Rosetta is in the past,' he ground out.

He felt her lean towards him and kiss his forehead. 'I know. You threatened to pepper poor Thomas with lead shot. Fortunately he didn't hear you, or you might not have found your meat served with such alacrity the next day.'

Alex opened his eyes. 'Caroline, *this* is why I am dangerous.'

She smiled at him in the candlelight. 'Silly. I said you *threatened* — you didn't actually do anything. In all your terrors and all your nightmares the only person you were ever endangering was yourself, tossing from side to side until you were like to fall out of bed. Once I had talked to you and soothed you, you went back to sleep.'

He relaxed, assimilating this as he worked one arm free of the sheets. She must be telling the truth. She would not be so unafraid if he had given her even the slightest indication that his raving self would overstep the mark. 'But I *kissed* you,' he whispered.

'Only because I was there.'

They were silent for a moment while he

traced her cheek. 'You are here now.'

'So I am,' she said contentedly.

She was just as soft, just as unafraid, just as giving as she had been in the coach. Alex tumbled headlong into the honesty of Caroline Fortune's kiss and knew, at last, that it was safe to sleep.

14

Caroline slid very gently from under the weight of Alexander's arm and wriggled out of his enveloping dressing-gown. She had slept as soundly as he, the candle had long guttered out, and soon the world would be waking.

Alexander would be all right now, she thought, as she sped on silent feet up to her own room, and though there was an ache in her chest that he would soon be out of her life, at least he knew he had nothing to fear.

As for her, she would carry the memory of his kisses within her forever.

At the stable, getting the horses ready for the day, she distracted herself by regaling the men with details of the alderman's dinner. There had always been this exchange of information between them: she described the goings-on in her world, they filled her in on the gossip in theirs. Frequently the two accounts tallied.

' . . . and Harry might at last be making progress with Louisa's father.' She paused with her foot in Flood's cupped hands, ready to be thrown up to Solange's back. 'I own I am concerned about Mr d'Arblay. Not that Louisa is likely to have anything to do with him for all he looks the gentleman and behaves so prettily around her, but he seemed out of all proportion annoyed last night.'

Flood gave her the boost to the saddle and rubbed the back of his hand across his mouth. 'Him again. Well now . . . He never has a feather to fly with and lives mostly on his lordship's credit, but we knew that. What else? Takes care always to be seen with the right people and never with the wrong ones. Leastwise, not when the gentry are looking.'

'The wrong ones?' said Caroline, arrested by his tone. 'What sort of wrong ones?'

Flood met her eyes. 'Maybe the ones Jem Jessop is seen with. The ones with generous hearts who help out coves what are getting behind with the rent. The ones not always fussed about the best horse necessarily winning.'

Solange moved, wanting to be off. Caroline patted her absently. 'You think he is deeper in debt than normal?'

'Could be.'

'Was Jessop on the hiring roster at the livery office?'

'Now there's a thought,' said Flood softly. 'A job in a lord's stable would be a nice bone to throw a hungry pack, wouldn't it? I'll make enquiries. You'd best go, Miss Caro. I'll send one of the lads down to the road if milord turns up again.'

'I don't believe he will. He was worn to threads last night. I daresay he'll sleep in half the morning.' She took a quick breath. 'And then he will be off to Cheveley.'

There was a tiny silence. 'Probably for the best, lass.'

Caroline nudged Solange forward. 'I know, Flood. I know.'

* * *

Alexander flatly refused to go in the carriage to Cheveley, directing his horse to be brought to Penfold Lodge for the three-mile journey instead. 'Will you accompany me?' he asked Caroline. 'You and your brother? I shall miss our rides together.'

Caroline's heart fluttered. 'Gladly,' she said. 'But will your hosts not think it strange? We hardly move in the same social circles, you know.'

'I shall put it down to your being an incorrigibly conscientious nurse.'

Did he mean because she had lain alongside him that he might sleep in peace? He hadn't mentioned those kisses this morning. He hadn't looked at her in any

281

particular way. She told herself she was being ridiculous. 'My brother, I know, will be more than happy to ride escort. Your mama has found herself a devoted slave in him.'

Alexander grunted. 'She has a retinue of devoted slaves all over England.'

'It is easy to see why. I like her very much.'

'Everybody always does. She scatters her affection as broadly and thickly as a farmer sows his grain, and reaps a like result.'

There was just the tiniest touch of irony in his voice. Caroline considered him thoughtfully. 'Her grace has a happy manner,' she said, 'but I do not believe she loves indiscriminately. She would not be as insistent on, say, Mr d'Arblay recuperating at Cheveley after a blow to the head as she is being with you.'

His shoulders twitched impatiently. 'There's nothing in that. Mama is enjoying one of her maternal phases.'

'And you do not like being fussed. Permit me to say, my lord, that you would like it less if she knew of your indisposition and merely sent you a few lines to say that she hoped you would be better soon.'

Alexander glared at her. 'I should thank heaven that she had at last learnt to act with moderation.'

Caroline rose. 'And you would then dash off a note to your father, asking if your mama was quite well. You may bamboozle yourself, if you must, but you do not fool me. I have some errands to run for Mrs Penfold. I will see you in the stable yard in an hour.' By which time she would have controlled this absurd impulse to cry. She was going to miss sparring with him.

★ ★ ★

As he had prophesied, Alex's mama was indeed in full-blown rapture on his arrival at the Duke of Rutland's estate at Cheveley. He lifted his eyebrows in a *What did I tell you?* fashion at Caroline. But Mama was also immensely civil to both Caroline and Harry, introducing them to various of Rutland's house guests and including them in the conversation. Watching, Alex realized it hadn't occurred to him that they would do other than acquit themselves sensibly, and so it proved. It seemed no time at all before the customary half-hour was up and they said they must go. The words hit Alex like a jabbing uppercut to his midriff.

Conscious of an audience, he took Caroline's hand in a formal hold and told her he would always be grateful for the care he had received at Penfold Lodge.

'Indeed, you were most welcome, my lord.'

Her words were as conventional as his own.

Alex lifted her fingers to his lips and pressed a kiss to them. Was it his imagination or did her hand tremble slightly? He held her eyes a tiny moment longer, then let her go.

Mama was talking already about plans for this week and what day they would leave for Abervale. Alex let the flow trickle past him, watching until Caroline and her brother left the room. When the door shut, he felt as if a small piece of the day had gone with them. He nodded to the company and was shown to his allotted bedchamber where he found his valet expressing satisfaction at being back in a proper nobleman's residence.

' . . . rising at a civilized hour, no more eating in the kitchen as if you were a commoner, a proper upper servants' room . . . '

Alex stared out of his window at spacious, wooded grounds without a horse or an honest working man in sight. He was doing this for Caroline, he repeated. He needed to give himself time. He was in no doubt about his own feelings, but he needed to be quite, quite sure that he was safe both in and out of company before he took the next step. A few days, that's all it would take. And meanwhile he could deal with this unexpected sense of loss. He would make the right adjustment in his head and pick up his old life again. In the background his valet was still blathering. That settled the matter. Alex would start by going downstairs in search of a glass of Madeira and informed male conversation.

★ ★ ★

Caroline discussed training schedules with Harry ready for next week's racing, retired at a decent hour, took Solange out for an early gallop — trusting that the Lord would overlook it being Sunday in view of the seriousness of next week's race — and then accompanied Mrs Penfold to church.

Unfortunately, her mother caught up with her in the churchyard. Even more unfortunately, she knew Lord Rothwell had removed to Cheveley. And even more unfortunately than that, she had discovered from some undisclosed source that her troublesome, plain, second daughter was somehow on visiting terms with the Duchess of Abervale.

'So, Caroline, it has been quite a while, has it not? I daresay you will be pleased enough to come home again tomorrow. I shall give orders to Cook to make up a batch of her best macaroons — which I flatter myself are *quite* the most superior in all Newmarket — and then if it chances to happen that her grace and Lord Rothwell should call to thank you for your aid with the nursing, as I daresay they will, we shall not be in the least disgraced. Selina has a new cerulean gown which may catch his lordship's eye and there is enough of the material left over to add a flounce to one of yours to give it a new touch.'

Caroline saw her freedom and next week's vital plans disappear behind the iron bars of a proper-young-lady's existence. 'You are all care, Mama,' she said with a regretful sigh, 'but I am afraid poor Mrs Penfold is so worn out with the extra work that I have promised her faithfully to remain a week or two until she has fully recruited her energies.'

Mrs Fortune's eyes sharpened as she directed them to where Martha Penfold was in conversation with a friend. 'She does not look worn out.'

Caroline's own eyes widened. 'It is Sunday, Mama. Naturally she makes an effort when she is at church. But I know as soon as we are back at Penfold Lodge, all she will be fit for is to lie on the sofa and have me read passages from the Bible to her.'

'Well, it is very inconvenient. By the time she is recovered, the Duchess and Lord Rothwell may have left the neighbourhood completely.'

Caroline thought she could probably vouch for it.

★ ★ ★

It was Monday afternoon of the Second Spring Meeting and in three days' time Solange would have to race. Caroline pulled her cap low over her brow and sat in a slumped, round-shouldered fashion astride the mare as she guided her through the racing crowd. Harry rode Rufus next to her — the better to calm Solange — and Flood walked close on her other side.

The grey mare was palpably nervous, with little shivers of tension running under her skin. Caroline was aware that her own unfamiliar lack of assurance was communicating itself to the horse. She castigated herself silently; she *must* be more composed. The crowds were not as strange to her as they were to Solange. She had been to meetings countless times before dressed as a boy and she had even raced at them. The trouble was that the last of those times had been some three or four years ago, before what curves she possessed had developed, and when her understanding of society's standards had been less informed than it was today. The freedom and sense of adventure of coming here with Bertrand and Harry was gone. All she could see now were people who might penetrate her disguise at any minute,

287

exposing her to the world's censure, possibly earning Harry a ban for using his sister as a jockey — and degrading her in Alexander's eyes. *Alexander*. Even through her fear of discovery, Caroline's heart lurched. Considering how hard she had wished him gone when he was first deposited on their doorstep, his absence from Penfold Lodge these past forty-eight hours had left the house feeling like a shell and herself only half alive. It was amazing how you could make yourself so busy you barely had time to sit down, yet still miss someone.

Solange fidgeted restively. Caroline hunched lower in the saddle. It wasn't surprising that the mare was nervous. All around them jostled the nobility and the gentry in their well-cut riding coats and faultless breeches, their horses glossy and their bearing confident. There were also curricles and phaetons cutting across their path, vendors of food and drink shouting their wares, noise everywhere. Somehow Caroline must find within herself the well-spring that enabled her to connect with Solange. In her mind's eye, she depopulated the heath, losing the bookmakers and legs gathered around the betting post, wiping from the picture the important-faced race judges and hurrying grooms. She concentrated on the mare's broad shoulders, on the feel of her honed muscles.

'Better,' grunted Flood.

Caroline continued to breathe deeply and evenly, keeping her eyes on Solange's neck, knowing she was doing it right at last. She could feel the horse becoming calmer with every pace.

'Fortune!' said a surprisingly glad voice close by them. 'What's this? More of your training?'

And now Caroline really daren't look up.

'Good day, Rothwell,' said Harry cheerfully. 'Yes, as you can see, I am doing my level best to rob you.'

'I will try not to hold it against you,' said Alexander with a laugh. 'It is a good idea. Don't want her bolting from the crowd on Thursday before she's even got to the starting line.'

'My thoughts exactly,' replied Harry.

'I see you're riding Rufus. Now, why do I get the impression that your sister has been discussing breeding programmes with you?'

'Ah well, she knows her stuff, does Caro. Good meeting today, isn't it? I won't keep you. Daresay I'll run across you again later.'

Alexander lowered his voice, but Caroline was so attuned to him she could make out the words clearly. 'Is your lad well? That's the least at ease I've ever seen him.'

Harry laughed. 'Oh, Brown is like Solange.

Not overly keen on people. He'll be all right on the day.'

'I bow to your experience. Is your sister . . . ' *Was that a catch in his voice?* 'Is your sister in good health?'

'Never better. She's bamboozled Mama into thinking Mrs P needs her. So she is fixed at Penfold Lodge for the present, happy as a grig. It makes the place more homely, you know?'

'Indeed I was very comfortable there. I . . . I am glad she is in good spirits.'

They moved on. Caroline didn't know whether she was happy to have been close to Alexander, glad he was well, pleased he had asked after her, or terrified in case he recognized her. A mix of all, she thought, and though every step they took increased the distance between them and made her safer, she felt an absurd impulse to cry.

'Hey, Alex!' called Giles d'Arblay's voice from quite a long way behind.

Caroline gave a start at the same time as Solange's muscles bunched. *Oh, you idiot*, she berated herself, *one lapse of concentration and see what happens!* She threw herself flat along the horse's neck, crooning encouragement into her ear as Solange tried to plunge left into Rufus, then right into Flood's rock-like reassurance. All Caroline's own agitation was subsumed in the need to keep her mount tranquil.

Calm, Solange, calm, she willed urgently. What sort of stupid idea had this been? Whose complacent idiocy had suggested it? With the throng on the heath this afternoon there would be fatalities for sure if Solange bolted. Balked, the mare gave a last long quiver, then snorted and relaxed. Caroline had never been so thankful in her life. She lay for a moment more against the long, warm neck, feeling the sweat drip from her brow onto Solange's mane, waiting for her heartbeat to return to normal.

'We'll do this again tomorrow,' she murmured to Harry as they walked on. 'I'll take her home now.'

Harry and Flood exchanged glances. 'Another quarter hour would be better if you can hold her,' rumbled Flood. 'We'll not go anywhere near milord.'

Caroline bit her lip; she knew she was being a coward. More work now meant less on Thursday. Solange came first. She had to. 'Very well,' she agreed. And after all, what with the very real fear of physical danger both to herself and the crowd around them just then, her worries about being unmasked as a female seemed cobweb-puny by comparison.

★ ★ ★

Out of the corner of his eye, Alex saw the lad Brown control Solange's sideways skitter. He found he was holding his breath at the way both Harry and the groom radiated sudden tension. Not Brown, though. Even as Alex watched, he became one with the animal, soothing and calming her. Odd how the boy was ungainly when walking her, but a thing of beauty at any speed. It must be as Fortune had said, he was awkward out of his own milieu. Alex knew an absurd impulse to go after them and call the bet off, but here was Giles, pushing his horse through the crowd.

'Ho, Alex, didn't you hear me?'

Alex turned. 'Giles. You are quite a stranger. I thought to have seen you these last two days at Cheveley.' Although he was just as happy that he hadn't.

Giles looked pleased with himself. 'I have been frying other fish. Yesterday, for example, I was taking tea after church with a certain goldsmith's daughter and her aunt. The trade connection is a trifle lowering, to be sure, but one has to make sacrifices.'

A shiver of distaste passed through Alex at Giles's cold-bloodedness. 'You are aware Miss Taylor considers herself engaged to young Fortune?'

292

His friend laughed. 'There's nothing in that. It is fathers who make matches, not pretty widgeons. One can always win *them* over in the bedchamber once the deed is done. And with this particular widgeon, it will not even be a hardship.'

'You are not serious?' said Alex, the appalling sentiment sticking in his craw.

'Of course I am. She's a gift. How often does one run across an heiress whose papa is in love with the aristocracy? A baronet's son may not be as good as a lord, but he was mightily impressed by my castle.'

'He wouldn't be if he saw it.'

The satisfied expression slipped. 'Dammit, Alex, it's all very well for you with a thriving estate to draw on for funds, I'm damn near rolled up.'

'My *funds* as you call them, require work and good husbandry to replenish. If you would only take time to add to the farms your godfather left you, you too would reap the benefit.'

'What? Go up to Yorkshire to dicker with a pack of thieves? You must be mad.' Giles rose in his saddle, craning to see over the crowd. 'Looks as if they'll be off soon. Osman's a cert for this one, don't you think? By the by, Alex, if today goes badly, I'll need to borrow a thousand until the quarter.'

Only wager what you can afford to lose.

'No,' said Alex slowly. 'No, I really think it is time you stood on your own feet. I am not going to be your emergency purse any more.'

Giles shrugged. 'As you like. But I don't know what else you are going to do with your money.'

Caroline's face appeared in Alex's mind. 'I may have some thoughts of marriage,' he said off-handedly. *Marriage.* The word tasted strange on his tongue. But the images it brought with it were catch-breath seductive.

Giles's laughter could be heard well above the crowd. 'No really, that's coming it too strong! What, you? Leg-shackled to one of those chattering, fawning, society ladies you despise? You'd be divorced within a day. Far better to lend me a couple of thousand than to tamely hand your bank-book into their pretty little claws.'

Alex's thoughts snapped back. 'A couple of thousand is it now? If you are that far in tick, you shouldn't bet.'

Already setting off for the start, Giles glanced at him in amazement. 'Stap me, that villain must have hit you harder than we knew. Come to Newmarket and not bet? Now I know you are mad.'

Giles's favoured horse didn't win, but there

was no sign of annoyance on his face as they moved back up the flat to the Rowley Mile marker for the next race. 'The meeting's young yet,' he said cheerfully. 'I fancy Domine Sampson next.'

Alex frowned, his attention caught. Wasn't Domine Sampson the horse Caroline and Harry had mentioned as having performed more poorly than expected at the previous meeting? He was about to drop a warning, but was distracted by catching sight of an unexpected face. 'Why is Jessop here?' he exclaimed. 'I left him no such orders. He should be at the White Hart still.'

'He brought my spare mount,' said Giles.

'What is wrong with your own man?'

'I let him go. Too unreliable. I knew you wouldn't mind me using Jessop while you were laid up.'

Alex felt another spurt of annoyance. First Giles was annexing his money, now his grooms. And he was unworried about losing his previous stake and proposed to throw good money after bad now. Yes, he had been the same ever since they were boys, but . . . 'You may keep Jessop,' he said abruptly. 'I will make you over the papers tonight.'

'Eh?' Paying for the man himself evidently hadn't been in Giles's plan. 'But then you'll be a groom short.'

'Not so. I am leaving Solange at Penfold Lodge.'

Giles roared with laughter a second time. 'Alex, your wits are turning! You are never imagining that greenhorn puppy really can turn your widowmaker into a race winner?'

It was fortunate that Chieftain was such a composed horse. A more highly-strung animal might have started trampling around, the way his rider was mangling the reins. 'It matters not,' said Alex curtly. 'Miss Caroline Fortune has expressed a wish to purchase her.'

'Ha! The chit's as soft in the head as her brother. I'd get the money off her before the race if I were you, Alex. You won't get it after.' He plunged into the ring of gentlemen around the betting post.

Alex nudged Chieftain away and over towards where the Duke of Rutland was holding court. To be sure, two days was not that long a test period to give oneself, but he thought he might usefully call on Caroline tomorrow. To thank her, of course. And to mention Giles visiting Miss Taylor. A friendly act, that was all. Nothing else.

Yet.

★　★　★

'My lord, this is an unexpected surprise.' Caroline could not mask the thrill of pleasure Alexander's entry into the morning room gave her.

'I hope I am not disturbing you?'

He did not look overly concerned that she might have better things to do. 'Not at all,' she said politely. 'Mrs Penfold is mastering a singularly complicated new stitch and I am wondering how best to account to my cousin for all the hay we have fed to the horses this month. What do you think? Should I hide it amongst the corn and the oats and lay the whole tally boldly before him, though he might suffer a seizure on his eyes leaping immediately to the total? Or should I lead up to it gradually with the final sum tucked over the page?'

'As I have never met your cousin, I cannot say. For myself I prefer to know straight away what I must deal with.'

'I should have guessed you would not hold with flummery.' It was absurd that she couldn't seem to think straight. There were so many things she wanted to talk to him of, but she had lost the knack of launching into them. 'My brother tells me he saw you yesterday. I hope you had better luck than he did.'

He hailed the subject with alacrity. Was it

possible that he was also finding conversation difficult? Caroline could not help but be gratified. 'No, I did not,' he said now, 'and I must take you both to task for sending me wrong. I am quite sure I remember you mentioned Grafton's Minuet as a sound horse and yet Lake's Domine Sampson trounced her yesterday and lost me my stake.'

Caroline chuckled. 'That will teach you not to be guided by anything other than your own good sense. We lost too.'

'As did several others. I tell you, Giles had to be very circumspect indeed last night since Grafton was dining at Cheveley with us.'

'Ah.' Caroline took a deep breath. She did not want to do this, to break the pleasure of seeing him again properly for the first time in three days, but she had her duty as a friend to think of. 'That leads me to something I would as lief not mention. It is fortunate you are here, my lord. I had a letter from Louisa this morning.'

But Alexander spoke at the same time. 'In actual fact I came to warn you — '

He broke off and she met his eyes, astonished. 'About Mr d'Arblay?'

'I . . . yes.'

Caroline's heart leapt as she hastily rearranged what she had been going to say. She had really not expected him to feel guilty on Mr d'Arblay's account. Oh, she was so glad she had misjudged him. She wasted a full minute praising him to herself. 'I beg your pardon. I know he is your friend, but I find I cannot repose any trust in him.'

He leant forward and removed from her hands the pen she had been fiddling with. 'Be easy, you will break it. I was going to tell you Giles has been laying siege to the alderman. He *has* been my friend for many years, and frequently a good companion. He may even be genuinely attached to Miss Taylor. But I fear he has a want of steadiness that would make him an unsuitable husband.'

It was an enormous admission from a man who was so much in the habit of being right. Caroline could not compound his sense of his own failings further. She was proud of him for admitting as much and indeed, for her purposes, it would suffice. She had been dreading pointing out to him, for example, that had Lady Jersey not arrived at that inn in Stamford, Giles would have been perfectly placed to dismiss Alexander's sister's suitor with a grand flourish himself and offer comfort. Almost certainly a lot more comfort than the spoilt young heiress bargained for. Giles going straight to the George while Alexander chased one false trail after another indeed! It smacked of so much contrivance,

Caroline was astonished Alexander hadn't seen it for himself. 'Will you talk to Louisa's father?' she asked.

He looked startled. 'I? Betray Giles to a man I hardly know? Such an undertaking would be unthinkable.'

Caroline's spirits fell. Of course it would be impossible. She kept forgetting that he had only recently come amongst them. Even so, she made one last attempt. 'It is well known in the town that you pay his bills. Just mentioning that fact to Alderman Taylor might be sufficient.'

His face twisted as if she had given him a draught of some particularly noxious medicine. 'Well known?'

'Yes. At least, it is to me because I talk to our grooms. In Newmarket we are sadly used to impecunious young men spending freely what they do not have, and have learnt to identify them and whether payment is likely to be forthcoming from *whatever* source. It will not be such common report in Bury St Edmunds though, so the alderman is unlikely to be aware of the situation.'

Profound distaste crossed Alexander's face. 'Caroline, I cannot.' He jumped up and took a hasty turn about the room.

Feeling wretched, Caroline glanced over at Mrs Penfold, absorbed in her knitting, then straightened her back and followed Alexander to where he was staring rigidly out of the far window. He didn't turn around.

'Have I done this?' he asked in a low, strained voice. 'Have I caused Giles to be this way because I do always settle his accounts?'

Caroline thought it very likely, but only said, 'It is understandable. You are his friend. You do not want to see Mr d'Arblay in a debtors' prison any more than I want to see Louisa trapped in an unhappy marriage. I am sorry. I did not mean to put you in an untenable position. Please consider the request unmade.'

He sighed. 'I suppose it would not be thought so very out of the ordinary for me to ride over and purchase a gold chain or some such for my mother?'

Caroline glowed with pride in him. 'Not out of the ordinary at all,' she said.

'Or . . . ' He hesitated. 'Or if you wished to visit your friend, I could offer you my escort?'

Caroline moistened her lips, her heart thudding. In truth, she would like that very much, but she remembered only too well what had happened the last time they were in a closed carriage together. Prospective Members of Parliament could have nothing to do with the daughters of gentleman trainers. She had already accepted that, hard though it was. Lord Rothwell would not be compromised simply because Miss Fortune was weak. 'That is kind of you indeed, but Louisa is to come to me in any event on Thursday. She is as anxious as we are about the race. Perhaps you should take your mama? I daresay she would enjoy the fine architecture of the town.'

Alexander looked at her with stark incredulity. 'Good God, Caroline, you have the most appalling suggestions of anyone I have ever met. If I take Mama, you must go too, or I shall run mad. Will ten o'clock tomorrow suit you?'

It was Caroline's turn to be startled. 'Why yes, but I . . . That is, we may not be back in time for you to get to the racing.'

'Giles would no doubt think it heresy, but it will not hurt me to miss one day.' He took polite leave of an abstracted Mrs Penfold. Caroline followed him into the hall. As the footman handed him his hat, he turned back. 'Do *you* think it heresy?' he asked.

Now where was his mind skipping to? Caroline blinked, bewildered. There was a confused hurry of feelings in her breast. Aside from the agitation that she would once more be in company with him the whole morning, there was also the knowledge that he had come to Newmarket for the racing, he had already missed a week of it, and he would miss more whilst performing a distasteful errand purely on her friend's account. A friend that he himself had no particular feelings for. He was a long way from the man he had seemed a month ago.

'No, Alexander,' she said, gathering her wits together. 'I think it is extremely good of you and not heresy at all.'

He gave a twisted smile. 'Thank you, though I am not sure I agree. Until tomorrow, then.' At the last moment, he took up her hand and kissed it.

Caroline was left staring at the closing door in more confusion than ever.

15

To say Alderman Taylor was delighted at the arrival of Lord Rothwell and the Duchess of Abervale in his establishment was somewhat of an understatement. He immediately sent for his daughter, refreshments, a more comfortable chair for her grace, and all the gold chains the display cases held.

He also repeatedly thanked Caroline *sotto voce* for bringing her patrons to Bury St Edmunds and told her what a happy day it was when she and Louisa first became friends.

The duchess was appreciative of everything in the shop, but appeared chiefly struck by her son's thoughtfulness in noticing that the chain she wore with her favourite locket had worn quite thin. 'I won't say it is unlike him,' she confided to Caroline, 'but I do begin to have hopes when he thinks it is better if I choose a present for myself, rather than him ordering any old article and my being expected to be pleased when it really won't do at all.'

'Perhaps he is growing up, ma'am. I believe all gentlemen do eventually.'

'Very likely. And see how he is drawing the dear alderman aside so that we can enjoy looking at these in peace. I do think this new fashion for not wearing all one's nicest items together is rather vexing, don't you?'

Caroline perceived that her real task was to dissuade her grace from buying up half the goldsmith's stock and thought she thoroughly deserved the treat of being gathered up with Louisa and her father when the business was concluded, and all being taken to a hotel for coffee and ices 'every bit as good as Gunter's' according to the duchess, before they drove home again.

'Thank you, my lord,' she said, when Alexander saw her to the Penfold Lodge door.

'I hope you are not too fatigued,' he said with a smile. 'I always think going on an outing with Mama is akin to being pulverized by meringues.'

'What an unnatural son you are. I found her grace quite delightful.' Then, as Alexander lifted an amused eyebrow, Caroline added honestly, 'But I do see that it is not the sort of thing one could do *every* day.'

'Not if one wants to remain sane and solvent,' he replied. 'I confess I enjoyed today, too. I will see you after the race tomorrow — if you will allow me to call?'

The race. Caroline's insides suddenly contracted. 'Certainly, my lord,' she said. 'I look forward to it.'

He hesitated. 'Caroline, win or lose, I would like you to know that I would retract the bet if I could.'

★　★　★

Thursday. The day of the race. Caroline felt sick with nerves. She rose at her usual hour, rode out as usual, went back to the kitchen with Harry as usual and had to flee the room as her stomach rebelled at the cooking odours. A tray of tea with some thin bread and butter was firmly sent after her.

It was a private match, so Solange had not had to be shown to the stewards in advance. Furthermore, it was to be held at the close of the meeting. While this gave Caroline much more time to imagine all possible disastrous scenarios, it did at least enable her to be in evidence at home beforehand to greet Alderman Taylor who was leaving Louisa at Penfold Lodge before going up to the heath himself with Harry, and also, sadly, to sustain a short call from her mother. Mrs Fortune had been most put out to learn — *from two different sources, Caroline. Two! I have never been so mortified* — that her daughter had tripped merrily off to Bury St Edmunds the day before with a party from Cheveley. She pointed out that it had been tiresomely thoughtless of Caroline not to drop a note around to Fortune House asking Selina to accompany her. It would have been the work of minutes. Had she no sense of what was due to her family? Caroline was suitably apologetic, Mama left, and the butler could at last be told the ladies were not at home to visitors.

Louisa accompanied Caroline upstairs. Caroline loved her friend dearly and appreciated the support Louisa thought she was giving, but she would much rather have got dressed in the Penfold Lodge racing colours by herself. Not that Louisa said anything, it was just that her cut-off gasp at the adapted underclothes that were all that would fit under the white breeches, and then the widening of her eyes betraying how tightly those breeches clung to Caroline's legs was more than a trifle unsettling.

'Can you breathe?' she asked, as Caroline doubled a shirt tightly around herself and buttoned up the close-fitting buff and crimson silk jacket.

'Enough,' said Caroline. She sat still whilst Louisa pinned her hair into place, then jammed on the black racing cap. Last of all, she wriggled into a concealing coat of Harry's for the ride up though the town. 'Wish me luck,' she said.

Louisa hugged her. 'I do.'

Flood had readied Solange and was waiting in the stable yard. Caroline rubbed some dirt into her face before resolutely meeting his eyes. 'I can do this,' she said.

'You can, lass.'

He threw her up into the saddle and together they walked under the arch and into the street. Caroline concentrated on Solange as she had never concentrated on a horse before. Carriages, other horses and pedestrians all passed by on the edges of her vision. She was the mare and the mare was her. She hardly even realized they had reached the start of the Rowley Mile until Flood's hand on the bridle halted them and she heard Harry's voice, oddly formal, saying, 'You agree this is the horse you sent me for training?'

And then Alexander replying, 'Oh yes, that's her all right.'

Caroline kept her shoulders slumped and her head down. How could he not recognize her? She felt Flood nudge her leg. 'Dismount for weighing-out, lad.'

She flushed, slid off and sat on the scale with her saddle. Still she kept her eyes downcast.

As she got back on Solange, she heard Giles d'Arblay pass a light remark wondering which mousehole Mr Harry Fortune had found his unfortunate rider in. The laughter which greeted this sally indicated that quite a crowd was lingering after the main races to see this one.

Solange shifted sideways with a whinny. Caroline gripped her with her knees, wondering which of them she was comforting. They moved to the start. Four other horses joined them, but all Caroline's attention was on the course ahead. Solange was packed with wiry, nervous energy; Caroline *had* to get her out in front where she wouldn't be jostled as soon as was possible. It seemed an interminable wait until the runner puffed up to say milord and the judges and all were in position at the finishing post.

Eight furlongs. Maybe two minutes of time.

'Go,' said the starter — and they were off.

There was no room left in Caroline for nerves or for sickness. The horse on the far right had started best but Solange was going well too. At least she didn't have to worry about guiding the mare around any bends, this course was a straight mile and as flat as anywhere for the first six furlongs. How long had passed? Ten seconds? Twenty? There were hoofbeats in her ears as a chestnut head edged into her vision. Grafton's half-thoroughbred, it had to be. 'Go on,' she crooned to Solange. 'Go on, girl.'

They must be at four furlongs by now. The horse on the far right was slowing, winded. Was Grafton's increasing on them though? Caroline crouched lower, urging the grey mare on. Five furlongs. Now the dip was in sight. The trick was to use the increased speed going down the incline to push the horse up the final rising furlong. 'Go, darling,' she whispered. 'It's just like our stretch of training ground. Go, go, go.' Caroline was almost flat now, melding herself to the horse's back. Was she edging further in front of the chestnut?

Six furlongs. Thundering down the dip, not, not, *not* thinking about uneven ground and broken legs. Seven furlongs and rising ground and Grafton's horse falling back. And going on, going on, going on . . .

Solange galloped at full stretch to the finishing post. Caroline blinked her eyes open to focus on the two figures she knew would be just past the mound of turf. Harry had swept his hat off and was throwing it in the air. Alexander was smiling almost as exultantly. She had won. She had won and he was happy about it, not chagrined. He didn't care that his bet was lost. She thought her heart would burst. She slowed Solange as she headed towards them, hardly able to believe her victory. For a split second she met Alexander's warm, laughing eyes . . .

And then behind him, his face as cold as a Fell winter, she saw Giles d'Arblay raise his arm.

'Look out, Alex!' he yelled and cracked his whip in the air.

Solange let out a sound that should never be forced out of an animal's throat and reared up almost vertical.

Caroline clung on with everything she had. Terror swept through her, whether hers or the mare's she didn't know. For one, two, three seconds Solange danced on her hind legs before thumping to the ground with her fores and thundering away across the heath.

Alive. Caroline was still alive and she was hanging on, but there were people everywhere, scattering, shouting, making Solange worse. Please God don't let them get in the way, don't let anyone indulge in well-meaning heroics. Please God, don't let anyone get killed. Please God, please God, please God . . .

They crossed the London Road in a headlong blur of speed. 'Straight on,' said Caroline to the horse. 'We'll go straight on away from everyone, then around the outside of the town towards Cheveley and get home from there. You're a wonderful horse, a splendid girl and I won't let them hurt you. I won't let anyone hurt you ever again.'

There were fewer people at last. The scrub and turf of the heath showed signs of giving way to fields. Solange slowed. Caroline's heartbeat gradually fell back to normal and she managed to unclench her hands from the reins.

Alive. She was alive and Solange was alive and the crowd on the heath was alive and even though eddies of tension whirled over the grey mare's hide it was just the normal easing down to an everyday hack. Nothing to worry about now. No rogue instincts. Normality.

But with normality came realization. Tears trickled down Caroline's cheeks. 'Oh, Solange,' she wept, as the full impact of their actions spread itself out in her head. 'Oh, Solange, darling, do you know what we've done? We were first past the post but we didn't weigh in. We've lost the race.'

$\star \quad \star \quad \star$

As the grey mare thundered away, terrified bystanders scrambling out of her path, Alex's mind whirred with disbelief. The lad — Brown — was Caroline! *Caroline!*

For one brief moment, in her jubilation at winning, she'd met his eyes full on. They were honey-brown. No one else Alex knew had eyes like that. No one had a face like that, under the concealing layer of dirt. She'd done it. She'd ridden Solange in order to win the wager. And she *had* won it. For one soaring, explosive moment he'd been so proud of her.

And then his heart had been ripped out and hurled into the far distance as if belted by some gigantic celestial cricket bat.

Alex screwed up his vision. Caroline had control of the mare again and was heading her away from the crowd, away from traffic, away from people. The horrific emptiness when Solange had reared and screamed and Alex thought Caroline would be flung to the ground like a rag doll and trampled had passed. He could breathe again. In a while he would have to think about the knowledge that had come crashing down on him during those endless few heartbeats, but for now he could simply stand and be amazed and be thankful.

'I knew it!' Beside him, Giles was exultant. 'The horse has bolted without the rider weighing in. That means it will have been distanced. The second horse wins. You can claim your wager, Alex. A thousand guineas!

313

Fortune will have to sell all his stock to cover it. That'll teach him to brush *me* off.'

It was as if Alex had never known Giles before. 'You knew Solange would bolt?' he said, in a remote voice that didn't sound like his own at all.

Giles was looking hither and thither amongst the crowd, hardly paying attention. 'I thought there was a good chance. You should thank me. Now we can both collect.'

'What of the rider?'

It wasn't surprising that Giles failed to spot any warning signs in Alex's mild, detached words. They were only just making it out of his mouth, let alone picking up enough impetus to infuse themselves with emotion.

'What of him?' he said with a laugh, beckoning to his groom. 'If he's any sense he'll drop off. And if it chances that he doesn't bounce, Fortune can use the fee he was going to pay him for a burial instead.'

The last vestiges of his boyhood friend's glamour fell away. Giles quite simply didn't exist any more. Alex strode to the judges' box, catching Harry by the arm and towing him along. 'It was a private match,' he said in an authoritative, carrying voice. Around him the crowd fell silent. Alex raised his voice still more. 'All here bear witness. I would like it made known that I accept completely and without reservation that Mr Harry Fortune has trained the grey mare Solange sufficiently well to win the race as per the terms of our wager. I therefore make no claim on him.'

Harry clasped his forearm, his face shining with relief and gratitude. 'Thank you, my lord. It was a foolish bet, but I could and would have paid you had you decided otherwise. This will make all the difference to us. Louisa is at Penfold Lodge. When I tell her, you will have her thanks as well.'

The judges conferred. The spokesman cleared his throat. 'A private match does not come under Jockey Club rules,' he announced. 'Solange passed the post first by a length. Lord Rothwell has declared himself satisfied with the weight. The result stands.'

The gentlemen around the ring of bookmakers burst into vociferous life. Alex looked at Harry. 'I must get after your sister,' he said, his voice pitched so only the pair of them could hear.

'Would you? Thank you. I have to find Louisa's father and take him back to Penfold Lodge.' Then Harry caught his breath as the purport of Alex's words sunk in. He paled. 'You knew it was Caro?'

'Not until she won. It was a damn good disguise. She's safe in that I saw her gain control of the horse, but what the devil were you doing letting her ride?' Latent anger threatened to tip him over the edge again.

Harry looked at him soberly. 'Being weak for the very last time in my life. She'll be heading for home. God speed, Rothwell.'

He plunged into the crowd. Alex turned too, hurrying for the enclosure where he'd left Chieftain. Out of the corner of his eye he saw Giles already driving his curricle fast towards the town, no doubt to drown his sorrows at the nearest inn. After a trick like that, if he had lost money on the race it was just too bad. Alex put him out of his mind. He had a far more important quest.

★   ★   ★

Rather than trample the Duke of Rutland's newly sown fields, Caroline directed Solange into the bridle-paths that bordered every hedge. The enormity of what she had done bowed her shoulders, regardless of the fact that as soon as Solange had reared, there was no other course of action Caroline could have taken. She let the mare drop to a slow walk, telling herself she was giving her a chance to cool down and recover from her exertions. Really, she was putting off the moment when she would have to enter the stable yard and tell the men she had both won — and lost.

A thousand guineas. It was an appalling sum. It would mean no new foals this year, and a severe set-back to her dreams of an independent competence. But she would pay it, she would keep Solange, and say goodbye to Lord Rothwell.

Lord Rothwell. Caroline jerked alert. He had said he would call on her after the race. She needed to get home and changed. But, picking up speed, she heard the sound of hoofbeats behind her. She cursed under her breath, thinking it must be one of Rutland's bailiffs, come to tell her she was trespassing. She would have to do her shy, stammering act again and hope the man didn't look too closely under the tears and the dirt.

'Imbecile girl!'

That was *not* one of his grace's bailiffs. Caroline's heart pitter-pattered.

'Dammit, Caroline, will you stop while I'm trying to scold you!'

'Don't shout. You'll set her off again,' she said, as a brown gelding came alongside. Her words set up a train of thought in the back of her mind.

'Then by all means dismount,' said Alexander, dangerously polite.

'Whoa, girl.' Caroline guided Solange to a small copse and slid off, using a branch for support as she looped the reins over it. Not for the world would she admit that her legs might not hold her up.

Alexander tethered Chieftain to the same tree. She had never appreciated before quite how tall he was, how imposing he appeared in his caped greatcoat, just how thunderously his eyebrows could draw together . . .

'God in Heaven, I thought I'd lost you,' he said, and crushed her to his lips.

. . . just how strong he was, just how safe his arms felt, just how much she wanted this moment to go on for ever.

But it couldn't. 'Alexander,' she managed to say, 'you're strangling me.'

He loosened his arms, but didn't let go, which was fortunate because she would certainly have fallen. Instead, with hands that didn't appear to belong to her any more than her legs did, she pulled at the stock around her neck.

'Let me,' he said, and then, with a shaky laugh, 'Dammit, I can't stand.'

He couldn't stand either? Did that mean . . . ? Did that mean . . . ?

Caroline's thoughts were in a whirl. She stared at him as they half-staggered, half-fell to a convenient tree stump. For ever afterwards, she would never be quite sure how she came to land on Alexander's lap. Her cap had fallen off during their embrace. Now she felt the pins in her hair working loose as Alexander undid the knot in her neckcloth.

'What did you think you were doing?' he asked.

'Making myself look like a man,' she said meekly.

This earned her a gentle slap on her posterior. 'Not the neckcloth, which I have to say my eight-year-old nephew could tie better than you. What did you think you were doing riding Solange?'

'She won't let anyone else on her back,' said Caroline. Again something flashed across her mind, something she knew was important, but which she couldn't for the life of her attend to whilst sitting on Alexander's lap dressed in breeches.

'There,' he said, unwinding a couple of yards of Harry's borrowed linen.

Caroline found she could breathe again. 'Oh, wonderful,' she said with real gratitude. 'How ever do gentlemen wear those things all the time?'

'Practice.' He settled her more comfortably and put his arms around her, then kissed her long and comprehensively. 'Caroline, could you not have told me? I thought we had become better friends than for you to go along with your brother's deception.'

Friends? Was that all this was? Did friends

cause each other's knees to tremble? Did friends spend quite so long with their lips locked together? 'It wasn't Harry's deception, it was mine,' she said. 'A thousand guineas may not be a large sum to you, but it is to us. I have my pride, Alexander.'

'Pride is one thing: putting yourself in danger is quite another.'

'Nonsense. There should not have been any danger. Yes, Solange is nervous with noise and crowds, but she has been a perfectly well-behaved, nice horse with me even with those distractions. I have been riding her both astride and side-saddle ever since you first brought her to Penfold Lodge.'

His arms tightened around her. 'You could have been killed,' he said into her hair.

Ah. Not just friends, then. Caroline's bones turned to honey and she moved her mouth blindly to meet his. 'I did not think so,' she said when the kiss ended. 'I was more worried about being unmasked. And not winning.' She took a deep breath. 'Which I didn't, since I failed to weigh in. We will arrange for the money to be paid to you tomorrow.'

Alexander cursed the money in language that until now Caroline had thought to be the prerogative of stable hands and grooms. 'It was a private match,' he said in a tone that brooked no argument. 'I declared myself happy with the result in front of half Newmarket. A great many of my friends will even now be discussing how best to have me committed.'

'Oh, Alexander.' In the ensuing interlude, the rest of Caroline's hair pins gave up the struggle.

'You are delectable,' he said, running his hand with delicious promise over her hip and leg, 'but you are shivering and I don't believe I am in much better shape myself. Let us get you and your horse safely back to Penfold Lodge.'

'And will you stay and eat with us?'

'Very willingly.' He found both their hats, eased hers on whilst she twisted her hair on top of her head to conceal it, then lifted her bodily into the saddle. 'Provided you wash your face first.'

'And clad myself as a young lady again. I know.'

His hand trailed lingeringly down the tightly fitting breeches. 'If you must.'

Caroline felt herself blush. Still, if he found her delectable looking as dreadful as she did now, it augured reasonably well for the future.

They were not very far from the road. Solange turned left eagerly, wanting her stable. 'See,' said Caroline, 'she knows she's going home. The men will wonder what has become of me. I should have been back long since. I was putting off telling them about the race and losing all that money.'

Alexander reached across and squeezed her hand. 'You will not have to worry about that ever again.'

They trotted on. Caroline was too full of feelings for words and, from the silence, Alexander was presumably in a like state. As they got near home, though, they heard shouting in the road.

Caroline frowned. 'That sounds like Harry. Oh, no. Now what can be amiss?'

'Whatever it is, you must not be seen,' said Alexander, and Caroline thrilled at his possessive tone. 'Can you get up to the stable and into the house without being spotted?'

'Easily. I'll slip off and walk Solange up through the archway so that her flank hides me. I can get in through the side door and change.'

Alexander nodded. 'Do that. I will distract everyone here.' They came cautiously around the corner to find an entire crowd in the road outside Penfold Lodge. 'Good God,' he said. 'Go.'

Caroline went.

16

'What the devil goes on here?' called Alex in an authoritative voice.

He might well ask. There were coaches and curricles drawn up outside the house and an unconscionable number of people milling around in the usually quiet road. Indeed, *milling* seemed to be the operative word, judging by one gentleman just getting up from the dirt and another squaring up to him before battle was rejoined. Alex found he was becoming extremely cross. He wanted to be with Caroline, exploring the lovely, wondrous thing that was happening between them. These people, whatever they were doing, were stopping him.

At his shout, one of the onlookers detached himself. It was Flood, the Penfold Lodge head groom. 'Did you find her, milord?' he asked in a barely audible rumble as he took Alex's reins.

Alex dismounted. 'She's at the stable now,' he replied in a similar mutter. 'You should never have let her ride. What's all this?'

Flood snorted. 'Your fine friend with an eye to what's Mr Harry's. I'll leave them to tell you. If you can stop Mr Harry a-killing of him, that is.' He turned and led Chieftain up to the yard.

Alex strode forward, grabbing the nearest combatant by the collar. It proved to be Harry Fortune, missing his hat, with his cheek grazed, his fists clenched, his eyes glittering, and his coat all over dust from the road.

'Well done, Alex,' said his opponent, darting towards them. 'Hold still and I'll break that pretty nose for him. See how the lady likes her plebeian paramour *then*.'

Giles? Alex was dumbfounded. What the deuce was happening?

Harry twisted out of Alex's grip. 'Oh will you? We'll see about that!'

'Desist, both of you!' roared Alex. He became aware of another altercation, in the doorway this time. Louisa Taylor, with knots of blue ribbons fluttering on her dress, was struggling with her stout, evidently distressed father.

'No, Papa, I will not go indoors. What do I care if fighting is not for a lady's eyes? If Harry is hurt, *I* am going to tend him and no other!'

'No one is going to be hurt,' said Alex forcefully. Sweet Heaven, it was a veritable circus! He swept the bystanders a glance.

Apart from the Penfold Lodge servants they were completely unknown to him. 'I regret to inform you all that the entertainment is over,' he announced. 'I would have one of the gentlemen pass round a hat, but they appear to have both lost them. I suggest you depart about your business, and everybody concerned in this matter remove inside where we can discuss any grievances in a civilized manner.'

The onlookers grumbled at the end of such a promising mill and drifted off. Most of the servants reluctantly remembered their duties, but a couple stayed in place.

'No,' said Harry Fortune between gritted teeth.

'I beg your pardon?' said Alex.

'No, I will not have Mr d'Arblay set so much as a toe inside my house.'

'Are you going to tell me why?' On the doorstep, he saw Miss Taylor had been joined by Caroline, washed and hastily dressed in her pink gown with a cherry ribbon in her hair. Despite the gravity of the situation, he felt his spirits lift.

Harry did not relax his stance for an instant. 'Certainly I will tell you. It is far from secret. Indeed, I would like the whole world to know what sort of hell-born scum Mr d'Arblay is.'

'No, Harry, let me explain to Lord Rothwell. I was the person primarily concerned, after all.' Louisa hurried down the path, shaking off her father, determined to have her say.

Giles brushed at his clothes. 'All a misunderstanding, Alex,' he said leisurely, just as if he was not sporting a split lip and an incipient black eye. 'Finished on the heath, are you? Bound for Cheveley now? I'll tell you about it on the way.'

Across their heads, Alex met Caroline's eyes. 'I don't think so, Giles,' he said with deliberation. He saw the tension leave her. She smiled, just for him, telling him she had perfect faith, now and for ever more, that he would be scrupulously honourable. He smiled back, feeling like a lion and lord of the world.

'We were waiting for news of the race,' said Louisa, rushing into speech, 'watching the window to the street as you can imagine, when there was a tremendous clattering of horses and Mr d'Arblay's curricle pulled up.'

Alex tried to move Caroline from the forefront of his mind and concentrate on her friend instead. He remembered seeing Giles driving hell-for-leather away from the heath. His glance at that gentleman was met with an indifferent shrug. It was unlike him to keep silent, but possibly he felt out-numbered. The two Penfold Lodge footmen who had remained were standing near him as watchful as cats at a mousehole.

'He jumped down,' continued Louisa, 'shouting at his groom to hold the horses, and then hammered on the door.'

Alex flicked a look at the curricle.

'No, that is one of Harry's men,' said Louisa. 'Mr d'Arblay's groom left the horses and ran away when Harry hit him, calling out that Mr d'Arblay hadn't heard the last of this and he'd collect what was owed later. Jessop, I think he's called.'

This became ever more interesting. Why would Fortune have hit Jessop as well as laying into Giles? And how could Giles owe money to a groom? 'Pray continue, Miss Taylor,' said Alex gravely.

Louisa clasped and unclasped her hands, obviously agitated. She took a deep breath. 'Mr d'Arblay said . . . he said Papa had had a seizure at the races and that he — Mr d'Arblay — had straight away volunteered to collect me and take me to him. And . . . and I would have gone, but I didn't quite see why Harry wouldn't have come for me. And I'm sorry, Papa, but even though Mr d'Arblay said there wasn't a moment to lose and you were calling for me and I wasn't to waste time putting on my warm cloak or my outdoor shoes or fetching my reticule, I . . . it just didn't feel right that it wasn't Harry. And I started to say as much — but not very well because I was so worried and muddled and confused — and Mr d'Arblay took my wrist and pulled me down the path. And I looked up to pray ask him to stop, and his groom was *laughing*.'

She pressed her lips together, working to regain control. Harry made an animal-sounding snarl. Alex could hardly fault him; he felt utter revulsion at whatever Giles had become. Caroline walked down the path and gripped her friend's hand in solidarity.

Louisa met Alex's eyes. 'And . . . and I think he knew that I wasn't going to go with him, because he pulled harder, really hurting, and said that Papa might be dying and that I must go and that he — Mr d'Arblay — had admired and revered me from the moment he first saw me and he knew I wasn't the sort of brave daughter who would ever let her father down. He was much stronger than I was, but I was so frightened and I was still holding back but slipping on the path because I only had indoor shoes on, and then . . . ' She stopped and looked with utter adoration at Harry Fortune. 'And then Harry came.'

'Bringing with him a very much alive papa,' said that gentleman grimly.

Louisa let go of Caroline's hand and went towards her beloved. 'Harry *flew* off the curricle seat,' she said. 'Mr d'Arblay's groom tried to trip him up, but Harry hit him without even *thinking* about it and then dragged Mr d'Arblay off me.' She buried her face in Harry's shirt, the rest of her words muffled. 'I was so scared, but he made it all right.'

Harry's arms came around her. 'Hush, love, you won't ever be scared again. I promise.'

'Very touching,' said Giles in a bored tone. 'My felicitations. One can see why you leapt to conclusions, of course, but I assure you I was never so delighted in my life to see Alderman Taylor in the curricle. Really sir, the likeness to that other poor gentleman who collapsed on the heath is remarkable.'

'You always did tell shocking tarradiddles, Giles,' said a clear voice.

Alex's head whipped around. With the crowd departed he was now able to distinguish the crest on the one coach still drawn up by the side of the road. A crest he knew very well indeed. 'Mama,' he said in resignation. 'It needed only this.'

'But he did, darling, you know he did. Right from a boy,' said the duchess, stepping down, with the aid of a footman, to join them. 'I fear I have been a sad failure as his godmother. Are you *very* wealthy, my dear?' she asked Louisa.

'She is. Or she would be with the right settlement,' said Alderman Taylor, advancing in his turn and making a low bow to the duchess. 'Abduction, young Fortune called it, and it's not so very far from the truth by what I'm hearing.' He poked Giles in the chest. 'I'm disappointed in you, young man. Fine feathers aren't the only things that make fine birds, you know. Castle indeed. I should have gone by what my book said about your family seat. Lack of care's in the blood, when all's said and done.'

Louisa raised a lovely, tear-stained face to her father. 'Harry's family has always worked hard, Papa,' she said tremulously. 'And Harry was only wild for a little while because he thought he would never be able to marry me.'

Fortune kept his arm around her and looked the alderman full in the eyes. 'Which I am more than ever determined to do now, sir, whether you cut her off or not. It's not gentlemanly, but I'll fight anyone you care to name to keep Louisa safe.'

'No more talk of violence in front of my daughter, if you please. It's high time you and I went indoors for a chat. It may be the done thing in Newmarket to discuss business in the street, but it isn't where I come from and I daresay it's not what her grace is used to either.'

'No indeed,' said the duchess. 'And I believe a tray of tea would not go amiss, don't you think? I *did* call to find out about the race. I suppose somebody knows the outcome?'

'I will come inside in a moment,' said Harry. He looked steadily at Alex, almost challenging him to do the right thing.

Alex felt his gut clench. This was it. 'Well, Giles?' he asked.

Giles raised an eyebrow as if surprised to be addressed. 'I was mistaken. I apologize for the distress I have caused. I assure you that it was most inadvertently done.' He surveyed his clothes ruefully and turned towards his curricle. 'Fortune won the bet, ma'am. Daresay I'll see you later, Alex.'

It was another defining moment. Alex had been having a lot of these just recently. He knew, beyond all doubt, that his oldest friend had just tried to forcibly abduct Louisa Taylor in order to get hold of her dowry. He also knew that Giles had offered a civilized, face-saving way for everyone to gloss over the events of the afternoon. But some time over the last day, or week, or month, Alex had changed.

'Why did you do it, Giles?' he asked quietly.

* * *

Yes! Caroline almost jumped in the air with delight. She met the duchess's eyes to see triumph in them too. She had been so afraid of this confrontation, so afraid Alexander would let his boyhood friend leave Penfold Lodge unchallenged. It was what four-dozen gentlemen out of fifty would do.

She watched as Giles d'Arblay registered Alexander's implacability. His eyes travelled dispassionately over the audience. It was astonishing how the veneer of charm had simply evaporated from the man. '*Not* in front of the assembled masses, I think. Dine with me tonight.'

No, willed Caroline. *Say no.*

'No,' said Alexander. 'But we can walk apart now, if you wish.'

There was just the tiniest flicker of calculation in Giles's face. Intent on them both as she was, it set up an instant warning in Caroline's head. 'Very well,' he agreed. 'To the paddocks, perhaps?'

Alexander looked at Harry. 'May we?'

'Provided you do not take your eyes off him,' said Harry, unsmiling.

'You will be able to see us,' snapped Giles. 'You do not need to fear for your precious livestock.' He swung away. Alexander followed him.

'Return inside with your father, love,' said Harry to Louisa. 'I am going to the stable to watch them.' And to Caroline. 'What is it, Caro?'

Caroline shivered, her eyes on the two men's backs. There was something, something important, but so much had happened today that . . . oh, why couldn't she *think*? 'I don't know,' she said in frustration. 'I don't trust him. There was something in his face just now . . . '

'I have always thought,' said the duchess, pausing on her way to the door, 'that Giles egged Alex on. I know, of course, that the boy's home life was appalling and he was with us more often than not. And I know I was guilty of encouraging the friendship when they were young because Alex was such a solemn little thing and Giles was full of fun. But looking back now, do you know I can't recall a single accident to Alex when Giles wasn't there? That dreadful time with the bridge, for instance. I found out from my eldest son long afterwards that it was Giles who had dared Alex to cross it when all the children had been expressly forbidden to.

And then there was the curricle race in the park when one of Alex's wheels came off and he broke his arm. It was Giles he was racing. And Giles *battens* on him so. It is really quite unhealthy. I do hope Alex will finally make the break with him.'

She rustled into the house. Caroline remained where she was, her eyes fixed on Alexander, walking up the stable path with Mr d'Arblay. His shoulders were stiff. She could tell his former friend was not making any headway with whatever explanation he had conjured up. Alexander stopped by the stable, she saw him making a flat-handed cutting gesture as if to say *we finish here*, but Giles walked on towards the paddocks.

Towards the paddock where Solange had been turned out.

And he was tapping his whip against his leg.

'No,' said Caroline aloud, her hand going to her mouth. She started to move, stray shards of information coalescing together, her head filling with image upon deadly image.

A hand upraised with a whip.

'She bolted with me once.'

Tremors in Solange's flank at d'Arblay's voice.

'Caro?' Harry was loping urgently beside her. 'Caro, what is it?'

334

'Never an accident when Giles wasn't there.'

A face in a loo mask pressed against a window.

'Look out, Alex!'

And, most damning of all, 'I, for instance, made out my will some years ago leaving my estate to Giles.'

A queer moan broke from Caroline's throat. She felt again the sickening sensation of clinging to a rearing horse. 'Quick, Harry. Oh, quick. I think he's going to kill Alexander!'

★ ★ ★

This was getting them nowhere. Giles had admitted to being far deeper in debt than Alex had any idea of. He'd seen a chance to cut short negotiations for Miss Taylor's hand and had taken it, but he still didn't show any remorse and had as good as said he'd do the same thing again if the opportunity arose. 'What does it matter that her father preferred you and she preferred the whelp?' he said impatiently. 'They would both have come around. It isn't as if I wouldn't have been the perfect husband and son-in-law. They would have had nothing to complain of.'

Alex could hardly contain his revulsion.

'But to get your way you were prepared to resort to abduction and violence!'

Giles shrugged. 'Only because they were being so cursed slow about doing the thing traditionally. You don't understand the fix I'm in, Alex. All you have to do is stretch out your hand to the nearest bank to be in funds. I don't have that option, damn their sanctimonious hides. Even with the crooked betting I'm not making enough to stave off ruin. And my creditors aren't the sort who will wait.'

'They will have to. I am not bailing you out ever again. In truth, I should have stopped long ago.' Alex was so eaten up with loathing of Giles — and disgust with himself that he hadn't seen, hadn't looked for, the change in him — that he almost missed the admission about *crooked betting*. Dear heaven, Sally Jersey had been right all along! Who would have thought it? And of course Giles had been with him on the course every time when he was looking for leads. Misdirection would have been simple. Alex felt ill at having been so easily gulled.

Giles strolled on, almost insulting in his assumption that Alex would follow. 'But you didn't ever stop bailing me out, did you? Face it, Alex, you need me. I'm your obverse, your other half. Lord Alexander Rothwell never puts a foot wrong because he pays the

Honourable Giles d'Arblay to do it for him.'

'That's not true. You're — you were — my friend. I feel . . . I felt . . . '

'Sorry for me?' Giles tossed the bitter words over his shoulder. 'Twist the knife some more, why don't you? Yes, you have always had everything, and I nothing. I used to be galled by your pity until I started using it.'

Where was he going? Did he intend making a break on foot across the fields? Out of the corner of his eye Alex saw Harry and Caroline hurrying along the path. He picked up his pace towards Giles. He felt tainted by association and didn't want Caroline to see him until he was clean again. In the paddock, Rufus lifted his head. Solange, brushed down now and cropping peacefully, followed him.

Alex tried again. 'There was no pity. We were friends, don't you see? I lent you money because I had it and you didn't. To begin with, that was enough.'

Giles hitched himself up to sit on the rail. Alex was whisked backwards to the past without warning. How many times had they roosted like this on paddock rails when they were children? Talking the day away. Closer than brothers. *Oh, Giles.*

'And more recently?' murmured his boyhood friend.

Caroline was running for some reason, her hair around her face, a hand pressed to her side. The sight of her reminded Alex that things were very different now. This was no time to be seduced by nostalgia. 'You've changed,' he said to Giles. 'That rider today — you really didn't care that he might have died when Solange bolted, did you?'

He got a disbelieving laugh. 'Why should I? He was a nothing. It would have been Fortune's fault if he'd died, claiming he could train the firebrand when he obviously couldn't.'

'He did a damn good job, considering how wild she was when she arrived.'

'Good God, Alex, what did they dose you with when you were here? Any half-baked trainer can produce the appearance of docility.'

'Like the ones you employ, perhaps? Fortune deserved to win that bet and you know it. He's worked wonders to even achieve getting Solange to the starting post without incident.'

Giles made a gesture as if he was weary of the whole discussion. 'Oh, yes, a miracle from a greenhorn. Do you know, I just can't see it. Are you telling me it was simply the crowd that spooked the horse? That if you went right up to her now, she wouldn't turn a hair?'

Alex glanced at Solange, grazing peacefully. 'I believe I probably could, yes.'

'Go on then,' jeered Giles. 'If you are so confident of your new friends. Prove it to me. And then I will go quietly away and never bother any of you again. I'll go to America. I've heard there are heiresses a-plenty for smart young aristocrats there.'

Alex could hear Caroline and Harry running past the stables now, but he needed to concentrate on Giles. Would he really go away? It was a mesmerizing thought. Alex would have to pay his debts, of course, and his passage too, belike, but it would be worth it just to cut this canker out of his life. 'You mean it?' he said, wanting to believe him.

A small smile played over Giles's mouth. He slid off the rail as if prepared to leave that minute. 'Oh yes. You go and stand right in front of the mare, and I promise you'll never hear from me again.'

'Very well.' Alex swung himself over the wooden barrier. He patted Rufus absently and walked over to Solange.

★ ★ ★

'Alexander, no!' screamed Caroline with the last of her breath. Her slippers were in shreds and her arms ached with the effort of keeping her skirts hoisted up enough to run, but she continued to pound forward, ignoring the pain in her feet. 'It was him,' she gasped, though what emerged was little more than a squeak. How could she have not told Alexander that she had seen Giles this afternoon raising his whip with hatred in his eyes? Those same eyes spared her a contemptuous look as she pelted up to the paddock now, but he dismissed her as finished. All his attention was on the brave, foolish, loyally-blind man walking towards Solange. He was four yards away from her, three yards away, two . . .

Caroline scrambled under the rail, stumbled across the field and, putting out a supreme effort, launched herself into Alexander's side just as Giles snapped his whip up and yelled, 'Look ou — '

'Not this time,' growled Harry, laying into him with a punishing right.

The world flicked out of kilter for a moment. When it came back Caroline was tumbled across Alexander where they had both fallen with the impetus of her last desperate push. Her breath was tearing her chest apart. Her lungs felt as if they were on fire.

He moved under her, more dumbfounded than winded. 'What the devil . . . ?'

'He was going to kill you,' she whispered, her throat raw.

'Giles? Nonsense.' But there was an edge of uncertainty to his voice.

'Alexander, he was. He is jealous of you. He hates you. And you made that stupid, stupid will. I realized it all just now. Down there by the house. It was him who coshed you. He pulled off your greatcoat hoping the rain would soak you and finish you off. It was him at the window that night, thinking there would be no one else in the room. Don't you see? He's been trying to kill you all your life!'

Her body shrieked in protest as Alexander raised himself to a sitting position, pulling her up with him. She was so weak and trembling that she simply folded into his chest. He had to put his arms around her to stop her falling. 'I knew something in Solange's past had caused her to hate men and fear shouting,' she went on, still taking great tearing breaths. 'Twice when I've been on her she's been anxious at the sound of Mr d'Arblay's voice, but I didn't make the connection. Today as we were coming towards you at the end of the race I saw him crack his whip and shout 'Look out, Alex', right before Solange lost control. He was about to do the same just now. You wouldn't have stood a chance against her hoofs at that range. You must see it. Why would he have trained her to rear at those exact words if he meant you no harm?

His face . . . Oh, Alexander, his face was terrible.'

Alexander's eyes, profoundly shocked, locked on hers. 'He gave Solange to me in payment of a debt,' he said, uttering the words as if he barely believed them. 'He'd been baiting me about my horsemanship so I got up on her right there and then to show him. He was quite a way behind me.' He swallowed, still looking at her with haunted eyes. 'Dear God. Oh, dear God, Caroline, I heard him shout just that, '*Look out, Alex!*' And then she bolted.'

Caroline's eyes filled with tears. 'Alexander, I'm so sorry.' She put her arms around him and wept for his betrayed trust.

She felt him hold her, felt him draw her close to his body. 'Don't cry. Dearest Caroline, don't cry.'

'I can't stop,' she sobbed.

She felt him give a shaky laugh. 'Try this then.' And then he was kissing her and the tears were drying on her cheeks and the fear when she thought she'd lose him was receding. 'My life,' he murmured. 'My salvation. Marry me, Caroline?'

'Yes,' she said. 'Oh yes.' Then after another head-spinning embrace, 'Unless you change your mind when you've had time to think about it.'

342

'Never,' he said. 'We'll tell your brother now. Then if I renege, he can call me out and beat me to a pulp as well as any other stray victims. Talking of which . . . '

They made to stand up, but — 'My feet,' she gasped, and collapsed again.

Alexander squatted to inspect one unbearably painful sole. 'Sweetheart,' he said huskily, 'you've run yourself ragged for me.'

'I had to. I couldn't not.'

'Put your arms around my neck, I'll carry you.'

He swept her up. Caroline's heart thumped. In spite of the pain in her feet she grinned shyly at him. 'I must run myself ragged again. This is nice.'

'Dear heart, it can be done *without* the lacerated flesh.'

He carried her across to where Harry was leaning on the rail, looking as white and nauseous as she'd felt earlier. Caroline's new-found joy wavered. 'What is it?' she said. 'Please don't tell me you disapprove.'

But Harry didn't even seem to have noticed them. 'It's d'Arblay.' His voice cracked on the words. 'I've killed him.'

Caroline's arms tightened around Alexander's neck. She heard his indrawn breath and looked down. Giles d'Arblay lay where he had fallen. She only now noticed that his head was at an odd angle.

'I hit him to stop him shouting the words,' said Harry, trembling violently. 'He fell back against the post and I told him to get up and finish the fight like a man. I . . . I kicked him even. But he didn't.' Without warning he was suddenly and violently sick.

Alexander held Caroline close to his body. She felt his heart beating into her side. He looked down at his one-time friend, his eyes unbearably sad. 'I saw you hit him in the road outside,' he said slowly. 'Everyone did. You both landed a number of punches. It was a fair fight. But after we came up here, all I saw was you and your sister running up with the news that Miss Taylor had accepted your suit. Giles and I were talking. He started backwards in shock, stumbled, and hit his head on that fence post.'

Caroline gazed into his tortured, honourable face. She didn't know how they would make this marriage work, how they would balance his preference for town and politics with her fondness for horses and the country, but she loved him with all her heart and she saw that he loved her equally deeply. Her heart swelled. She was quite, quite sure that together they could do anything they set their minds to. 'I saw the same,' she said. 'Harry shouted 'Congratulate me, Rothwell'. Mr d'Arblay stumbled backwards and simply didn't get up again. Such . . . such a tragic end to a happy day.'

Alexander looked down again. Tears glimmered in his eyes. 'All that bright promise,' he said softly. 'All tarnished. All gone to waste. It's better this way, Fortune, believe me. I am much in your debt. Is Rutland the local JP? We'll get word to him straight away.' He beckoned to Flood, waiting on the path, then turned resolutely aside. 'Come back to the house now and find us all a drink. Not that I am saying my bride-to-be is starting to get heavy, you understand . . . '

That startled Harry out of his stupor. 'Bride-to-be? Really? Why, that's splendid! Oh but Caro, Mama will be insufferable!'

There was a horrified silence.

'Unless we don't tell her,' said Alexander thoughtfully. 'I suppose the two of you — and Miss Taylor and the alderman — wouldn't care to make a visit to Abervale? To rid today's events from our minds, perhaps. We have a very fine chapel there, and I am particularly well acquainted with the local bishop. I can always ask for your father's consent by letter and send my attorney to sort out the marriage articles.'

'Splendid idea,' said Harry. 'I'll go and tell Louisa to pack.'

Flood trod stolidly up with a length of sacking. Alexander gave him the right story for when the magistrate's man should arrive.

'Aye,' said the head groom. 'I thought that was the way of things from what I could see from the yard. You take Miss Caro back to the house and leave it to me, milord.'

As he carried her down the path, Caroline looked at her not-very-far-in-the-future husband. 'I don't think I've said this yet. I love you, Alexander.'

He kissed her gently. 'And I love you.'

He laughed. It was a wonderful sound. Caroline smiled, her heart lightening to hear him. 'What is it?'

'I was thinking what a *fortunate* wager I made last month.'

The tragedy would come back and haunt his dreams, Caroline knew. But she would be lying by his side to soothe him to sleep, then and always. Now she looked at his joyous face, so different from the impatient, arrogant noble who strode into her life just four weeks ago, and felt profound thanks and a great burgeoning love. 'That is a dreadful play on words. Take me home at once,' she said severely.

He tightened his hold and kissed her. 'Oh, yes.'

We do hope that you have enjoyed reading this large print book.

Did you know that all of our titles are available for purchase?

We publish a wide range of high quality large print books including:
Romances, Mysteries, Classics
General Fiction
Non Fiction and Westerns

Special interest titles available in large print are:
The Little Oxford Dictionary
Music Book
Song Book
Hymn Book
Service Book

Also available from us courtesy of Oxford University Press:
Young Readers' Dictionary
(large print edition)
Young Readers' Thesaurus
(large print edition)

For further information or a free brochure, please contact us at:
Ulverscroft Large Print Books Ltd.,
The Green, Bradgate Road, Anstey,
Leicester, LE7 7FU, England.
Tel: (00 44) **0116 236 4325**
Fax: (00 44) **0116 234 0205**

FAIR DECEPTION

Jan Jones

Fate seems to intervene when Kit Kydd rescues Susanna Fair from abduction. Kit must appear settled to be made his great-aunt's heir, and Susanna is an actress. By pretending to be engaged during a visit to Lady Penfold, Kit can protect Susanna from further danger. But Lady Penfold lives in the horse-racing town of Newmarket, which holds the secret of Susanna's scandalous past. And the dishonourable Rafe Warwick has wagered two thousand guineas on making Susanna his mistress. Now how will she cope with her theatre company's request to make a final public performance . . . and falling in love with Kit?

WINDS OF HONOUR

Ashleigh Bingham

The Honourable Phoebe Pemberton is beautiful and wealthy, but is the daughter of the late, disgraceful Lord Pemberton and Harriet Buckley . . . Phoebe escapes her mother's plans to teach her the family business of wringing profits from the mills. She dreams of running away, and, when she learns of her mother's schemes for Phoebe's marriage as part of a business transaction, she calls on her friend Toby Grantham for help . . . But Harriet's vengeful fury is aroused, leaving Phoebe tangled in a dark and desperate venture.

SCANDAL AT THE DOWER HOUSE

Marina Oliver

When Catarina's elderly husband dies, she moves to the Dower House where things are about to change dramatically with the arrival of Catarina's young sister Joanna. Tricked by her cousin Matthew into a sham marriage, Joanna is now pregnant and alone. Catarina has a plan to hide her sister's disgrace, but then tragedy strikes suddenly at the Dower House. What will be the fate of Joanna's unwanted child?

CHEF

Jaspreet Singh

Kip Singh is timorous and barely twenty when he arrives for the first time at General Kumar's camp, nestled in the shadow of the mighty Siachen Glacier that claimed his father's life. He is placed under the supervision of Chef Kishen, a fiery, anarchic mentor who guides Kip towards the heady spheres of food and women. As a Sikh, Kip feels secure in his allegiance to India, the right side of this interminable conflict. Until, one oppressively close day, a Pakistani 'terrorist' with long, flowing hair is swept up on the banks of the river and changes everything.

MATHILDA SAVITCH

Victor Lodato

Fear doesn't come naturally to Mathilda Savitch. She looks directly at things that others cannot bring themselves to mention: for example, the fact that her beloved sister is dead; pushed in front of a train by a man still at large. Her grief-stricken parents have been basically sleepwalking ever since, and Mathilda is going to shock them back to life. Her strategy? Being bad. She decides to investigate the catastrophe, sleuthing through her sister's secret possessions — anything she can ferret out. But Mathilda risks a great deal — she must leave behind everything she loves in order to discover the truth.